MAKE ROOM! MAKE ROOM!

"Stick around and wait for me, we'll walk back together," Shirl's new friend said to her, as they stood in line waiting for their water rations. "It's getting late and plenty of punks would like to grab the water; they can always sell it."

"Yes, I'll wait for you, that's a good idea," Shirl said, suddenly feeling very alone.

"Cards," the patrolman said and Shirl handed him the three Welfare cards, hers, Andy's and Sol's. He held them to the light, then handed them back to her. "Six quarts," he called out to the valve man.

"That's not right," Shirl said.

"Reduced ration today, lady, keep moving, there's a lot of people waiting."

MAKE ROOM! MAKE ROOM!

HARRY HARRISON

A BERKLEY MEDALLION BOOK
published by
BERKLEY PUBLISHING CORPORATION

To
TODD and MOIRA
For your sakes, children,
I hope this proves to be a work of fiction.

Published by arrangement with
Doubleday & Company, Inc.

BERKLEY MEDALLION EDITION, JULY, 1967

BERKLEY MEDALLION BOOKS are published by
Berkley Publishing Corporation
15 East 26th Street, New York, N.Y. 10010

Berkley Medallion Books ® TM 757,375

Printed in the United States of America

PROLOGUE

In December, 1959, The President of the United States, Dwight D. Eisenhower, said: "This government . . . will not . . . as long as I am here, have a positive political doctrine in its program that has to do with this problem of birth control. That is not our business." It has not been the business of any American government since that time.

In 1950 the United States—with just 9.5 per cent of the world's population—was consuming 50 per cent of the world's raw materials. This percentage keeps getting bigger and within fifteen years, at the present rate of growth, the United States will be consuming over 83 per cent of the annual output of the earth's materials. By the end of the century, should our population continue to increase at the same rate, this country will need more than 100 per cent of the planet's resources to maintain our current living standards. This is a mathematical impossibility—aside from the fact that there will be about seven billion people on this earth at that time and—perhaps—they would like to have some of the raw materials too.

In which case, what will the world be like?

MONDAY, AUGUST 9, 1999

NEW YORK CITY—

—stolen from the trusting Indians by the wily Dutch, taken from the law-abiding Dutch by the warlike British, then wrested in turn from the peaceful British by the revolutionary colonials. Its trees were burned decades ago, its hills leveled and the fresh ponds drained and filled, while the crystal springs have been imprisoned underground and spill their pure waters directly into the sewers. Reaching out urbanizing tentacles from its island home, the city has become a megalopolis with four of its five boroughs blanketing half of one island over a hundred miles long, engulfing another island, and sprawling up the Hudson River onto the mainland of North America. The fifth and original borough is Manhattan: a slab of primordial granite and metamorphic rock bounded on all sides by water, squatting like a steel and stone spider in the midst of its web of bridges, tunnels, tubes, cables and ferries. Unable to expand outward, Manhattan has writhed upward, feeding on its own flesh as it tears down the old buildings to replace them with the new, rising higher and still higher—yet never high enough, for there seems to be no limit to the people crowding here. They press in from the outside and raise their families, and their children and their children's children raise families, until this city is populated as no other city has ever been in the history of the world.

On this hot day in August in the year 1999 there are—give or take a few thousand—thirty-five million people in the City of New York.

PART ONE

1

The August sun struck in through the open window and burned on Andrew Rusch's bare legs until discomfort dragged him awake from the depths of heavy sleep. Only slowly did he become aware of the heat and the damp and gritty sheet beneath his body. He rubbed at his gummed-shut eyelids, then lay there, staring up at the cracked and stained plaster of the ceiling, only half awake and experiencing a feeling of dislocation, not knowing in those first waking moments just where he was, although he had lived in this room for over seven years. He yawned and the odd sensation slipped away while he groped for the watch that he always put on the chair next to the bed, then he yawned again as he blinked at the hands mistily seen behind the scratched crystal. Seven . . . seven o'clock in the morning, and there was a little number 9 in the middle of the square window. Monday, the ninth of August, 1999—and hot as a furnace already, with the city still imbedded in the heat wave that had baked and suffocated New York for the past ten days. Andy scratched at a trickle of perspiration on his side, then moved his legs out of the patch of sunlight and bunched the pillow up under his neck. From the other side of the thin partition that divided the room in half there came a clanking whir that quickly rose to a high-pitched drone.

"Morning . . ." he shouted over the sound, then began coughing. Still coughing he reluctantly stood and crossed the room to draw a glass of water from the wall tank; it came out in a thin, brownish trickle. He swallowed it, then rapped the dial on the tank with his knuckles and the needle bobbed up and down close to the *Empty* mark. It needed filling, he would have to see to that before he signed in at four o'clock at the precinct. The day had begun.

A full-length mirror with a crack running down it was fixed to the front of the hulking wardrobe and he poked his

7

face close to it, rubbing at his bristly jaw. He would have to shave before he went in. No one should ever look at himself in the morning, naked and revealed, he decided with distaste, frowning at the dead white of his skin and the slight bow to his legs that was usually concealed by his pants. And how did he manage to have ribs that stuck out like those of a starved horse, as well as a growing potbelly—both at the same time? He kneaded the soft flesh and thought that it must be the starchy diet, that and sitting around on his chunk most of the time. But at least the fat wasn't showing on his face. His forehead was a little higher each year, but wasn't too obvious as long as his hair was cropped short. You have just turned thirty, he thought to himself, and the wrinkles are already starting around your eyes. And your nose is too big—wasn't it Uncle Brian who always said that was because there was Welsh blood in the family? And your canine teeth are a little too obvious so when you smile you look a bit like a hyena. You're a handsome devil, Andy Rusch, and when was the last time you had a date? He scowled at himself, then went to look for a handkerchief to blow his impressive Welsh nose.

There was just a single pair of clean undershorts in the drawer and he pulled them on; that was another thing he had to remember today, to get some washing done. The squealing whine was still coming from the other side of the partition as he pushed through the connecting door.

"You're going to give yourself a coronary, Sol," he told the gray-bearded man who was perched on the wheelless bicycle, pedaling so industriously that perspiration ran down his chest and soaked into the bath towel that he wore tied around his waist.

"Never a coronary," Solomon Kahn gasped out, pumping steadily. "I been doing this every day for so long that my ticker would miss it if I stopped. And no cholesterol in my arteries either since regular flushing with alcohol takes care of that. And no lung cancer since I couldn't afford to smoke even if I wanted to, which I don't. And at the age of seventy-five no prostatitis because . . ."

"Sol, please—spare me the horrible details on an empty stomach. Do you have an ice cube to spare?"

"Take two—it's a hot day. And don't leave the door open too long."

Andy opened the small refrigerator that squatted against

the wall and quickly took out the plastic container of margarine, then squeezed two ice cubes from the tray into a glass and slammed the door. He filled the glass with water from the wall tank and put it on the table next to the margarine. "Have you eaten yet?" he asked.

"I'll join you, these things should be charged by now."

Sol stopped pedaling and the whine died away to a moan, then vanished. He disconnected the wires from the electrical generator that was geared to the rear axle of the bike, and carefully coiled them up next to the four black automobile storage batteries that were racked on top of the refrigerator. Then, after wiping his hands on his soiled towel sarong, he pulled out one of the bucket seats salvaged from an ancient 1975 Ford, and sat down across the table from Andy.

"I heard the six o'clock news," he said. "The Eldsters are organizing another protest march today on relief headquarters. *That's* where you'll see coronaries!"

"I won't, thank God, I'm not on until four and Union Square isn't in our precinct." He opened the breadbox and took out one of the six-inch-square red crackers, then pushed the box over to Sol. He spread margarine thinly on it and took a bite, wrinkling his nose as he chewed. "I think this margarine has turned."

"How can you tell?" Sol grunted, biting into one of the dry crackers. "Anything made from motor oil and whale blubber is turned to begin with."

"Now you begin to sound like a naturist," Andy said, washing his cracker down with cold water. "There's hardly any flavor at all to the fats made from petrochemicals and you know there aren't any whales left so they can't use blubber—it's just good chlorella oil."

"Whales, plankton, herring oil, it's all the same. Tastes fishy. I'll take mine dry so I don't grow no fins." There was a sudden staccato rapping on the door and he groaned. "Not yet eight o'clock and already they are after you."

"It could be anything," Andy said, starting for the door.

"It could be but it's not, that's the callboy's knock and you know it as well as I do and I bet you dollars to doughnuts that's just who it is. See?" He nodded with gloomy satisfaction when Andy unlocked the door and they saw the skinny, bare-legged messenger standing in the dark hall.

"What do you want, Woody?" Andy asked.

"I don' wan' no-fin," Woody lisped over his bare gums. Though he was in his early twenties he didn't have a tooth in his head. "Lieutenan' says bring, I bring." He handed Andy the message board with his name written on the outside.

Andy turned toward the light and opened it, reading the lieutenant's spiky scrawl on the slate, then took the chalk and scribbled his initials after it and returned it to the messenger. He closed the door behind him and went back to finish his breakfast, frowning in thought.

"Don't look at me that way," Sol said, "I didn't send the message. Am I wrong in guessing it's not the most pleasant of news?"

"It's the Eldsters, they're jamming the Square already and the precinct needs reinforcements."

"But why you? This sounds like a job for the harness bulls."

"Harness bulls! Where do you get that medieval slang? Of course they need patrolmen for the crowd, but there have to be detectives there to spot known agitators, pickpockets, purse-grabbers and the rest. It'll be murder in that park today. I have to check in by nine, so I have enough time to bring up some water first."

Andy dressed slowly in slacks and a loose sport shirt, then put a pan of water on the windowsill to warm in the sun. He took the two five-gallon plastic jerry cans, and when he went out Sol looked up from the TV set, glancing over the top of his old-fashioned glasses.

"When you bring back the water I'll fix you a drink——or do you think it is too early?"

"Not the way I feel today, it's not."

The hall was ink black once the door had closed behind him and he felt his way carefully along the wall to the stairs, cursing and almost falling when he stumbled over a heap of refuse someone had thrown there. Two flights down a window had been knocked through the wall and enough light came in to show him the way down the last two flights to the street. After the damp hallway the heat of Twenty-fifth Street hit him in a musty wave, a stifling miasma compounded of decay, dirt and unwashed humanity. He had to make his way through the women who already filled the steps of the building, walking carefully so that he didn't step on the children who were playing below. The sidewalk was still in shadow but so jammed with people that he walked in the street, well away from the curb to avoid the rubbish and litter banked high there. Days of heat had softened the tar so that it gave underfoot, then clutched at the soles of his shoes. There was the usual line leading to the columnar red water point on the corner of Seventh Avenue, but it broke up with angry shouts and some waved fists just as he reached it. Still muttering, the crowd dispersed and Andy saw that the duty patrolman was locking the steel door.

"What's going on?" Andy asked. "I thought this point was open until noon?"

The policeman turned, his hand automatically staying close to his gun until he recognized the detective from his own precinct. He tilted back his uniform cap and wiped the sweat from his forehead with the back of his hand.

"Just had the orders from the sergeant, all points closed for twenty-four hours. The reservoir level is low because of the drought, they gotta save water."

"That's a hell of a note," Andy said, looking at the key still in the lock. "I'm going on duty now and this means I'm not going to be drinking for a couple of days. . . ."

After a careful look around, the policeman unlocked the door and took one of the jerry cans from Andy. "One of these ought to hold you." He held it under the faucet while it filled, then lowered his voice. "Don't let it out, but the word is that there was another dynamiting job on the aqueduct upstate."

"Those farmers again?"

"It must be. I was on guard duty up there before I came to this precinct and it's rough, they just as soon blow you up with the aqueduct at the same time. Claim the city's stealing their water."

"They've got enough," Andy said, taking the full container. "More than they need. And there are thirty-five million people here in the city who get damn thirsty."

"Who's arguing?" the cop asked, slamming the door shut again and locking it tight.

Andy pushed his way back through the crowd around the steps and went through to the backyard first. All of the toilets were in use and he had to wait, and when he finally got into one of the cubicles he took the jerry cans with him; one of the kids playing in the pile of rubbish against the fence would be sure to steal them if he left them unguarded.

When he had climbed the dark flights once more and
opened the door to the room he heard the clear sound of ice
cubes rattling against glass.

"That's Beethoven's Fifth Symphony that you're playing," he said, dropping the containers and falling into a
chair.

"It's my favorite tune," Sol said, taking two chilled
glasses from the refrigerator and, with the solemnity of a
religious ritual, dropped a tiny pearl onion into each. He
passed one to Andy, who sipped carefully at the chilled
liquid.

"It's when I taste one of these, Sol, that I almost believe
you're not crazy after all. Why do they call them Gibsons?"

"A secret lost behind the mists of time. Why is a Stinger a
Stinger or a Pink Lady a Pink Lady?"

"I don't know—why? I never tasted any of them."

"I don't know either, but that's the name. Like those
green things they serve in the knockjoints, Panamas.
Doesn't mean anything, just a name."

"Thanks," Andy said, draining his glass. "The day looks
better already."

He went into his room and took his gun and holster from
the drawer and clipped it inside the waistband of his pants.
His shield was on his key ring where he always kept it and he
slipped his notepad in on top of it, then hesitated a moment.
It was going to be a long and rough day and anything might
happen. He dug his nippers out from under his shirts, then
the soft plastic tube filled with shot. It might be needed in
the crowd, safer than a gun with all those old people milling
about. Not only that, but with the new austerity regulations
you had to have a damn good reason for using up any ammunition. He washed as well as he could with the pint of
water that had been warming in the sun on the window sill,
then scrubbed his face with the small shard of gray and gritty soap until his whiskers softened a bit. His razor blade was
beginning to show obvious nicks along both edges and, as he
honed it against the inside of his drinking glass, he thought
that it was time to think about getting a new one. Maybe in
the fall.

Sol was watering his window box when Andy came out,
carefully irrigating the rows of herbs and tiny onions.
"Don't take any wooden nickels," he said without looking

up from his work. Sol had a million of them, all old. What in the world was a wooden nickel?

The sun was higher now and the heat was mounting in the sealed tar and concrete valley of the street. The band of shade was smaller and the steps were so packed with humanity that he couldn't leave the doorway. He carefully pushed by a tiny, runny-nosed girl dressed only in ragged gray underwear and descended a step. The gaunt women moved aside reluctantly, ignoring him, but the men stared at him with a cold look of hatred stamped across their features that gave them a strangely alike appearance, as though they were all members of the same angry family. Andy threaded his way through the last of them and when he reached the sidewalk he had to step over the outstretched leg of an old man who sprawled there. He looked dead, not asleep, and he might be for all that anyone cared. His foot was bare and filthy and a string tied about his ankle led to a naked baby that was sitting vacantly on the sidewalk chewing on a bent plastic dish. The baby was as dirty as the man and the string was tied about its chest under the pipestem arms because its stomach was swollen and heavy. Was the old man dead? Not that it mattered, the only work he had to do in the world was to act as an anchor for the baby and he could do that job just as well alive or dead.

Christ but I'm morbid this morning, Andy thought, it must be the heat, I can't sleep well and there are the nightmares. It's this endless summer and all the troubles, one thing just seems to lead to another. First the heat, then the drought, the warehouse thefts and now the Eldsters. They were crazy to come out in this kind of weather. Or maybe they're being driven crazy by the weather. It was too hot to think and when he turned the corner the shimmering length of Seventh Avenue burned before him and he could feel the strength of the sun on his face and arms. His shirt was sticking to his back already and it wasn't even a quarter to nine.

It was better on Twenty-third Street in the long shadow of the crosstown expressway that filled the sky above, and he walked slowly in the dimness keeping an eye on the heavy pedicab and tugtruck traffic. Around each supporting pillar of the roadway was a little knot of people, clustered against it like barnacles around a pile, with their legs almost among

the wheels of the traffic. Overhead there sounded a waning
rumble as a heavy truck passed on the expressway and he
could see another truck ahead parked in front of the
precinct house. Uniformed patrolmen were slowly climbing
into the back and Detective Lieutenant Grassioli was
standing next to the cab with a noteboard, talking to the
sergeant. He looked up and scowled at Andy and a nervous
tic shook his left eyelid like an angry wink.

"It's about time you showed up, Rusch," he said, making
a check mark on the noteboard.

"It was my day off, sir, I came as soon as the callboy
showed up." You had to put up a defense with Grassy or he
walked all over you: he had ulcers, diabetes and a bad liver.

"A cop is on duty twenty-four hours a day so get your
chunk into the truck. And I want you and Kulozik to bring
in some dips. I got complaints from Centre Street coming
out of my ears."

"Yes, sir," Andy said to the lieutenant's back as he
turned toward the station house. Andy climbed the three
steps welded to the tailgate and sat down on the board
bench next to Steve Kulozik, who had closed his eyes and
started to doze as soon as the lieutenant had left. He was a
solid man whose flesh quivered somewhere between fat and
muscle, and he was wearing wrinkled cotton slacks and a
short-sleeved shirt just like Andy's, with the shirt also
hanging over the belt to conceal the gun and holster. He
opened one eye halfway and grunted when Andy dropped
down beside him, then let it droop shut again.

The starter whined irritably, over and over, until finally
the low-quality fuel caught and the diesel engine slowly
thudded to life, shuddered and steadied as the truck pulled
away from the curb and moved east. The uniformed
policemen all sat sideways on the benches so they could
catch some of the breeze from the truck's motion and at the
same time watch the densely populated streets: the police
weren't popular this summer. If anything was thrown at
them they wanted to see it coming. Sudden vibration
wracked the truck and the driver shifted to a lower gear and
leaned on his horn, forcing a path through the swarming
people and hordes of creeping man-powered vehicles. When
they came to Broadway progress slowed to a crawl as people
spilled over into the roadway next to Madison Square with
its flea market and tent city. It was no better after they had

turned downtown since the Eldsters were already out in force and heading south, and were haltingly slow in getting out of the truck's way. The seated policemen looked out at them indifferently as they rolled by, a slowly surging mass: gray heads, bald heads, most of them with canes, while one old man with a great white beard swung along on crutches. There were a large number of wheelchairs. When they emerged into Union Square the sun, no longer blocked by the buildings, burned down unrelentingly upon them.

"It's murder," Steve Kulozik said, yawning as he swung down from the truck. "Getting all these old gaffers out in the heat will probably kill off half of them. It must be a hundred degrees in the sun—it was ninety-three at eight o'clock."

"That's what the medics are for," Andy said, nodding toward the small group of men in white who were unrolling stretchers next to the Department of Hospitals trailer. The detectives strolled toward the rear of the crowd that already half filled the park, facing toward the speaker's platform in the center. There was an amplified scratching sound and a quickly cut-off whine as the public address system was tested.

"A record-breaker," Steve said, his eyes searching the crowd steadily while they talked. "I hear the reservoirs are so low that some of the outlet pipes are uncovered. That and the upstate rubes dynamiting the aqueduct again. . . ."

The squeal from the loudspeaker dissolved into the echoing thunder of an amplified voice.

". . . Comrades, Fellows and Dames, members all of the Eldsters of America, I ask your attention. I had ordered some clouds for this morning but it sure looks like the order never got through. . . ."

An appreciative murmur rolled over the park, there were a few handclaps.

"Who's that talking?" Steve asked.

"Reeves, the one they call Kid Reeves because he's only sixty-five years old. He's business manager of the Eldsters now and he'll be their president next year if he keeps going like this. . . ." His words were drowned out as Reeves's voice shattered the hot air again.

"But we have clouds enough in our lives so perhaps we can live without these clouds in the sky." This time there was an angry edge to the crowd's grumbling answer. "The authorities have seen to it that we cannot work, no matter how fit or able we are, and they have fixed the tiny, insulting, miserable handout that we are supposed to live on and at the same time see to it that money buys less and less every year, every month, almost every day. . . ."

"There goes the first one," Andy said, pointing to a man at the back of the crowd who fell to his knees, clutching his chest. He started forward but Steve Kulozik held him back.

"Leave it for them," he said, pointing to the two medics who were already pushing forward. "Heart failure or heat stroke and it's not going to be the last. Come on, let's circulate the crowd."

". . . once again we are called upon to unite . . . forces that would keep us poverty ridden, starving, forgotten . . . the rising costs have wiped out . . ."

There seemed to be no connection between the small figure on the distant platform and the voice booming around them. The two detectives separated and Andy slowly worked his way through the crowd.

". . . we will not accept second best, or third or fourth best as it has become, nor will we accept a dirty corner of the hearth to drowse and starve in. Ours is a vital segment—no, I'll say *the* vital segment of the population—a reservoir of age and experience, of knowledge, of judgment. Let City Hall and Albany and Washington act—or beware, because when the votes are counted they will discover . . ."

The words broke in crashing waves about Andy's head and he paid them no attention as he pushed between the painfully attentive Eldsters, his eyes alert and constantly moving, threading a path through the sea of toothless gums, gray-whiskered cheeks and watery eyes. There were no dips here, the lieutenant had been wrong about that, the pickpockets knew better than to try and work a crowd like this. Dead broke, these people, all of them. Or if they had a little change it was locked in one of those old clasp purses and sewn to their underwear or something.

There was a movement in the crowd and two young boys pushed through laughing to each other, locking their bare scratched legs about each other's in a tumbling game, seeing who would fall.

"That's enough," Andy said, standing in front of them. "Slow down and out of the park, boys, there's nothing for you here."

"Who says! We can do what we wanna. . . ."

"The law says," Andy snapped at them and slid the blackjack out of his pocket and lifted it warningly. "Move!"

They turned without a word and made their way out of the crowd and he followed just far enough to make sure that they were gone. Kids, he thought as he slid the tube of shot away, maybe just ten or eleven years old, but you had to watch them closely and you couldn't let them give you any crap and you had to be careful because if you turned your back and there were enough of them they would pull you down and cut you up with pieces of broken glass like they did to poor damned Taylor.

Something seemed to possess the old people, they were beginning to move back and forth and, when the amplified voice was silent for an instant, distant shouting could be heard from beyond the speakers' platform. It sounded like trouble and Andy forced his way toward it. Reeves's voice suddenly broke off and the shouts were louder and there was the sharp sound of falling broken glass. A new voice boomed from the loudspeakers.

"This is the police. I am asking you all to disperse, this meeting is over, and you will go north out of the Square—"

An enraged howl drowned the speaker and the Eldsters surged forward, carried on waves of emotion. Their screaming died and words could be made out again, the amplified voice of Reeves, the original speaker.

". . . Folks . . . easy now . . . I just want you to hold on . . . can't blame you for getting disturbed but it's not the way you think at all. The captain here has explained the situation to me and I can see, from where I'm standing, that this has nothing to do with our meeting. There's some kind of trouble over there on Fourteenth Street—NO!—don't move that way, you'll only get hurt, the police are there and they won't let you pass and there, I see them coming now, uptown there, the choppers, and the police have mentioned flying wire. . . ."

A moan followed the last words and the crowd shuddered, the restless movement reversed and they slowly began drifting uptown, out of Union Square, away from Fourteenth Street. The old people in this crowd knew all about flying wire.

Andy was past the speakers' platform and the crowd was thinner, he could now see the milling mob that jammed Fourteenth Street and he began to move quickly toward it.

There were policemen along the outer edge of it, clearing a space near the park, and the nearest one raised his night stick and shouted:

"Stay back there, buddy, or you're going to be in trouble."

He nodded when Andy showed him his badge, then turned away.

"What's up?" Andy asked.

"Got a real riot brewing here and it's gonna get worse before it's better—get back there you!" He rapped his stick on the curb and a bald man on aluminum crutches stopped and wavered a moment, then turned back into the park. "Klein's had one of those lightning-flash sales, you know, they suddenly put up signs in the windows and they got something that sells out quick, they done it before with no trouble. Only this time they had a shipment of soylent steaks—" He raised his voice to shout over the roar of the two approaching green and white copters. "Some chunk-head bought hers and went around the corner and ran into one of those roving TV reporters and blabbed the thing. People are pouring in from all over hell and gone and I don't think half the streets are blocked yet. Here's the wire now to seal off this side."

Andy pinned his badge to his shirt pocket and joined the patrolmen in pushing the crowd back as far as possible. The mob didn't protest; they looked up and shuddered away from the flapping roar of the copters, jamming together like cattle. The copters came low and the bales of wire fell from their bottoms. Rusty iron bales of barbed wire that thudded and clanked down hard enough to burst their sealed wrapping.

This was not ordinary barbed wire. It had a tempered-steel core of memory wire, metal that no matter how it was twisted or coiled would return to its original shape when the restraints were removed. Where ordinary wire would have lain in a heaped tangle this fought to regain its remembered form, moving haltingly like a blind beast as the strains and stresses were relieved, uncoiling and stretching along the street. Policemen wearing heavy gloves grabbed the ends and guided it in the right direction to form a barrier down the middle of the road. Two expanding coils met and fought a mindless battle, locking together and climbing into the air only to fall and struggle again and squirm on in a writhing union. When the last strand stopped scratching across the pavement the street was blocked by a yard-high and a yard-wide wall of spiked wire.

But the trouble wasn't over; people were still pushing in from the south along the streets that had not yet been sealed off by the wire. For the moment it was a screaming, pushing impasse because, though more wire would stop the influx, in order to drop the wire the crowd had to be pushed back and a clear space made. The police were shoved back and forth in the face of the surging mob and above their heads the copters buzzed about like angry bees.

A sudden exploding crash was followed by shrill screams. The pressure of the jammed bodies had burst one of the plate-glass show windows of Klein's and soft flesh was being jammed onto the knives of glass; there was blood and moans of pain. Andy fought his way against the tide toward the window; a woman with staring eyes and blood running from an open gash on her forehead bumped into him, then was carried away. Closer in, Andy could barely move and above the shouting of the voices he could hear the shrill of a police whistle. There were people climbing through the broken window, even walking on the bleeding bodies of the injured, grabbing at the boxes piled there. It was the back of the food department. Andy shouted as he came closer, he could barely hear his own voice in the uproar, and clutched at a man with his arms full of packages who forced his way out of the window. He couldn't reach him—but others could and the man writhed and fell under the grabbing hands, his packages eddying away from him.

"Stop!" Andy shouted. "Stop!" as helplessly as though he were locked in a nightmare. A thin Chinese boy in shorts and much-mended shirt crawled out of the window almost at his fingertips, holding a white box of soylent steaks against his chest, and Andy could only stretch his hands out helplessly. The boy looked at him, saw nothing, looked away and bending double to hide his burden began to wriggle along the edge of the crowd against the wall, his thin body forcing a way. Then only his legs were visible, muscles knotted as if he were fighting a rising tide, feet straining half out of the auto-tire-soled sandals. He was gone and Andy forgot him as he reached the broken window and pulled himself up beside the patrolman in the torn shirt who had preceded him there. The patrolman swung his night stick at the clutching arms and cleared a space. Andy joined him and skillfully sapped a looter who tried to break out between them, then pushed the unconscious body and spilled bundles back into the store. Sirens wailed and a splashing of white spray rose above the mob as the riot trucks began rumbling their way inward with water nozzles streaming.

2

Billy Chung managed to work the plastic container of soylent steaks up under his shirt and, when he bent half double, it wasn't easily noticeable. For a while he could still move, then the press became too much and he sheltered against the wall and pushed back at the forest of legs that hammered him and jammed his face against the hot dusty brick. He did not try to move and a knee caught him in the side of the head and half stunned him and the next thing he was aware of was a cool spray of water on his back. The riot trucks had arrived and their pressure hoses were breaking up the crowd. One of the columns of water swept over him, plastered him against the wall and went past. The push of the crowd was gone now and he tremblingly got to his feet, looking around to see if anyone had noticed his bundle, but no one had. The remnants of the mob, some of them bloody and bruised, all of them soaking wet, streamed past the lumbering riot trucks. Billy joined them and turned down Irving Place, where there were fewer people, and he looked desperately around for a hiding place, a spot where he could have a few moments of privacy, the hardest thing to find in this city. The riot was over and in a little while somebody would notice him and wonder what he had under his shirt and he would get it, but good. This wasn't his territory, there weren't even any Chinese in this neighborhood, they would spot him, they would see him. . . . He ran a bit but started to pant heavily and slowed down to a fast walk. There had to be something.

There. Repairs or something against one of the buildings,

a deep hole dug down to the foundation with pipes and a pool of muddy water at the bottom. He sat down next to the broken edge of the concrete sidewalk, leaned against one of the barriers that ringed the hole, bent forward and glanced around out of the corners of his eyes. No one looking at him, but plenty of people near, people coming out of the houses or sitting on the steps to watch the bedraggled mob move by. Running footsteps and a man came down the middle of the street holding a large parcel under his arm, glaring around with his fist clenched. Someone tripped him and he howled as he went down and the nearest people fell on him clutching for the crackers that spilled on the ground. Billy smiled, for the moment no one was watching him, and slid over the edge, going up to his ankles in the muddy bottom. They had dug around a foot-thick and corroded iron pipe making a shallow cave into which he backed. It wasn't perfect but it would do, do fine, only his feet could be seen from above. He lay sideways on the coolness of the earth and tore open the box.

Look at that—look at that, he said over and over again to himself and laughed as he realized he was beginning to drool and had to spit away the excess saliva. Soylent steaks, a whole boxful, each flat and brown and big as his hand. He bit into one, choked and wolfed it down, forcing crumbling pieces into his mouth with his dirty fingers until it was so full he could hardly swallow, chewing at the lovely softness. How long had it been since he had eaten anything like this?

Billy ate three of the soybean and lentil steaks that way, pausing every now and then between bites and poking his head cautiously out, brushing the lanky black hair from his eyes as he looked upward. No one was watching him. He took more out of the box, eating them slowly now, and only stopped when his stomach was stretched out tautly, and grumbling at the unusual condition of being stuffed so full. While he licked the last of the crumbs from his hands he worked on a plan, already feeling unhappy because he had eaten so many of the steaks. Loot was what he needed and steaks were loot and he could have stuffed his gut as well with weedcrackers. Hell. The white plastic box was too obvious to carry and too big to hide completely under his shirt, so he had to wrap the steaks in something. Maybe his handkerchief. He pulled this out, a dirty and crumpled rag cut from old sheeting, and wrapped it around the remaining ten steaks, tying the corners so they wouldn't fall out. When he tucked this under the waistband of his shorts it did not make too obvious a bulge, though it pressed uncomfortably against his full stomach. It was good enough.

"What you doing down that hole, kid?" one of the blowzy women seated on the nearby steps asked when he climbed back to the street.

"Blow it out!" he shouted as he ran for the corner followed by their harpy screams. Kid! He was eighteen years old even though he wasn't so tall, he was no kid. They thought they owned the world.

Until he got to Park Avenue he hurried, he didn't want to get any of the local gangs after him, then walked uptown with the slow-moving traffic until he reached the Madison Square flea market.

Crowded, hot, filled with a roar of many voices that hammered at the ears and noisome with the smell of old dirt, dust, crowded bodies; a slowly shifting maelstrom of people moving by, stopping at stalls to finger the ancient suits, dresses, chipped crockery, worthless ornaments, argue the price of the small tilapia dead with gaping mouths and startled round eyes. Hawkers shouted the merits of their decaying wares and people streamed along, carefully leaving room for the two hard-eyed policemen who walked side by side watching everything—but keeping to the main pathway that bisected the Square and led to the patched grayness of the old Army pyramidal tents of the long-established temporary tent city. The police stayed out of the narrow paths that twisted away through the jungle of pushcarts, stands and shelters that jammed the Square, the market where anything could be bought, anything sold. Billy stepped over the blind beggar who sprawled across the narrow opening between a concrete bench and the rickety stall of a seaweed vendor and worked his way inward. He looked at the people there, not at what they were selling, and finally stopped before a pushcart loaded with a jumble of ancient plastic containers, mugs, plates and bowls, with their once-bright colors scratched and grayed by time.

"Hands off!" The stick crashed down on the edge of the cart and Billy jerked his fingers away.

"I'm not touching your junk," he complained.

"Move on if you're not buying," the man said, an Oriental with lined cheeks and thin white hair.

"I'm not buying, I'm selling." Billy leaned closer and whispered so that only the man could hear. "You want some soylent steaks?"

The old man squinted at him. "Stolen goods, I suppose," he said tiredly.

"Come on—you want them or not?"

There was no humor in the man's fleeting smile. "Of course I want them. How many do you have?"

"Ten."

"A D and a half a piece. Fifteen dollars."

"Shit! I'll eat them myself first. Thirty D's for the lot."

"Don't let greed destroy you, son. We both know what they are worth. Twenty D's for the lot. Period." He fished out two worn ten-dollar bills and held them folded in his fingers. "Let's see what you have."

Billy pushed the stuffed handkerchief across and the man held it under the cart and looked inside. "All right," he said, and still with his hands beneath the cart transferred them to a square of heavy, wrinkled paper and handed back the cloth. "I don't need that."

"The loot now."

The man handed it over slowly, smiling now that the transaction was finished. "Do you ever come to the Mott Street club?"

"Are you kidding?" Billy grabbed for the money and the man released it.

"You should. You're Chinese, and you brought these steaks to me because I'm Chinese too and you knew you could trust me. That shows you're thinking right. . . ."

"Knock it off, will you, grandpa." He hit himself in the chest with his thumb. "I'm Taiwan and my father was a general. So one thing I know—have nothing to do with you downtown Commie Chinks."

"You stupid punk—" He raised his stick but Billy was already gone.

Things were going to change now, yes they were! He did not notice the heat as he dodged automatically through the milling crowds, seeing the future ahead and holding tight to the money in his pocket. Twenty D's—more than he had ever owned at one time in his life. The most he had ever had before was three-eighty that he had lifted from the apartment across the hall the time they had left their window open. It was hard to get your hands on cash money, and cash money was the only thing that counted. They never saw any at home. The Welfare ration cards took care of everything, everything that kept you alive and just alive enough to hate it. You needed cash to get on and cash was what he had now. He had been thinking about this for a long time.

He turned into the Chelsea branch of Western Union on Ninth Avenue. The pasty-faced girl behind the high counter looked up and her glance slid away from him and out the wide front window to the surging, sunlit traffic beyond. She dabbed at the sweat droplets on her lip with a crumpled handkerchief, then wiped the creases under her chin. The operators, bent over their work, didn't look up. It was quiet here with just the distant hum of the city through the open door, the sudden lurching motion as a teletype clattered loudly. On a bench against the rear wall six boys sat looking at him suspiciously, their searching eyes ready to fill with hatred. As he went toward the dispatcher he could hear their feet shifting on the floor and the squeak of the bench. He had to force himself not to turn and look as he waited, imitating patience, for the man to notice him.

"What do you want, kid?" the dispatcher said, finally looking up, speaking through tight, pursed lips reluctant to give anything away, even words. A man in his fifties, tired and hot, angry at a world that had promised him more.

"Could you use a messenger boy, mister?"

"Beat it. We got too many kids already."

"I could use the work, mister, I'd work any time you say. I got the board money." He took out one of the ten-dollar bills and smoothed it on the counter. The man's eyes glared at it quickly, then jerked away again. "We got too many kids."

The bench creaked and footsteps came up behind Billy and a boy spoke, his voice thick with restrained anger.

"Is this Chink bothering you, Mr. Burgger?" Billy thrust the money back into his pocket and held tightly to it.

"Sit down, Roles," the man said. "You know my rule about trouble or fighting."

He glared at the two boys and Billy could guess what the rule was and knew that he wouldn't be working here unless he did something quickly.

"Thank you for letting me talk to you, Mr. Burgger," he said, innocently, as he felt back with his heel and jammed his weight down on the boy's toes as he turned. "I won't bother you any more—"

The boy shouted and pain burst in Billy's ear as the fist lashed out and caught him. He staggered and looked shocked but made no attempt to defend himself.

"All right, Roles," Mr. Burgger said distastefully. "You're through here, get lost."

"But—Mr. Burgger . . ." he howled unhappily. "You don't know this Chink. . . ."

"Get out!" Mr. Burgger half rose and pointed angrily at the gaping boy. "Out!"

Billy moved to one side, unnoticed and forgotten for the moment, and knew enough not to smile. It finally penetrated to the boy that there was nothing he could do and he left—after hurling a look of burning malice at Billy—while Mr. Burgger scratched on one of the message boards.

"All right, kid, it looks like you maybe got a job. What's your name?"

"Billy Chung."

"We pay fifty cents every telegram you deliver." He stood and walked to the counter holding the board. "You take a telegram out you leave a ten-buck board deposit. When you bring the board back you get ten-fifty. That clear?"

He laid the board down on the counter between them and his eyes glanced down to it. Billy looked and read the chalked words: *fifteen cent kickback*.

"That's fine with me, Mr. Burgger."

"All right." The heel of his hand removed the message. "Get on the bench and shut up. Any fighting, any trouble, any noise, and you get what Roles got."

"Yes, Mr. Burgger."

When he sat down the other boys stared at him suspiciously but said nothing. After a few minutes a dark little boy, even smaller than he, leaned over and mumbled, "How much kickback he ask?"

"What do you mean?"

"Don't be a chunkhead. You kick back or you don't work here."

"Fifteen."

"I told you he would do it," another boy whispered fiercely. "I told you he wouldn't keep it at ten. . . ." He shut up abruptly when the dispatcher glared in their direction.

After this the day rolled by with hot evenness and Billy was glad to sit and do nothing. Some of the boys took telegrams out, but he was never called. The soylent steaks were sitting like lead in his stomach and twice he had to go back to the dark and miserable toilet in the rear of the building. The shadows were longer in the street outside but the air still held the same breathless heat that it had for the past ten days. Soon after six o'clock three more boys trickled in and found places on the crowded bench. Mr. Burgger looked at the group with his angry expression, it seemed to be the only one he had.

"Some of you kids get lost."

Billy had had enough for the first day so he left. His knees were stiff from sitting and the steaks had descended far enough so he began to think about dinner. Hell, he grimaced sourly, he knew what they would have for dinner. The same as every other night and every other year. On the waterfront there was a little breeze from the river and he walked slowly along Twelfth Avenue and felt it cool upon his arms. Behind the sheds here, with no one in sight for the moment, he pried open one of the wire clips that held on the tire sole of his sandal and slipped the two bills into the crack. They were his and his only. He tightened the clip and climbed the steps that led to the *Waverly Brown* which was moored to Pier 62.

The river was invisible. Secured together by frayed ropes and encrusted chains the rows of ancient Victory and Liberty ships made up an alien and rusty landscape of odd-shaped superstructures, laundry-hung rigging, supports, pipes, aerials and chimneys. Beyond them was the single pier of the never-completed Wagner Bridge. This view did not seem strange to Billy because he had been born here after his family and the other Formosa refugees had settled into these temporary quarters, hastily constructed on the ships that had been rotting, unwanted, at their mooring up the river at Stony Point ever since the Second World War. There had been no other place to house the flood of newcomers and the ships had seemed a brilliant inspiration at the time; they would certainly do until something better was found. But it had been hard to find other quarters and more ships had been gradually added until the rusty, weed-hung fleet was such a part of the city that everyone felt it had been there forever.

Bridges and gangways connected the ships and occasionally there would be a glimpse of foul, garbage-filled water between them. Billy worked his way over to the *Columbia Victory,* his home, and down the gangway to apartment 107.

"About time you got in," his sister Anna said. "Everyone's through eating and you're lucky I saved you anything." She took his plate from a high shelf and put it on the table. She was only thirty-seven yet her hair was almost gray, her back bent into a permanent stoop, her hope of leaving the family and Shiptown was long since gone. She was the only one of the Chung children who had been born in Formosa, though she had been so young when they left that her memories of the island were just vague and muted echoes of a pleasant dream.

Billy looked down at the damp slices of oatmeal and the brown crackers and felt his throat close up: the steaks were still clear in his memory, spoiling him for this. "I'm not hungry," he said, pushing it away.

His mother had caught the motion and turned from the TV set, the first time she had bothered to notice him since he had come in.

"What is the matter with the food? Why are you not eating the food? That is good food." Her voice was thin and high-pitched with a rasping whine made more obvious because she spoke in intonated Cantonese. She had never bothered to learn more than a few words of English and the family never spoke it at home.

"I'm not hungry." He groped for a lie that would satisfy her. "It's too hot. Here, you eat it."

"I would never take food from my children's mouths. If you won't eat it the twins will." While she talked she kept looking at the TV screen and the thunder of its amplified voices almost drowned out hers, throbbing against the shriller screeches of the seven-year-old boys who were fighting over a toy in the corner. "Here, give it to me. I'll have just a bite myself first, I give most of my food to the children." She put a cracker to her mouth and began to chew it with quick, rodentlike motions. There was little chance that the twins would see any of it since she was a specialist in consuming crumbs, leftover scraps, odds and ends; the pudgy roundness of her figure showed that. She took a second cracker from the dish without moving her eyes from the screen.

The heat and the nausea he was still feeling choked at Billy's throat. He was suddenly aware of the closeness of the steel-walled compartment, his brothers' whining voices, the scratchy roar of the TV, his sister rattling the plates as she cleared up. He went into the other room, the only other room they had, and pulled the heavy metal door shut after him. It had been a locker of some kind, it was only six foot square and was almost completely filled by the bed on which his mother and sister slept. A window had been made in the hull, just a rectangular opening with the ragged thirty-year-old marks of the cutting torch still clear around the edge. In the winter they bolted a cover over it, but now he could lean his arms on the opening and look across the crowded ships to the distant lights on the New Jersey shore. It was almost dark, yet the air on his face felt just as hot as it had all day.

When the sharp edges of the metal began to cut into his arms he went and washed up in the basin of murky water behind the door. There wasn't much of it, but he scrubbed his face and arms and plastered his hair back as well as he could in the tiny mirror fixed to the wall, then turned quickly away and pulled down the corners of his mouth. His face was so round and young and when he relaxed, his mouth always had a slight curve so that he seemed to be smiling, and that was not how he felt. His face lied about him. With the last of the water he rubbed down his bare legs and removed most of the dirt and mud; at least he felt cooler now. He went and lay on the bed and looked at the photograph of his father on the wall, the only decoration in the room. Captain Chung Pei-fu of the Koumintang Army. A career soldier who had dedicated his life to war and who had never fought a battle. Born in 1940, he had grown up on Formosa and had been one of the second-generation soldiers in Chiang Kai-shek's time-marking, aging army. When the Generalissimo had died suddenly at the age of eighty-four Captain Chung had had no part in the palace revolutions that had finally pushed General Kung to the top. And when the disastrous invasion of the mainland had finally taken place he had been in the hospital, ill with malaria, and had stayed there during the Seven Deadly Days. He had been one of the very first people airlifted to safety when the island fell—even before his family. In the photograph he looked stern and military, not unhappy the way Billy had always known him. He had committed suicide the day after the twins had been born.

Like a vanishing memory the photograph faded from sight in the darkness, then appeared again, dimly seen, as the small light bulb brightened and dimmed as the current fluctuated. Billy watched as the light faded even more, until just the filament glowed redly, then went out. They were cutting the current earlier tonight, or probably something was wrong again. He lay in the suffocating darkness and felt the bed grow hot and sodden under his back, and the walls of the iron box closed in on him until he could stand it no more. His moist fingers groped along the door until they found the handle and when he went into the other room it was no better, worse if anything. The flickering greenish light of the TV screen played over the shining faces of his mother, his sister, his two brothers, transforming their gape-jawed and wide-eyed faces into those of newly drowned corpses. From the speaker beat the tattoo of galloping hoofs and the sound of endless six-shooter gunfire. His mother squeezed mechanically on the old generator flashlight that had been wired to the set, so that it could be played when the house current was off. She noticed him when he tried to go by and held out the generator to him, still contracting mechanically.

"You will squeeze this, my hand is tired."

"I'm going out. Let Anna do it."

"You will do what I say," she shrilled. "You will obey me. A boy must obey his mother." She was so angry she forgot to work the generator and the screen went black and the twins began crying at once, while Anna called to them to be quiet and added to the confusion. He did not go out—he fled—and did not stop until he was on deck, breathing hoarsely and covered with sweat.

There was nothing to do, no place to go, the city pressed in around him and every square foot of it was like this, filled with people, children, noise, heat. He gagged over the rail into the darkness but nothing came up.

Automatically, scarcely aware he was doing it, he threaded his way through the black maze to the shore then hurried toward the wide-spaced street lights of Twenty-third Street: it was dangerous to be in the darkness of the

city at night. Maybe he should take a look into Western
Union, or maybe he better not bother them so soon? He
turned into Ninth Avenue and looked at the yellow and blue
sign and chewed his lip uncertainly. A boy came out and
hurried away with a message board under his arm; that
made room for another one. He would go in.

When he turned into the doorway his heart thudded as he
saw that the bench was empty. Mr. Burgger looked up from
his desk and the anger was as fresh on his face as it had been
that afternoon.

"It's a good thing you made up your mind to come back
or you just wouldn't have had to bother coming back. Everything is moving tonight, I don't know why. Get this delivered." He finished scrawling an address on the cover, then
slipped the gummed-paper seal through the hole in the
hinged boards and licked it and sealed it shut. "Cash on the
counter." He slapped the board down.

The clip wouldn't unbend and Billy broke a fingernail
when he had to work the money out and unroll one of the
bills and slide it across the scratched wood. He held tight to
the other bill, clutched at the board and hurried out,
stopping with his back to the wall as soon as he was out of
sight of the office. There was enough light from the
illuminated sign to read the address:

Michael O'Brien
Chelsea Park North
W. 28 St.

He knew the address and, though he had passed the
buildings an untold number of times, he had never been
inside the solid cliff of luxury apartments that had been built
in 1976 after a spectacular bit of corruption had permitted
the city to turn Chelsea Park over to private development.
They were walled, terraced and turreted in new-feudal style,
which appearance perfectly matched their function of
keeping the masses as separate and distant as possible.
There was a service entrance in the rear, dimly lit by a wire-
caged bulb concealed in a carved stone cresset, and he
pressed the button beneath it.

"This entrance is closed until oh-five hundred hours," a
recorded voice clattered at him and he held the board to his
chest in a quick spasm of fear. Now he would have to go

around to the front entrance with its lights, the doorman, the people there; he looked down at his bare legs and tried to brush away some of the older stains. He was clean enough now, but there was nothing he could do about the ragged and patched clothing. Normally he never noticed this because everyone else he met was dressed the same way, it was just that things were different here, he knew that. He didn't want to face the people in this building, he regretted that he had ever worked to get this job, and he walked around the corner towards the brilliantly lit entrance.

A pondlike moat, now just a dry receptacle for rubbish, was crossed by a fixed walkway tricked out to look like a drawbridge, complete with rusty chains and a dropped portcullis of spike-ended metal bars backed by heavy glass. Walking the brightly lit path of the bridge was like walking into the jaws of hell. The bulky figure of the doorman was silhouetted behind the bars ahead, hands behind his back, and he did not move even after Billy had stopped, just inches away on the other side of the barred glass, but kept staring down at him coldly with no change of expression. The door did not open. Not trusting himself to say anything, Billy held up the message board so the name could be seen on the outside. The doorman's eyes flicked over it and he reluctantly touched one of the decorative whorls and a section of bars and glass slid aside with a muffled sigh.

"I got a message here. . . ." Billy was unhappily aware of the uncertainty and fear in his voice.

"Newton, front," the doorman said and jerked his thumb at Billy to enter.

A door opened on the far side of the lobby and there was a rumble of masculine laughter, suddenly cut off as a man came out and closed the door behind him. He was dressed in a uniform like the doorman's, deep black with gold buttons, but with only a curl of red braid on each shoulder rather than the other's resplendent frogging. "What's up, Charlie?" he asked.

"Kid with a telegram, I never saw him before." Charlie turned his back on them and resumed his watchdog position before the door, his duty done.

"The board is good," Newton said, twisting it from Billy's grasp before he realized what was happening, and running his fingers over the indented Western Union trademark. He handed it back and when Billy took it he quickly patted his shirt and shorts, under the arms and in the crotch.

"He's clean," then he laughed, "except I gotta go wash my hands now."

"All right, kid," the doorman said without turning, his back still to Billy, "bring it up and get down here again, quick."

The guard had his back turned too as he walked away leaving Billy alone in the center of the lobby, in the middle of the stretch of figured carpet with no sign of what to do or where to go next. He wanted to ask directions but he couldn't, the automatic contempt and superiority of the men had disarmed him, driven him down so that all he wanted to do was find a place to hide. A gliding hiss from the far end of the room drew his numbed attention and he saw an elevator door slide open in the base of what he had taken to be a giant church organ. The operator was looking at him and Billy started forward, the telegram board held before him as though it were a shield against the hostility of the environment.

"I got a message here for Mr. O'Brien." His voice quavered and almost cracked. The operator, a boy no older than he was, produced a half-authentic sneer; he was young but was already working hard at learning the correct staff manners.

"O'Brien, 41-E, and that's on the fifth floor in case you don't know anything about apartment houses." He stood, blocking the elevator entrance, and Billy was uncertain what to do next.

"Should I . . . I mean, the elevator . . ."

"You ain't stinking up this elevator for the tenants. The stairs are down that way."

Billy felt the angry eyes following him as he walked down the hall and some of the anger caught in him. Why did they have to act like that? Just working in a place like this didn't mean they lived here. That would be a laugh—them living in a place like this. Even that fat chunk of a doorman. Five flights—he was panting for breath before he had reached the second and had to stop and wipe off some of the sweat when he got to the fifth. The hall stretched away in both directions, with alcoved doors opening off of it and an occasional suit of armor standing guard over its empty length. His skin prickled with sweat; the air was breathless and hot.

He started in the wrong direction and had to retrace his steps when he found out that the numbers were decreasing toward zero. Number 41-E was like all the others without a button or knocker, just a small plate with the gilt script word *O'Brien* on it. The door opened when he touched it and, after looking in first, he entered a small, darkly paneled chamber with another door before him; a sort of medieval airlock. He had a feeling of panic when the door closed behind him and a voice spoke, apparently from thin air.

"What do you want?"

"A telegram, Western Union," he said and looked around the empty cubicle for the source of the voice.

"Let me see your board."

It was then he realized that the voice was coming from a grille above the inner door, next to the glassy eye of a TV pickup. He held up the board so that it could be seen by the orthicon. This must have satisfied the unseen watcher because there was the click of the circuit going dead and shortly after that the door opened before him, letting out a wave of chilled air.

"Let me have it," Michael O'Brien said, and Billy handed him the board and waited while the man broke the seal with his thumb and opened the hinged halves.

Though he was in his late fifties, iron gray, carrying an impressive paunch and a double row of jewels, O'Brien still bore the marks of his early years on the West Side docks. Scars on his knuckles and on the side of his neck—and a broken nose that had never been set correctly. In 1966 he had been a twenty-two-year-old punk, as he was fond of saying when he told the story, with nothing on his mind but booze and broads and a couple of days' stevedoring a week to pay for the weekends, but when he had walked into a roundhouse swing in a brawl at the Shamrock Bar and Grill it had changed his life for him. While recovering in St. Vincent's (the nose had healed quickly enough but he had fractured his skull on the floor) he had taken a long look at his life and decided to make something of it. What it was he made he never added when he told the story, but it was common knowledge that he had become involved with ward politics, the disposal of hijacked goods from the docks and a number of other things that were best not to mention in his hearing. In any case his new interests paid better than stevedoring and he had never regretted a moment of it. Six

foot two, and swaddled in an immense and colorful dressing
gown like a circus elephant, he could have been ludicrous,
but wasn't. He had seen too much, done too much, was too
sure of his power ever to be laughed at—even though he
moved his lips when he read and frowned in concentration
while he spelled out the telegram.

"Wait there, I want to make a copy of this," he said when
he came to the end. Billy nodded, happy to wait as long as
possible in the air-cooled, richly decorated hall. "Shirl,
where the hell is the pad?" O'Brien shouted.

There was a mumbled answer from the door on the left
and O'Brien opened it and went into the room. Billy's eyes
automatically followed him through the lit doorway to the
white-sheeted bed and the woman lying there.

She lay with her back turned, unclothed, red hair
sweeping across the pillow, her skin a whitish pink with a
scattering of brown freckles across the shoulders. Billy
Chung stood unmoving, his breath choked in his throat; she
wasn't ten feet away. She crossed one leg over the other, ac-
centuating the round swell of buttock. O'Brien was talking
to her but the words came through as meaningless sounds.
Then she rolled over toward the open door and saw him.

There was nothing he could do, he could not move and he
could not turn his eyes away. She *saw* him looking at her.

The girl on the bed smiled at him, then reached out a
slender arm to the door, her breasts rose full and round,
pink tipped—the door swung shut and she was gone.

When O'Brien opened the door and came out a minute
later she was no longer on the bed.

"Any answer?" Billy asked as he took back the message
board. Did his voice sound as strange to this man as it did to
him?

"No, no answer," O'Brien said as he opened the hall
door. Time seemed to be moving slowly now for Billy, he
clearly saw the door as it opened, the shining tongue of the
lock, the flat piece of metal on the wall with the hanging
wires. Why were these important?

"Aren't you gonna give me a tip, mister?" he asked, just
to occupy a moment more.

"Beat it, kid, before I boot your chunk."

He was in the hall and the heat hit him doubly hard after
the cool apartment, pressing on his skin and meeting the
spreading warm that suffused the lower part of his body,

just the kind of feeling he had the first time he got near a girl; he rested his head against the wall. Even in the pictures they passed around he had never seen a girl like this. All the ones he had banged had been glimpsed briefly in a dim light or not at all, thin limbs, gray skins, dirty as he, with ragged underclothing.

Of course. A single lock on the inner door guarded by the burglar alarm above. But the alarm was disconnected, he had seen the dangling wires. He had learned about things like this when Sam-Sam had run the Tigers, they had broken into stores and done a couple of jobs of burglary before the cops shot Sam-Sam. A sharp jimmy would open that door in a second. But what did this have to do with the girl? She had smiled, hadn't she? She could be there waiting when the old bastard went to work.

It was a lot of crap and he knew it, the girl wouldn't have anything to do with him. But she had smiled? The apartment was different, a quick job before the wiring was fixed, he knew the layout of the building—if only there was a way of getting by those chunkheads at the front door. This had nothing to do with the girl, this was for cash. He went quietly down the stairs, looking carefully before turning the corner on the ground floor and hurrying on to the basement.

You had to ride your luck. He didn't meet anyone and in the second room he entered he found a window that also had a disconnected burglar alarm on it. Maybe the whole building was like that, they were rewiring it or it had broken and they couldn't fix it, it didn't matter. The window was covered with dust and he reached up and drew a heart in the film of dust so he could recognize it from the outside.

"You took a long time, kid," the doorman said when he came up.

"I had to wait while he copied the message and wrote an answer, I can't help it." He whined the lie with unsuspected sincerity, it was easy.

The doorman didn't ask to look at the board. With a pneumatic hiss the portcullis opened and he went across the empty drawbridge to the dark, crowded, dirty and stifling street.

3

Behind the low hum of the air-conditioner, so steady a
sound that the ear accepted it and no longer heard it, was
the throbbing rumble of the city outside, beating like a great
pulse, more felt than heard. Shirl liked that, liked its
distance and the closed-in and safe feeling the night and
thickness of the walls gave her. It was late, 3:24 the glowing
numbers on the clock read, then changed soundlessly to
3:25 while she watched. She shifted position and beside her
in the wide bed Mike stirred and mumbled something in his
sleep and she lay perfectly still, hoping he wouldn't wake
up. After a moment he settled down, pulling the sheet over
his shoulders, his breathing grew slow and steady again and
she relaxed. The motion of the air was drying the
perspiration from her skin, a cool feeling the length of her
uncovered body, strangely satisfying. Before he had come
to bed and wakened her she had had a few hours' sleep and
that seemed to be enough. Moving slowly, she stood and
walked over in front of the flow of air so that it washed her
body in its stream. She ran her hands over her skin, wincing
when they touched her sore breasts. He was always too
rough and it showed on her kind of skin; she'd be black-and-
blue tomorrow, then she'd have to put heavy makeup on to
cover the marks. Mike got angry if he saw her with any
blemishes or bruises, though he never seemed to think of
that when he was hurting her. Above the air-conditioner the
curtains were open a crack and the darkness of the city
looked in, the widely separated lights like the eyes of
animals; she quickly closed the curtains and patted them so
they would stay shut.

Mike gave a deep, throaty gargle, a startling sound when
you weren't used to it, but Shirl had heard it often enough.
When he snored like that it meant he was really sound
asleep—maybe she could take a shower without his
knowing it! Her bare feet were noiseless on the rug and she
closed the bathroom door so slowly it never made a click.

There! She switched on the fluorescents and smiled around at the plast-marble interior and the gold-covered fixtures with highlights glinting everywhere. The walls were sound-proof but if he wasn't really deeply asleep he might hear the water knocking in the pipes. A sudden fear hit her and she gasped and stood on tiptoe to look at the water me-ter. Yes, her breath escaped in a relaxed sigh, he had turned it on. With water costing what it did Mike turned it off and locked it during the day, the help had been stealing so much, and he had forbidden her to take any more showers. But he always took showers and if she sneaked one once in a while he couldn't tell from the dial.

It was cool and lovely and she stayed in it longer than she had meant to; she looked guiltily at the meter. After she had dried herself she used the towel to mop up every drop of water in the tub and on the walls and floor, then buried the towel in the bottom of the hamper where he would never see it. Her skin tingled and she felt wonderful. She smiled to herself as she patted on dusting powder. You're twenty-three, Shirl, and your dress size hasn't changed since you were nineteen. Except in the bust maybe, she was using a bigger bra, but that was all right because men liked it that way. She took a clean housecoat from the cupboard and slipped it on.

Mike was still sawing away when she passed through the bedroom, he seemed to be exhausted these days, probably tired from carrying around all that weight in this heat. In the year she had been living here he must have put on twenty pounds, most of it around the middle it looked like, but it didn't seem to bother him and she tried not to notice it. She turned on the TV to warm up, and then went into the kitchen to make a drink. The expensive stuff, the beer and the single bottle of whiskey, were for Mike only, but she didn't mind, she really didn't care what she drank as long as it tasted nice. There was a bottle of vodka, Mike could get all of that they needed, and it tasted good mixed with the orange concentrate. If you added some sugar.

A man's head filled the fifty-inch screen mouthing unheard words, looking right out at her; she pulled the gaping front of her housecoat closed and buttoned it. She smiled at herself when she did it, as she always did, because even though she knew the man couldn't see her it made her uncomfortable. The remote-box was on the arm of the couch and she curled up next to it with the drink and tapped the button. On the next channel was an auto race and on the next an old John Barrymore picture that looked jerky and ancient and she didn't like it. She went through most of the channels this way until she settled, as she usually did, on Channel 19, the Woman's Own Channel, which showed nothing but soap-opera serials, one serial at a time with all the episodes compacted together into a single great, glutinous chunk sometimes running up to twenty-four hours. This was one she hadn't seen before and when she plugged the earphone into the remote she discovered why, it was a British serial of some kind. The people all had strange accents and some of the things they did were a little hard to follow, but it was interesting enough. A woman had just given birth, sweating and without makeup, when she tuned in and the woman's husband was in jail but the news had come he had just escaped, and the man who was the father of the baby—a blue baby, they had just discovered—was her husband's brother. Shirl took a sip of the drink and snuggled down comfortably.

At six o'clock she turned off the set, washed and dried her glass and went in to get her clothes. Tab came on duty at seven and she wanted to get the shopping done as early as possible, before the worst of the heat. Quietly, so as not to wake Mike, she found her clothes and took them into the living room to dress. Panties and the net bra and her gray sleeveless dress, it was old enough and faded enough to go shopping in. No jewelry and of course no makeup, there was no point in looking for trouble. She never ate breakfast, that was a good way to watch calories, but she did have a cup of black kofee before she left. It was just seven when she checked to see if her key and money were in her purse, took the big shopping bag from the drawer and let herself out.

"Good morning, miss," the elevator boy said, opening the door with a flourish and giving her a smile that displayed a row of not too good teeth. "Looks like another scorcher today."

"It's eighty-two already, the news said."

"That's not the half of it." The door closed and they whined down the shaft. "They take that temperature on top of the building and I bet down near the street it's a lot more than that."

"You're probably right."

In the lobby the doorman Charlie saw her when the elevator opened and he spoke into his concealed microphone. "Going to be another hot one," he said when she came up.

"Morning, Miss Shirl," Tab said, coming out of the guardroom. She smiled, happy to see him as she always was, the nicest bodyguard she had ever known—and the only one who had never made a pass at her. She liked him not because of that but because he was the kind of man who would never even think of a thing like that. Happily married with three kids, she had heard all about Amy and the boys, he just wasn't that kind of man.

He was a good bodyguard though. You didn't have to see the iron knucks on his left hand to know he could take care of himself; though he wasn't tall, the width of his shoulders and the swelling muscles on his arms told their own story. He took the purse from her, buttoning it into his deep side pocket, and carried the shopping bag. When the door opened he went out first, bad party manners but good bodyguard manners. It was hot, even worse than she had expected.

"No weather report from you, Tab?" she asked, blinking through the heat at the already crowded street.

"I think you've heard enough of them already, Miss Shirl, I know I must have collected about a dozen on the way over this morning." He didn't look at her while he talked, his eyes swept the street automatically and professionally. He usually moved slowly and talked slowly and this was deliberate because some people expected a Negro to be that way. When trouble began it usually ended an instant later, since he firmly believed it was the first blow that counted and if you did that correctly there was no need for a second one, or more.

"After anything special today?" he asked.

"Just shopping for dinner and I have to go to Schmidt's."

"Going to take a cab crosstown and save your energy for the battle?"

"Yes—I think I will this morning." Cabs were certainly cheap enough, she usually walked just because she liked it, but not in this heat. There was a waiting row of pedicabs already, with most of the drivers squatting in the meager

shade of their rear seats. Tab led the way to the second one
in line and steadied the back so that she could climb in.

"What's the matter with me?" the first driver asked
angrily.

"You got a flat tire, that's what's the matter with you,"
Tab said quietly.

"It's not flat, just a little low, you can't—"

"Shove off!" Tab hissed and raised his clenched fist a few
inches; the sharpened iron spikes gleamed. The man
climbed quickly into his saddle and pedaled off down the
street. The other drivers turned away and said nothing.
"Gramercy Market," he told the second driver.

The cab driver pedaled slowly so that Tab could keep up
without running, yet the man was still sweating. His
shoulders went up and down right in front of Shirl and she
could see the rivulets of perspiration running down his neck
and even the dandruff on his thin hair; being this close to
people bothered her. She turned to look at the street. People
shuffling by, other cabs moving past the slower-moving
tugtrucks with their covered loads. The bar on the corner of
Park Avenue had a sign out saying BEER TODAY—2
P.M. and there were some people already lined up there. It
seemed a long wait for a glass of beer, particularly at the
prices they were charging this summer. There never was
very much, they were always talking about grain allotments
or something, but in the hot weather it was gone as soon as
they got it in, and at fantastic prices. They turned down
Lexington and stopped at the corner of Twenty-first Street
and she got out and waited in the shade of the building while
Tab paid the driver. A hoarse roar of voices came from the
stalls in the food market that had smothered Gramercy
Park. She took a deep breath and, with Tab close beside her
so that she could rest her hand on his arm, she crossed the
street.

Around the entrance were the weedcracker stalls with
their hanging rows of multicolored crackers reaching high
overhead, brown, red, blue-green.

"Three pounds of green," she told the man at the stand
where she always shopped, then looked at the price card.
"Another ten cents a pound!"

"That's the price I gotta pay, lady, no more profit for
me." He put a weight on the balance scale and shook
crackers onto the other side.

"But why should they keep raising the price?" She took a broken piece of cracker from the scale and chewed it. The color came from the kind of seaweed the crackers were made from and the green always tasted better to her, less of the iodiney flavor than the others had.

"Supply and demand, supply and demand." He dumped the crackers into the shopping bag while Tab held it open. "The more people there is the less to go around there is. And I hear they have to farm weed beds farther away. The longer the trip the higher the price." He delivered this litany of cause and effect in a monotone voice like a recording that has been played many times before.

"I don't know how people manage," Shirl said as they walked away, and felt a little guilty because with Mike's bankroll she didn't have to worry. She wondered how she would get along on Tab's salary, she knew just how little he earned. "Want a cracker?" she asked.

"Maybe later, thanks." He was watching the crowd and deftly shouldered aside a man with a large sack on his back who almost ran into her.

A guitar band was slowly working its way through the crowded market, three men strumming homemade instruments and a thin girl whose small voice was lost in the background roar. When they came closer Shirl could make out some of the words, it had been the hit song last year, the one the El Troubadors sang.

"... on earth above her ... As pure a thought as angels are ... to know her was to love her."

The words couldn't possibly fit this girl and her hollow chest and scrawny arms, not ever. For some reason it made Shirl uncomfortable.

"Give them a dime," she whispered to Tab, then moved quickly to the dairy stand. When Tab came after her she dropped a package of oleo and a small bottle of soymilk—Mike liked it in his kofee—into the bag.

"Tab, will you please remind me to bring the bottles back—this is the fourth one now! And with a deposit of two dollars apiece I'll be broke soon if I don't remember."

"I'll tell you tomorrow, if you're going shopping then."

"I'll probably have to. Mike is having some people in for

dinner and I don't know how many yet or even what he wants to serve."

"Fish, that's always good," Tab said, pointing to the big concrete tank of water. "The tank is full."

Shirl stood on tiptoe and saw the shoals of tilapia stirring uneasily in the obscured depths.

"Fresh Island 'lapia," the fish woman said. "Come in last night from Lake Ronkonkoma." She dipped in her net and hauled out a writhing load of six-inch fish.

"Will you have them tomorrow?" Shirl asked. "I want them fresh."

"All you want, honey, got more coming tonight."

It was hotter and there was really nothing else that she needed here, so that left just one more stop to make.

"I guess we better go to Schmidt's now," she said and something in her voice made Tab glance at her for a moment before he returned to his constant surveillance of the crowd.

"Sure, Miss Shirl, it'll be cooler there."

Schmidt's was in the basement of a fire-gutted building on Second Avenue, just a black shell above street level with a few squatters' shanties among the charred timber. An alleyway led around to the back and three steps went down to a heavy green door with a peephole in the center. A body-guard squatted in the shade against the wall, only customers were allowed into Schmidt's, and lifted his hand in a brief greeting to Tab. There was a rattle of a lock and an elderly man with sweeping white hair climbed the steps one at a time.

"Good morning, Judge," Shirl said. Judge Santini and O'Brien saw a good deal of each other and she had met him before.

"Why, a good morning to you, Shirl." He handed a small white package to his bodyguard, who slipped it into his pocket. "That is I wish it was a good morning but it is too hot for me, I'm afraid, the years press on. Say hello to Mike for me."

"I will, Judge, good-by."

Tab handed her purse to her and she went down and knocked on the door. There was a movement behind the tiny window of the peephole, then metal clanked and the door swung open. It was dark and cool. She walked in.

"Well if it ain't Miss Shirl, hiya honey," the man at the

door said as he swung it shut and pushed home the heavy steel bolt that locked it. He settled back on the high stool against the wall and cradled his double-barreled shotgun in his arms. Shirl didn't answer him, she never did. Schmidt looked up from the counter and smiled a wide, porcine grin.

"Why hiya, Shirl, come to get a nice little something for Mr. O'Brien?" He planted his big red hands solidly on the counter and his thick body, wrapped in blood-spattered white cloth, half rested on the top. She nodded but before she could say anything the guard called out.

"Show her some of the sweetmeat, Mr. Schmidt, I'll bet she goes for that."

"I don't think so, Arnie, not for Shirl." They both laughed loudly and she tried to smile and picked at the edge of the sheet of paper on the counter.

"I'd like steak or a piece of beef, if you have any," she said, and they laughed again. They always did this, knowing how far they could go without causing trouble. They knew about her and Mike and never did or said anything that would cause trouble with him. She had tried to tell him about it once, but there was no one thing she could tell him that they did that was wrong, and he had even laughed at one of their jokes and told her that they were just playing around and not to worry, that you couldn't expect party manners from meatleggers.

"Look at this, Shirl." Schmidt clanked open the box door on the wall behind him and took out a small flayed carcass. "Good leg of dog, nicely hung, good and fat too."

It did look good, but it was not for her so there was just no point in looking. "It's very nice, but you know Mr. O'Brien likes beef."

"Harder to get these days, Shirl." He moved deeper into the box. "Trouble with suppliers, jacking up the price, you know how it is. But Mr. O'Brien has been trading here with me for ten years and as long as I can get it I'm going to see he gets his share. How's that?" He came out and kicked the door shut, holding up a small piece of meat with a thin edging of white fat.

"It looks very good."

"Little over a half pound, big enough?"

"Just right." He took it from the scale and began to wrap it in pliofilm. "That'll set you back just twenty-seven ninety."

"Isn't that . . . I mean more expensive than last time?"
Mike always blamed her when she spent too much on food,
as if she were responsible for the prices, yet he still insisted
on eating meat.

"That's how it is, Shirl. Tell you what I'll do though, give
me a kiss and I'll knock off the ninety cents. Maybe even
give you a piece of meat myself." He and the guard laughed
uproariously at this. It was just a joke, like Mike said, there
was nothing she could say; she took the money from her
purse.

"Here you are, Mr. Schmidt, twenty . . . twenty-five . . .
twenty-eight." She took the tiny slate from her purse and
wrote the price on it and placed it next to the money.
Schmidt looked at it, then scratched an initial S under it with
a piece of blue chalk he always used. When Mike
complained about the price of meat she would show this to
him, not that it ever helped.

"Dime back," he smiled and slid the coin across the
counter. "See you again soon, Shirl," he called out as she
took up the package and started for the door.

"Yeah, soon," the guard said as he opened the door just
wide enough for her to slide through. As she passed him he
ran his hand across the tight rear of her dress and the closing
of the door cut off their laughter.

"Home now?" Tab asked, taking the package from her.

"Yes—I guess so, a cab too, I guess."

He looked at her face and started to say something, then
changed his mind. "Cab it is." He led the way to the street.

After the cab ride she felt better, they were slobs but no
worse than usual and she wouldn't have to go back there
until next week. And, as Mike said, you didn't expect party
manners from meatleggers. They and their little-boy dirty
jokes from grammar school! You almost had to laugh at
them, the way they acted. And they did have good meat, not
like some of the others. After she cooked the steak for Mike
she would fry some oatmeal in the fat, it would be good. Tab
helped her out of the cab and picked up the shopping bag.

"Want me to bring this up?"

"You better—and you could put the empty milk bottles
in it. Is there any place you could leave them in the
guardroom so we wouldn't forget them tomorrow?"

"Nothing to it, Charlie has a locked cabinet that we use, I
can leave them there."

Charlie had the door open for them and the lobby felt cooler after the heat of the street. They didn't talk while they rode up in the elevator; Shirl rummaged through her purse for the key. Tab went down the hall ahead of her and opened the outer door but stopped so suddenly that she almost bumped into him.

"Will you wait here a second, please, Miss Shirl?" he said in a low voice, placing the shopping bag silently against the wall.

"What is it . . . ?" she started, but he touched his finger to his lips and pointed to the inner door. It was open about an inch and there was a deep gouge in the wood. She didn't know what it meant but it was trouble of some kind, because Tab was in sort of a crouch with his fist with the knucks raised before him and he opened the door and entered the apartment that way.

He wasn't gone long and there were no sounds, but when he came back he was standing up straight and his face was empty of all expression. "Miss Shirl," he said, "I don't want you to come in but I think it would be for the best if you just took a look in the bedroom."

She was afraid now, knowing something was terribly wrong, but she followed him obediently, through the living room and into the bedroom.

It was strange, she thought that she was just standing there, doing nothing when she heard the scream, until she realized that it was her own voice, that she was the one who was screaming.

4

As long as it had been dark, Billy Chung found the waiting bearable. He had huddled in a corner against the cool cellar wall and had almost dozed at times. But when he noticed the first grayness of approaching dawn at the window he felt a sudden sharp spasm of fear that steadily grew worse. Would they find him hiding here? It had seemed so easy last night and everything had worked out so well. Just the way it had been when the Tigers had pulled those jobs. He had known just where to go to buy an old tire iron, and no questions asked, and just a dime more to have the end sharpened. Getting into the moat around the apartment buildings had been the only tricky part, but he hadn't been seen when he had dropped over the edge and he was sure no one had been looking when he had jimmied open the cellar window with the tire iron. No, if he had been seen they would have grabbed him by now. But maybe in the daylight they would be able to spot the jimmy marks on the window? He shivered at the thought and was suddenly conscious of the loud thudding of his heart. He had to force himself to leave the shadowed corner and to work his way slowly along the wall until he was next to the window, trying to see through the dust-filmed glass. Before he had closed the window behind him he had rubbed spit, and soot from the ledge, into the marks the tire iron had made; but had it worked well enough? The only clear spot on the window was the heart he had drawn in the dust and by moving his head around he looked through it and saw that the splintered grooves were obscured. Greatly relieved, he hurried back to his corner, but within a few minutes his fears returned, stronger than ever.

Full daylight was streaming through the window now—how long would it be before he was discovered? If anyone came in through the door all they had to do was look his way and they would see him; the small pile of old and cobwebbed boards behind which he cowered could not hide him completely. Shivering with fear, he pushed back against the concrete wall so hard that its rough surface bit through the thin fabric of his shirt.

There was no way to measure this kind of time. For Billy each moment seemed endless—yet he also felt that he had spent a lifetime in this room. Once footsteps approached, then passed the door, and during those few seconds he found out that his earlier fear had been only a small thing. Lying there, shaking and sweating at the same time, he hated himself for his weakness, yet could do nothing about it. His nervous fingers picked at an old scab on his shinbone until it tore away and the wound began to bleed. He pressed his rag of a handkerchief over it and the seconds crept slowly by.

Getting himself to leave the cellar proved to be even

harder than staying. He had to wait until the people in the apartment upstairs went out for the day—or did they go out? Another stab of fear. He had to wait but he could only estimate the time by looking at the angle of the sun through the clouded window and by listening to the sound of traffic in the street outside. By waiting as long as he could, then putting it off a little longer at the thought of the corridors outside, he reached the point when he felt that it was safe to leave. The jimmy went inside the waistband of his shorts where it couldn't be seen, and he brushed off as much dust as he could before turning the handle on the door.

Voices and the sound of hammering came from some distant part of the cellar, but he saw no one on the way to the stairs. As he climbed the third flight he heard rapid footsteps coming down toward him, and he just managed to go back to the floor below and hide in the corridor until they passed. This was the last alarm and a minute later Billy was on the fifth floor looking at the golden lettering of *O'Brien* once again.

"I wonder if maybe she's still home?" he whispered half aloud and smiled to himself. "She's trouble—you want cash," he added, but his voice was hoarse. There was a clear and insistent memory of those round breasts, rising toward him.

When the outer door was opened it sounded some signal inside the apartment, that was what had happened last night. This was all right, he had to be sure no one was inside before he tried to break in. Before his nerve failed completely he pushed the door open and stepped inside, closing it again behind him and leaning his back against it.

Someone might still be home. He felt his face grow damp at the thought and looked at the TV pickup, then swiftly away. If she asks me I'll say something about Western Union, about a message. The walls of the tiny, empty chamber pressed in on him and he shifted from one foot to the other waiting for the crackle of the loudspeaker.

It remained silent. He tried to guess how long a minute was, then counted to sixty and knew that he had counted too fast and counted it again. "Hello," he said, and just in case the TV thing wasn't working he knocked on the door, timidly at first, then more loudly as his confidence grew.

"No one home?" he called as he took out the tire-iron jimmy and slipped the sharpened end into the jamb of the closed door just below the handle. When it had been pushed in as far as it would go he pulled hard with both hands. There was a small cracking sound and the door swung open. Billy stepped through, almost on tiptoe, ready to turn and run.

The air was cool, the apartment dim and silent. Ahead, at the end of the long hall, he could see a room and part of a dark TV set. Just at his left hand was the closed door of the bedroom, the bed where she had been lying was just beyond it. Maybe she was still there, asleep, he would go in and not wake her at once but . . . he shivered. Shifting the tire iron to his left hand he slowly opened the door.

Rumpled sheets, tangled and empty. Billy walked by the bed and didn't look at it again. What else had he expected? A girl like that wouldn't want someone like him. He cursed and pried open the top drawer in the large dresser, splintering and cracking it with the iron. It was filled with smooth underclothes, pink and white and softer than he had ever felt when he ran his hand over them. He threw them on the floor.

One by one he treated all the other drawers the same way, hurling their contents about, but putting aside those items of clothing he knew could be sold for a high price in the flea market. A sudden banging brought back the fear that had been displaced by anger for the moment, and he stood frozen. It took a long moment before he recognized it as water in a pipe somewhere in the wall. He relaxed a bit, was in better control now and, for the first time, noticed the jewelry box on the end table.

Billy had it in his hand and was looking at the pins and bracelets and wondering if they were real and how much he could get for them when the bathroom door opened and Mike O'Brien walked into the room.

For a moment he did not see Billy, he just stopped and gaped at the ruin of the dresser and the scattered clothing. He was wearing his dressing gown, spattered with dark spots of water, and was drying his hair with a towel. Then he saw Billy, standing rigid with terror, and hurled the towel away.

"You little bastard!" Mike roared. "What the hell are you doing here!"

He was like a mountain of death approaching, with his great face flushed from the shower and reddened even more by rage. He stood two heads taller than Billy and there was muscle under the fat on his meaty arms, and all he wanted to do was break the boy in two.

Mike reached out with both hands and Billy felt the wall against his back. There was a weight in his right hand and he swung in panic, lashing out wildly. He hardly realized what had happened when Mike fell at his feet, not uttering a sound; there was just the heavy thud of his body hitting the floor.

Michael J. O'Brien's eyes were open, open wide and staring, but they were not seeing. The tire iron had caught him on the side of the temple, the sharp point cracking through the thin bone there and going on into his brain, killing him instantly. There was very little blood since the tire iron remained, a projecting blade handle stuck fast in the wound.

It was just by chance, a combination of circumstances, but Billy was not caught or recognized when he was leaving the building. He fled in blind panic and did not meet anyone on the stairs, but he missed a turning and found himself near the service entrance. A new tenant was moving in and at least a score of men, dressed in the same sort of ragged garments he wore, were carrying in furniture. The single uniformed attendant on duty was watching the people who entered the building and paid no attention at all when Billy walked out behind two of the others.

Billy was almost to the waterfront before he realized that in his flight he had left everything behind. He leaned his back to a wall, then slid slowly down until he squatted on his heels panting with exhaustion, wiping the sweat from his eyes so he could see if anyone had followed him. No one was taking any notice of him, he had escaped. But he had killed a man—and all for nothing. He shuddered, in spite of the heat, and gasped for air. Nothing, it had all been for nothing.

5

"Just like that? You want us to drop whatever we're doing and come running, just like that?" Lieutenant Grassioli's angry question lost some of its impact when he ended it with a deep belch. He took a jar of white tablets from the top drawer of his desk, shook two of them out into his hand and looked at them distastefully before putting them into his mouth. "What happened over there?" The words were accompanied by a dry, grating sound as he chewed the tablets.

"I don't know, I wasn't told." The man in the black uniform stood in an exaggerated position of attention, but there was the slightest edge of rudeness to his words. "I'm just a messenger, sir, I was told to go to the nearest police station and deliver the following message. 'There has been some trouble. Send a detective at once.'"

"Do you people in Chelsea Park think you can give orders to the police department?" The messenger didn't answer because they both knew that the answer was yes and it was better left unspoken. A number of very important private and public individuals lived in these buildings. The lieutenant winced at the quick needle of pain in his stomach. "Send Rusch here," he shouted.

Andy came in a few moments later. "Yes, sir?"

"What are you working on?"

"I have a suspect, he may be the paper hanger who has been passing all those bum checks in Brooklyn, I'm going to . . ."

"Put him on ice. There's a report here I want you to follow up."

"I don't know if I can do that, he's . . ."

"If I say you can do it—*do it*. This is my precinct, not yours, Rusch. Go with this man and report to me personally when you come back." The belch was smaller this time, more of a punctuation than anything else.

"Your lieutenant has some temper," the messenger said when they were out in the street.

"Shut up," Andy snapped without looking at the man. He had had another bad night and was tired. And the heat wave was still on; the sun almost unbearable when they left the shadow of the expressway and walked north. He squinted into the glare and felt the beginning of a headache squeeze at his temples. There was trash blocking the sidewalk and he kicked it angrily aside. They turned a corner and were in shadow again, the crenelated battlements and towers of the apartment buildings rose like a cliff above them. Andy forgot the headache as they walked across the drawbridge; he had only been inside the place once before, just in the lobby. The door opened before they reached it and the doorman stepped aside to let them in.

"Police," Andy said, showing his badge to the doorman. "What's wrong here?"

The big man didn't answer at first, just swiveled his head to follow the retreating messenger until he was out of earshot. Then he licked his lips and whispered: "It's pretty bad." He tried to look depressed but his eyes glittered with excitement. "It's . . . murder . . . someone's been killed."

Andy wasn't impressed; the City of New York averaged seven murders a day, and ten on good days. "Let's go see about it," he said, and followed the doorman toward the elevator.

"This is the one," the doorman said, opening the hall door of apartment 41-E; cool air surged out, fresh on Andy's face.

"That's all," he said to the disappointed doorman, "I'll take it from here." He walked in and at once noticed the jimmy grooves on the inner doorjamb, looked beyond them to the long length of hall where the two people sat on chairs backed to the wall. A full bag of groceries leaned against the nearest chair.

They were alike in their expressions with fixed round eyes, shocked at the sudden impact of the totally unexpected. The girl was an attractive redhead, nice long hair and a delicate pink complexion. When the man got quickly to his feet Andy saw that he was a bodyguard, a chunky Negro.

"I'm Detective Rusch, 12-A Precinct."

"My name is Tab Fielding, this is Miss Greene—she lives here. We just came back from shopping a little while ago and I saw the jimmy marks on the door. I came in by myself and went in there." He jerked his thumb at a nearby closed door. "I found him. Mr. O'Brien. Miss Greene came in a minute later and saw him too. I looked through the whole place but there was no one else here. Miss Shirl— Miss Greene—stayed here in the hall while I went to call the police, we've been here ever since. We didn't touch anything inside."

Andy glanced back and forth at them and suspected the story was true; it could be checked easily enough with the elevator boy and the doorman. Still, there was no point in taking chances.

"Will you both please come in with me."

"I don't want to," the girl said quickly, her fingers tightening on the sides of the chair. "I don't want to see him like that again."

"I'm sorry. But I'm afraid I can't leave you out here alone."

She didn't argue any more, just stood up slowly and brushed at the wrinkles in her gray dress. A very good-looking girl, Andy realized as she walked by him. The bodyguard held the door open and Andy followed them both into the bedroom. Keeping her face turned toward the wall, the girl went quickly to the bathroom and closed the door behind her.

"She'll be all right," Tab said, noticing the detective's attention. "She's a tough enough kid but you can't blame her for not wanting to see Mr. O'Brien, not like that."

For the first time Andy looked at the body. He had seen a lot worse. Michael O'Brien was still as impressive in death as he had been in life: sprawled on his back, arms and legs spread wide, mouth agape and eyes open and staring. The length of iron projected from the side of his head and a thin trickle of dark blood ran down the side of his neck to the floor. Andy knelt and touched the bared skin on his forearm; it was very cool. The air-conditioned room would have something to do with that. He stood and looked at the bathroom door.

"Can she hear us in there?" he asked.

"No, sir. It's soundproofed, the whole apartment is."

"You said she lives here. What does that mean?"

"She is—was Mr. O'Brien's girl. She's got nothing to do with this, no reason to have anything to do with it. He was her cracker and marge—" Realization hit and his shoulders slumped. "Mine too. We both gotta look for a new job now." He retired into himself, looking with great unhappiness at a suddenly insecure future.

Andy glanced around at the disordered clothing and the splintered dresser. "They could have had a fight before she went out today, she might have done it then."

"Not Miss Shirl!" Tab's fists clenched tight. "She's not the kind of person who could do this sort of thing. When I said tough I meant she could roll with things, you know, get along with the world. She couldn't of done this. It would have to be before I met her downstairs, I wait for her in the lobby, and she came down today just like she always does. Nice and happy, she couldn't of acted like that if she had just come from *this*." He pointed angrily at the mountainous corpse that lay between them.

He didn't say so but Andy agreed with the bodyguard. A good-looking bird like this one didn't have to kill anyone. What she did she did for D's and if a guy gave her too much trouble she'd just walk out and find someone else with money. Not murder.

"What about you, Tab, did you knock the old boy off?"

"Me?" He was surprised, not angry. "I wasn't even up in the building until I came back with Miss Shirl and found him." He straightened up with professional pride. "And I'm a bodyguard. I have a contract to protect him. I don't break contracts. And when I kill anyone it's not like *that*—that's no way to kill anyone."

Every minute in the air-conditioned room made Andy feel better. The drying sweat was cool on his body and the headache was almost gone. He smiled. "Off the record— strictly—I agree with you. But don't quote me until I make a report. It looks like a break and entry, O'Brien walked in on whoever was burglaring the place and caught that thing in the side of his head." He glanced down at the silenced figure. "Who was he—what did he do for a living? O'Brien's a common name."

"He was in business," Tab said flatly.

"You're not telling me much, Fielding. Why don't you run that through again."

Tab glanced toward the closed door of the bathroom and shrugged. "I don't know exactly what he did—and I have enough brains not to bother myself about it. He had something to do with the rackets, politics too. I know he had a lot of top-brass people from City Hall coming here——"

Andy snapped his fingers. "O'Brien—he wouldn't be Big Mike O'Brien?"

"That's what they called him."

"Big Mike . . . well, there's no loss then. In fact we could lose a few more like him and not miss any of them."

"I wouldn't know about that." Tab looked straight ahead, his face expressionless.

"Relax. You're not working for him any more. Your contract has just been canceled."

"I been paid to the end of the month. I'll finish my job."

"It was finished at the same time as the guy on the floor. I think you better look after the girl instead."

"I'm going to do that." His face relaxed and he glanced at the detective. "It's not going to be easy for her."

"She'll get by," Andy said flatly. He took out his notepad and stylo. "I'll talk to her now, I need a complete report. Stick around the apartment until I see her and the building employees. If their stories back you up there'll be no reason to keep you."

When he was alone with the body, Andy took the polythene evidence bag from his pocket and worked it down over the iron without touching it, then pulled the weapon free of the skull by holding on to it through the bag, as low down as possible; it came away easily enough and there was only a slow trickle of blood from the wound. He sealed the bag, then took a pillowcase from the bed and dropped the bag and tire iron into this. There would be no complaints now if he carried the bloody iron in the street—and if he worked it right he could get to keep the pillowcase. He spread a sheet over the body before knocking on the bathroom door.

Shirl opened the door a few inches and looked out at him. "I want to talk to you," he said, then remembered the body on the floor behind him. "Is there another room—?"

"The living room. I'll show you."

She opened the door all the way and came out, once more walking close to the wall without looking down at the floor. Tab was sitting in the hall, and he watched them silently as they passed.

"Make yourself comfortable," Shirl said. "I'll be with you in just a moment." She went into the kitchen.

Andy sat on the couch, it was very soft, and put his notepad on his knee. Another air-conditioner hummed in the window and the floor-to-ceiling curtains were closed almost all the way, so that the light was dim and comfortable. The television set was a monster. There were pictures on the walls (they looked like real paintings), books, a dining table and chairs in some kind of red wood. Very nice for someone.

"Do you want a drink?" Shirl called out from the kitchen, holding up a tall glass. "This is vodka."

"I'm on duty, thanks all the same. Some cold water will do fine."

She brought the two glasses in on a tray and, instead of handing his glass to him, pressed it against the side of the couch near his hand. When she let go the glass remained there, defying gravity. Andy pulled at it and it came free with a slight tug; he saw that there were rings of metal worked into the glass, so there must be magnets concealed under the fabric. Very elegant. For some reason this annoyed him and, after drinking some of the cold, flavorless water, he put the glass on the floor by his foot.

"I would like to ask you some questions," he said, making a tick mark on the notepad. "What time did you leave the apartment this morning?"

"Just seven o'clock, that's when Tab comes on duty. I wanted to do the shopping before it was too hot."

"Did you lock the door behind you?"

"It's automatic, it locks itself, there's no way to leave it open unless you block it with something."

"Was O'Brien alive when you left?"

She looked up at him angrily. "Of course! He was asleep, snoring. Do you think that *I* killed him?" The anger in her face turned to pain as she remembered what was lying in the other room; she took a quick gulp from her drink.

Tab's voice came from the doorway. "When I touched Mr. O'Brien's body it was still warm. Whoever killed him must have done it just a little while before we came in—"

"Go sit down and don't come in here again," Andy said sharply, without turning his head. He took a sip of the ice water and wondered what he was getting excited about. What difference did it make who had polished off Big Mike? It was a public service. The odds were all against this girl having done it. What motive? He looked at her closely and she caught his eye and turned away, pulling her skirt down over her knees as she did.

"What I think doesn't matter," he said, but the words didn't even satisfy him. "Look, Miss Greene, I'm just a cop doing my job. Tell me what I want to know so I can write it down and give it to the lieutenant, so he can make a report. Personally, I don't think that you had anything to do with this killing. But I still have to ask the questions."

It was the first time he had seen her smile and he liked it. Her nose wrinkled and it was a broad friendly grin. She was a cute kid and she would make out, oh yes, she would make out with anyone who had the D's. He looked back at his notepad and slashed a heavy line under *Big Mike*.

Tab closed the door behind Andy when he left, then waited a few minutes to be sure he wasn't coming back. When he went into the living room he stood so that he could watch the hall door and would know the moment it was opened.

"Miss Shirl, there's something you should know."

She was on her third large drink, but the alcohol did not seem to be having any effect. "What is that?" she asked tiredly.

"I'm not trying to be personal or anything, and I don't know anything about Mr. O'Brien's will . . ."

"You can put your mind at rest. I've seen it and everything goes to his sister. I'm not mentioned in it—and neither are you."

"I wasn't thinking about myself," he said coldly, his face suddenly hard. She was sorry at once.

"Please, I didn't mean it that way. I'm just being—I don't know, bitchy. Everything happening at once like this. Don't be angry at me, Tab—please. . . ."

"I guess you were being a little bitchy." He smiled for a moment before he dug into his pocket. "I figured it would be something like that. I have no complaints about Mr. O'Brien as an employer, but he took care of his money. Didn't throw it around, that's what I mean. Before the detective came I went through Mr. O'Brien's wallet. It was in his jacket. I left a few D's there but I took the rest— here." He pushed his hand out with a folded wad of bills in it. "It's yours, yours by right."

"I couldn't . . ."

"You *have* to. Things are going to be rough, Shirl. You're going to need it more than his family. There's no record of it. It's yours by right."

He put the money on the end table and she looked at it. "I suppose I should. That sister of his has enough without this. But we better split it—"

"No," he said flatly, just as the dull buzz of the announcer signaled that someone had opened the outer door from the hall.

"Department of Hospitals," a voice said and Tab could see two men in white uniforms on the TV screen inset near the door. They were carrying a stretcher. He went to let them in.

6

"How long you gonna be, Charlie?"

"That's my business—you just hold the fort until I get back," the doorman grunted, and looked the uniformed guard over with what he liked to think was a military eye. "I seen a lot better-looking gold buttons in my time."

"Have a heart, Charlie, you know they're just plastic. They'll fall to pieces if I try to rub on them."

In the loosely organized hierarchy of employees in Chelsea Park, Charlie was the unquestioned leader. It wasn't a matter of salary—this was probably the smallest part of his income—but a matter of position and industry. He was the one who saw the tenants most often and he lost nothing by this advantage. His contacts outside the buildings were the best and he could get anything the residents wanted—for a price. All the tenants liked him and called him Charlie. All the employees hated him and he had never heard what they called him.

Charlie's basement apartment came with the job, though the management would have been more than a little surprised at the number of improvements that had been made. An ancient air-conditioner wheezed and hammered and lowered the temperature at least ten degrees. Two decades of cast-off and restored furniture contributed a note of mixed color, while an impressive number of locked cabinets covered the walls. These contained a large collection of packaged food and bottled drink none of which Charlie touched himself, but instead resold at a substantial markup to the tenants. Not the least of the improvements was the absence of both a water and an electric meter; the building management unsuspectedly financed both of these major expenses for Charlie.

Two keys were needed to open the door and both were chained to his belt. He went in and hung his uniform coat carefully in the closet, then put on a clean but much-patched sport shirt. The new elevator boy was still asleep in the big double bed and he kicked the frame of the bed with his number-fourteen shoe.

"Get up. You go to work in an hour."

Reluctantly, still half asleep, the boy crawled out of the bedclothes and stood there, naked and slim, scratching at his ribs. Charlie smiled in pleasant memory of the previous night and smacked the boy lightly on his lean buttock.

"You're going to be all right, kid," he said. "Just take care of old Charlie, and Charlie will take care of you."

"Sure, Mr. Charlie, sure," the boy said, forcing interest into his voice. This whole thing was new to him and he still didn't like it very much, but it got him the job. He smiled coyly.

"That's enough of that," Charlie said and slapped the boy again, but this time hard enough to leave a red print on the white skin. "Just make sure the door is locked behind you when you go, and keep your mouth shut on the job." He went out.

The street was a lot hotter than he had thought it would be, so he whistled for a cab. This morning's work should net him enough to pay for a dozen cabs. Two empty pedicabs raced for his business and he sent the first one away because the driver was too runty and thin: Charlie was in a hurry and he weighed 240 pounds.

"Empire State Building, Thirty-Fourth Street entrance. And make some time."

"In this weather?" the driver grunted, standing on the pedals and lurching the creaking machine into motion. "You want to kill me, general?"

"Die. It won't bother me. I'll give you a D for the trip."

"You want me to die by starving, maybe? That much won't take you as far as Fifth Avenue."

They haggled the price most of the trip, twisting their way through the crowded streets, shouting to be heard above the unending noise of the city, a sound they were both so used to that they weren't even aware of it.

Because of the power shortage and lack of replacement parts there was only one elevator running in the Empire State Building, and this one went only as high as the twenty-fifth floor. After that you walked. Charlie climbed two flights and nodded to the bodyguard who sat at the foot of the stairs to the next floor. He had been here before and the man knew him, as did the three other guards at the head of the stairs. One of them unlocked the door for him.

With his shoulder-length white hair Judge Santini bore a strong resemblance to an Old Testament prophet. He didn't sound like one.

"Crap, that's what it is, crap. I pay a goddamn fortune for flour just so I can get a good bowl of pasta and what do you turn it into?" He pushed the plate of spaghetti away distastefully and dabbed the sauce from his lips with the large napkin he had tucked into his shirt collar.

"I did the best I could," his wife shouted back. She was small and dark and twenty years younger than he. "You want somebody to make spaghetti for you by hand, you should have married a *contadina* from the old country with broken arches and a mustache. I was born right here in the city on Mulberry Street, just like you, and all I know about spaghetti is you buy it from the grocery store—"

The shrill ring of the telephone cut through her words and silenced her instantly. They both looked at the instrument on the desk, then she turned and hurriedly left the room, closing the door behind her. There weren't many calls these days and what few came through were always important and about business she did not want to hear. Rosa Santini enjoyed all the luxuries that life provided, and what she didn't know about the judge's business wasn't going to bother her.

Judge Santini stood, wiped his mouth again and laid the napkin on the table. He didn't hurry, not at his age he didn't, but neither did he dawdle. He sat down at the desk, took out a blank notepad and stylo and reached for the phone. It was an old instrument with the cracked handpiece held together by wrappings of friction tape, while the cord was frayed and spliced.

"Santini speaking," he said and listened carefully, his eyes widened. "Mike—Big Mike—my God!" After this he said little, just yes and no, and when he hung up his hands were shaking.

"Big Mike," Lieutenant Grassioli said, almost smiling; even a mindful twinge from his ulcer didn't depress him as it usually did. "Someone did a good day's work." The bloodstained jimmy lay on the desk before him and he admired it as though it were a work of art. "Who did it?"

"The chances are that it was a break and entry that went wrong," Andy said, standing on the other side of the desk. He read from his notepad, quickly summing up all the relevant details. Grassioli grunted when he finished and pointed to the traces of fingerprint powder on the end of the iron.

"What about this? Prints any good?"

"Very clear, lieutenant. Thumb and first three fingers of the right hand."

"Any chance that the bodyguard or the girl polished the old bastard off?"

"I'd say one in a thousand, sir. No motive at all—he was the one who kept them both eating. And they seemed to be really broken up, not about him I don't think, but about losing their meal ticket."

Grassioli dropped the jimmy back into the bag and handed it across the desk to Andy. "That's good enough. We'll have a messenger going down to BCI next week so send the prints along then and a *short* report on the case. Get the report on the back of the print card—it's only the tenth of the month and we're already almost through our paper ration. We should get prints of the bird and the bodyguard to go with it—but the hell with that, there's not enough time. File and forget it and get back to work."

While Andy was making a note on his pad the phone rang; the lieutenant picked it up. Andy wasn't listening to the conversation and was halfway to the door when Grassioli covered the mouthpiece and snapped, "Come back here, Rusch," then turned his attention to the phone.

"Yes, sir, that's right," he said. "There seems no doubt that it was a break and entry, the killer used the same jimmy for the job. A filed-down tire iron." He listened for a moment and his face flushed. "No, sir, no we couldn't. What else could we do? Yes, that's SOP. No, sir. Right away, sir. I'll have someone get on it now, sir."

"Son of a bitch," the lieutenant added, but only after he had hung up the receiver. "You've done a lousy job on this case, Rusch. Now get back on it and see if you can do it right. Find out how the killer got into the building—and if it really was break and entry. Fingerprint those two suspects. Get a messenger down to Criminal Identification with the prints and have them run through, I want a make on the killer if he has a record. Get moving."

"I didn't know Big Mike had any friends?"

"Friends or enemies, I don't give a damn. But someone is putting the pressure on us for results. So wrap this up as fast as possible."

"By myself, lieutenant?"

Grassioli chewed the end of his stylo. "No, I want the report as soon as possible. Take Kulozik with you." He belched painfully and reached into the drawer for the pills.

Detective Steve Kulozik's fingers were short and thick and looked as though they should be clumsy; instead they were agile and under precise control. He held Shirl's right thumb with firm pressure and rolled it across the glazed white tile, leaving a clear and unsmudged print inside the square marked R THMB. Then one by one, he pressed the rest of her fingers to the ink pad and then to the tile until all the squares were full.

"Could I have your name, miss?"

"Shirl Greene, that's spelled with an *e* on the end." She stared at the black-stained tips on her fingers. "Does this make me a criminal now, with a record?"

"Nothing like that at all, Miss Greene." Kulozik carefully printed her name with a thin grease pencil in the space at the bottom of the tile. "These prints aren't made public, they're just used in conjunction with this case. Could I have your date of birth?"

"October twelfth, 1977."

"I think that's all we need now." He slid the tile into a plastic case along with the ink pad.

Shirl went to wash the ink from her hands, and Steve was packing in the fingerprint equipment when the door announcer buzzed.

"Do you have her prints?" Andy asked when he came in.

"All finished."

"Fine, then all that's left is to get the prints from the bodyguard, he's waiting downstairs in the lobby. And I found a window in the cellar that looks like it was pried open, better check that for latent prints too. The elevator operator will show you where it is."

"On my way," Steve said, shouldering the equipment case.

Shirl came out as Steve was leaving. "We have a lead now, Miss Greene," Andy told her. "I found a window in the basement that has been pried open. If there are any fingerprints on the glass or frame and they match the ones found on the jimmy, it will be fairly strong evidence that whoever did the killing broke into the building that way. And we'll compare the jimmy marks with the ones on the door here. Do you mind if I sit down?"

"No," she said, "of course not."

The chair was soft and the murmuring air-conditioner made the room an island of comfort in the steaming heat of the city. He leaned back and some of the tension and fatigue drained away; the door announcer buzzed.

"Excuse me," Shirl said and went to answer it. There was a murmur of voices in the hallway behind him as he flipped the pages in his notepad. The plastic cover was buckled on one of the sheets and some of the lettering was fading, so he went over it again with his stylo, pressing hard so that it was sharp and black.

"You get outta here, you dirty whore!"

The words were screamed in a hoarse voice, rising shrilly like a scraped fingernail on glass. Andy climbed to his feet and jammed the notepad into his side pocket. "What's going on out there?" he called.

Shirl came in, flushed and angry, followed by a thin gray-haired woman. The woman stopped when she saw Andy and pointed a trembling finger at him. "My brother dead and not even buried yet and this one is carrying on with another man . . ."

"I'm a police officer," Andy said, showing her his buzzer. "Who are you?"

She drew herself up, a slight movement that did nothing to increase her height; years of bad posture and indifferent diet had rounded her shoulders and hollowed her chest. Scrawny arms dangled from the sleeves of the much worn, mud-colored housedress. Her face, filmed now with sweat, was more gray than white, the skin of a photophobic city dweller; the only coloring in it appeared to be the grime of the streets. When she spoke her lips opened in a narrow slit, delivered the words like metal stampings from a press, then closed instantly afterward lest they deliver one item more than was needed. Only the watery blue eyes held any motion or life, and they twitched with anger.

"I'm Mary Haggerty, poor Michael's sister and only living relation by blood. I've come to take care of Michael's things, he's left them all to me in his will, the lawyer told me that, and I have to take care of them. That whore'll have to get out, she's taken enough from him. . . ."

"Just a minute." Andy broke into the shrill babble of words and her mouth snapped shut while she breathed rapidly through flared righteous nostrils. "Nothing can be touched or taken from this apartment without police permission, so you don't have to worry about your possessions."

"You can't say that with her here," she squawled and turned on Shirl. "She'll steal and sell everything that's not nailed down. My good brother . . ."

"Your good brother!" Shirl shouted. "You hated his guts and he hated yours, and you never came near this place as long as he was alive."

"Shut up!" Andy broke in, coming between the two women. He turned to Mary Haggerty. "You can go now. The police will let you know when the things in this apartment are available."

She was shocked. "But—you can't do that. I have my rights. You can't leave that whore here alone."

Andy's patience was cracking. "Watch your language, Mrs. Haggerty. You've used that word enough. Don't forget what *your* brother did for a living."

Her face went white and she took a half step backward. "My brother was in business, a businessman," she said weakly.

"Your brother was in the rackets, and that means girls among other things." Without her anger to hold her erect she slumped, deflated, thin and bony; the only round thing in her body was her abdomen, swollen from years of bad diet and bearing too many children.

"Why don't you go now," he said. "We'll get in touch with you as soon as possible."

The woman turned and left without another word. He was sorry that he had lost his temper and said more than he should, but there was no way to take back the words now.

"Did you mean that—what you said about Mike?" Shirl asked, after the door had closed. In a plain white dress and with her hair pulled back she looked very young, even innocent, despite the label Mary Haggerty had given to her. The innocence seemed more realistic than the charges.

"How long did you know O'Brien?" Andy asked, fending the question off for the moment.

"Just about a year, but he never talked about his business. I never asked, I always thought it had something to do with politics, he always had judges and politicians visiting him."

Andy took out his notebook. "I'd like the names of any regular visitors, people he saw in the last week."

"Now you are asking the questions—and you haven't answered mine." Shirl smiled when she said it, but he knew she was serious. She sat down on a straight-backed chair, her hands folded in her lap like a schoolgirl.

"I can't answer that in too much detail," he said. "I don't know that much about Big Mike. About all I can tell you for certain is that he was some sort of a contact man between the syndicate and the politicians. Executive level I guess you would call it. And it has been thirty years at least since the last time he was in court or behind bars."

"Do you mean—he was in jail?"

"Yes, I checked on it, he's got a criminal record and a couple of convictions. But nothing recently, it's the punks who get caught and sent up. Once you operate in Mike's circle the police don't touch you. In fact they help you—like this investigation."

"I don't understand. . . ."

"Look. There are five, maybe ten killings in New York every day, a couple of hundred felonious assaults, twenty, thirty cases of rape, at least fifteen hundred burglaries. The police are understaffed and overworked. We don't have time to follow up any case that isn't open and shut. If someone gets murdered and there are witnesses, okay, we go out and pick the killer up and the case is closed. But in a case like this, frankly, Miss Greene, we usually don't even try. Unless we get a make on the fingerprints and have a record on the killer. But the chances are that we don't. This city has a million punks who are on the Welfare and wish they had a square meal or a TV or a drink. So they try their hand at burglary to see what they can pick up. We catch a few and send them upstate on work gangs, breaking up the big parkways with pickaxes to reclaim the farmland. But most of them get away. Once in a while there is an accident, maybe someone comes in while they are pulling a job, surprises them while they are cleaning out the place. If the burglar is armed there may be a killing. Completely by accident, you understand, and the chances are ninety-nine out of a hundred that something like this happened to Mike O'Brien. I took the evidence, reported the case—and it should have died there. It would have if it had been anyone else. But as I said, Big Mike had plenty of political contacts and one of them put on some pressure to make a more complete investigation, and that is why I am here. Now— I've told you more than I should, and you'll do me a big favor if you forget all about it."

"No, I won't tell anyone. What happens next?"

"I ask you a few more questions, leave here, write up a report—and that will be the end of it. Lots of other work is piling up behind me and the department has already put more time into the investigation than it can afford."

She was shocked. "Aren't you going to catch the man who did it?"

"If the fingerprints are on file, we might. If not—we haven't got a chance. We won't even try. Aside from the reason that we have no time, we feel that whoever did Mike in performed a social service."

"That's terrible!"

"Is it? Perhaps." He opened his notepad and was very official again. He had finished with the questions by the time Kulozik came back with latent prints from the cellar window and they left the building together. After the cool apartment the air in the street hit like the blast from an open furnace door.

7

It was after midnight, a moonless night, but the sky outside the wide window could not equal the rich darkness of the polished mahogany of the long refectory table. The table was centuries old, from a monastery long since destroyed, and very valuable, as were all the furnishings in the room: the sideboard, the paintings, and the cut-crystal chandelier that hung in the center of the room. The six men grouped around the end of the table were not valuable at all, except in a financial sense, although in that way they were indeed very well off. Two of them were smoking cigars, and the cheapest cigar you could buy cost at least ten D's.

"Not every word of the report if you please, Judge," the man at the head of the table said. "Our time is limited and just the results will be all we need." If anyone there knew his real name they were careful not to mention it. He was now called Mr. Briggs and he was the man in charge.

"Surely, Mr. Briggs, that will be easy enough," Judge Santini said, and coughed nervously behind his hand. He never liked these sessions at the Empire State Building. As a judge he shouldn't be seen here too often with these people. Besides, it was a long climb and he had to think about his ticker. Particularly in this kind of weather. He took a sip of water from the glass in front of him and moved his glasses forward on his nose so that he could read better.

"Here is what it boils down to. Big Mike was killed instantly by a blow on the side of the head, done with a sharpened tire iron that was also used to break into the apartment. Marks made on a jimmied-open basement window match the ones on the door and they both fit the jimmy, so it looks as though whoever did it got in that way. There were clear fingerprints on the iron and on the basement window, the same prints. So far the prints appear to be of a person unknown, they do not match any of the fingerprints on file in the Bureau of Criminal Identification, nor are they the prints of O'Brien's bodyguard or girl friend, the ones who found the body."

"Who do the fuzz think done it?" one of the listeners asked from around his cigar.

"The official view is—ah, death by misadventure you might say. They think that someone was burgling the apartment and Mike walked in and surprised him, and Mike was killed in the struggle."

Two men started to ask questions but shut up instantly when Mr. Briggs began to speak. He had the gloomy, serious eyes of a hound dog, with the matching sagging lower lids and loose dewlaps on his cheeks. The pendant jowls waggled when he talked.

"What was stolen from the apartment?"

Santini shrugged. "Nothing, from what they can tell. The girl claims that nothing is missing and she ought to know. The room was taken apart, but apparently the burglar was jumped before he finished the job and then he ran in a panic. It could happen."

Mr. Briggs pondered this, but he had no more questions. Some of the others did and Santini told them what was known. Mr. Briggs considered for a while then silenced them with a raised finger.

"It appears that the killing was accidental, in which case it is of no importance to us. We will need someone to take over Mike's work—what is it, Judge?" he asked, frowning at the interruption.

Santini was sweating. He wanted the matter settled so he could go home, it was after 1 A.M. and he was tired. He wasn't used to being up this late any more. But there was a fact that he had to mention, it might be important and if it was noticed later and it came out that he had known about it and said nothing . . . it would be best to get it over with.

"There is one thing more I ought to tell you. Perhaps it means something, perhaps not, but I feel we should have all the information in front of us before we—"

"Get on with it, Judge," Mr. Briggs said coldly.

"Yes, of course. It's a mark that was on the window. You must understand that all the basement windows are coated with dust on the inside and that none of the others were touched. But on the window that was jimmied open, through which we can presume the killer entered the building, there was a design traced in the dust. A heart."

"Now what the hell is that supposed to mean?" one of the listeners growled.

"Nothing to you, Schlacter, since you are an American of German extraction. Now I am not guaranteeing that it means anything, it may just be a coincidence, meaningless, it could be anything. But just for the record, just to get it down, the Italian word for heart is *cuore*."

The atmosphere in the room changed instantly, electrified. Some of the men sat up and there was a rustle of shifting bodies. Mr. Briggs did not move, though his eyes narrowed. "Cuore," he said slowly. "I don't think he has enough guts to try and move into the city."

"He's got his hands full in Newark. He got burned once coming here, he's not going to try it again."

"Maybe. But he's half out of his head I hear. On the LSD. He could do anything. . . ."

Mr. Briggs coughed and they were all quiet on the instant. "We are going to have to look into this," he said. "Whether Cuore is trying to move into our area or whether someone is trying to stir up trouble and blaming it on him; either way we want to find out. Judge, see to it that the police continue the investigation."

Santini smiled but his fingers were knotted tightly together under the table. "I'm not saying no, mind you, not saying it can't be done, just that it would be very difficult. The police are very shorthanded, they don't have the personnel for a full-scale investigation. If I try to pressure them they'll want to know why. I'll have to have some good answers. I can have some people work on this, make some calls, but I don't think we can get enough pressure to swing it."

"*You* can't get enough pressure, Judge," Mr. Briggs said in his quietest voice. Santini's hands were trembling now. "But I never ask a man to do the impossible. I'll take care of this myself. There are one or two people I can personally ask to help out. I want to know just what is happening here."

8

Through the open window rolled the heat and stench, the sound of the city, a multivoiced roar that rose and fell with the hammered persistence of waves breaking on a beach; an endless thunder. In sudden punctuation against this background of noise there came the sound of broken glass and a jangled metallic crash; voices rose in shouts and there was a long scream at the same instant.

"What? What . . . ?" Solomon Kahn grumbled, stirring on the bed and rubbing his eyes. The bums, they never shut up, never let you grab a little nap. He got up and shuffled to the window, but could see nothing. They were still shouting—what could have made the noise? Another fire escape falling off? That happened often enough, they even showed it on TV if there was a gruesome picture to go with it. No, probably not, just kids breaking windows again or something. The sun was down behind the buildings but the air was still hot and foul.

"Some lousy weather," he muttered as he went to the sink. Even the boards in the floor were hot on the soles of his bare feet. He sponged off some of the sweat with a little water, then turned the TV on to the Music-Time station. A jazz beat filled the room and the screen said 18:47, with 6:47 P.M. underneath in smaller numerals for all the yuks who had dragged through life without managing to learn the twenty-four-hour clock. Almost seven, and Andy was on day duty today, which meant he should have been through by six, though they never left on time. Anyway, it was time to get the chow going.

"For this the Army gave me a fine fifteen-grand education as an aviation mechanic," he said, patting the stove. "Finest investment they ever made." The stove had started life as a gas burner, which he had adapted for tank gas when they had closed off the gas mains, then had installed an electric heating element when the supplies of tank gas had run out. By the time the electric supplies became too erratic—and expensive—to cook with, he had installed a pressure tank with a variable jet that would burn any inflammable liquid. It had worked satisfactorily for a number of years, consuming kerosene, methanol, acetone and a number of other fuels, balking only slightly at aviation gas while sending out a yard-long streamer of flame that had scorched the wall just before he could adjust it. His final adaptation had been the simplest—and most depressing. He had cut a hole in the back of the oven and run a chimney outdoors through another hole hammered through the brick wall. When a solid-fuel fire was built on the rack inside the oven, an opening in the insulation above it let the heat through to the front ring.

"Even the ashes stink like fish," he complained as he shoveled out the thin layer of powdery ash from the previous day. These he threw out the window in an expanding gray cloud and was gratified when he heard a cry of complaint from the window on the floor below. "Don't you like that?" he shouted back. "So tell your lousy kids not to play the TV at full blast all night and maybe I'll stop dumping the ashes."

This exchange cheered him, and he hummed along with *The Nutcracker Suite* which had replaced the nameless jazz composition—until a burst of static suddenly interrupted the music, drowning it out. He mumbled curses under his breath as he ran over and hammered on the side of the TV set with his fist. This had not the slightest effect. The static continued until he reluctantly turned the TV off. He was still muttering angrily when he bent to fire up the stove.

Sol placed three oily gray bricks of seacoal on the rack and went over to the shelf for his battered Zippo lighter. A good lighter that, bought in the PX when?—must be fifty years ago. Of course most of the parts had been replaced since that time, but they didn't make lighters like this any more. They didn't make lighters at all any more. The seacoal spluttered and caught, burning with a small blue flame. It stank—of fish—and so did his hands now: he went and rinsed them off. The stuff was supposed to be made of cellulose waste from the fermentation vats at the alcohol factory, dried and soaked with a low-grade plankton oil to keep it burning. Rumor had it that it was really made of dried and pressed fish guts from the processing plants, and he preferred this to the official version, true or not.

His miniature garden was doing well in the window box.

He plucked the last of the sage and spread it out on the table to dry, then lifted the plastic sheeting to see how the onions were doing. They were coming along fine and would be ready for pickling soon. When he went to rinse off his hands in the sink he looked quizzically at his beard in the mirror.

"It needs trimming, Sol," he told his image. "But the light is almost gone so it can wait until morning. Still, it wouldn't hurt none to comb it before you dress for dinner." He ran a comb through his beard a few times, then tossed the comb aside and went to dig a pair of shorts out of the wardrobe. They had started life many years earlier as a pair of Army suntan trousers, and since then had been cut down and patched until they bore little resemblance to the original garment. He was just pulling them on when someone knocked on the door. "Yeah," he shouted, "who is it?"

"Alcover's Electronics," was the muffled answer.

"I thought you died or your place burned down," Sol said, throwing the door open. "It's only been two weeks since you said you would do a rush job on this set—which I paid for in advance."

"That's the way the electron hops," the tall repairman said calmly, swinging his valise-sized toolbox onto the table. "You got a gassy tube, some tired components in that old set. So what can I do? They don't make that tube any more, and if they did I couldn't buy it, it would be on priority." His hands were busy while he talked, hauling the TV down to the table and starting to unscrew the back. "So how do I fix the set? I have to go down to the radio breakers on Greenwich Street and spend a couple of hours shopping around. I can't get the tube, so I get a couple of transistors and breadboard up a circuit that will do the same job. It's not easy, I tell you."

"My heart bleeds for you," Sol said, watching suspiciously as the repairman took the back off the set and extracted a tube.

"Gassy," the man said, looking sternly at the radio tube before he threw it into his toolbox. From the top tray he took a rectangle of thin plastic on which a number of small parts had been attached, and began to wire it into the TV circuit. "Everything's makeshift," he said. "I have to cannibalize old sets to keep older ones working. I even have to melt and draw my own solder. It's a good thing that there must have been a couple of billion sets in this country, and a

lot of the latest ones have solid state circuits." He turned on
the TV and music blared across the room. "That will be four
D's for labor."

"Crook!" Sol said. "I already gave you thirty-five D's.
. . ."

"That was for the parts, labor is extra. If you want the little luxuries of life you have to be prepared to pay for them."

"The repairs I need," Sol said, handing over the money.
"The philosophy I do not. You're a thief."

"I prefer to think of myself as an electronic grave rob-
ber," the man said, pocketing the bills. "If you want to see
the thieves you should see what I pay to the radio breakers."
He shouldered his toolbox and left.

It was almost eight o'clock. Only a few minutes after the
repairman had finished his job a key turned in the lock and
Andy came in, tired and hot.

"Your chunk is really dragging," Sol said.

"So would yours if you had a day like mine. Can't you
turn on a light, it's black as soot in here." He slumped to the
chair by the window and dropped into it.

Sol switched on the small yellow bulb that hung in the
middle of the room, then went to the refrigerator. "No
Gibsons tonight, I'm rationing the vermouth until I can
make some more. I got the coriander and orris root and the
rest, but I have to dry some sage first, it's no good without
that." He took out a frosted pitcher and closed the door.
"But I put some water in to cool and cut it with some alky
which will numb the tongue so you can't taste the water, and
will also help the nerves."

"Lead me to it!" Andy sipped the drink and managed to
produce a reluctant smile. "Sorry to take it out on you, but I
had one hell of a day and there's more to come." He sniffed
the air. "What's that cooking on the stove?"

"An experiment in home economics—and it was free for
the taking on the Welfare cards. You may not have noticed
but our food budget is shot to pieces since the last price
increase." He opened a canister and showed Andy the
granular brown substance inside. "It is a new miracle
ingredient supplied by our benevolent government and
called ener-G—and how's *that* for a loathsomely cute
name? It contains vitamins, minerals, protein, carbohy-
drates. . . ."

"Everything except flavor?"

"That's about the size of it. I put it in with the oatmeal, I doubt if it can do any harm because at this moment I am beginning to hate oatmeal. This ener-G stuff is the product of the newest wonder of science, the plankton whale."

"The *what?*"

"I know you never open a book—but don't you ever watch TV? They had an hour program on the thing. A conversion of an atomic submarine, cruises along just like a whale and sucks in plankton, all the microscopic sea things that you will be very surprised to find out the mighty whales live on. All three whales that're left. The smallest life forms supporting the biggest, there's a moral there someplace. Anyway—the plankton gets sucked in and hits a sieve and the water gets spit out and the plankton gets pressed into little dry bricks and stored in the sub until it is full up and can come back and unload. Then they futz around with the bricks of plankton and come up with ener-G."

"Oh, Christ, I bet it tastes fishy."

"No takers," Sol sighed, then served up the oatmeal.

They ate in silence. The ener-G oatmeal wasn't so bad as they had expected, but it wasn't very good, either. As soon as he was finished Sol washed the taste of it out of his mouth with the alcohol-and-water mixture.

"What's this you said about more work to come?" he asked. "They have you doing a double shift today?"

Andy went back to the window; there was a bit of air stirring the damp heat now that the sun had set. "Just about, I'm going on special duty for a while. You remember the murder case I told you about?"

"Big Mike, the gonif? Whoever chopped him did a service to the human race."

"My feelings exactly. But he's got political friends who are more interested in the case than we are. They have some connections, they pulled a few strings and the commissioner himself called the lieutenant and told him to get a man on the investigation full time and find the killer. It was my name on the report so I caught the assignment. And Grassy, oh, he is a sweet bastard, he didn't tell me about it until I was signing out. He gave me the job then and a strong suggestion that I get on to it tonight. Like now," he said, standing and stretching.

"It'll be a good deal, won't it?" Sol asked, stroking his beard. "An independent position, your own boss, working your own hours, being covered with glory."

"That isn't what I'll be covered with unless I come up with an answer pretty fast. Everyone is watching and they are putting on the pressure. Grassy told me I had to find the killer soonest or I would be back in uniform on a beat in Shiptown."

Andy went into his room and unlocked the padlock on the bottom drawer of the dresser. He had extra rounds of ammunition here, some private papers and equipment, including his issue flashlight. It was the squeeze-generator type and it worked up a good beam when he tested it.

"Where to now?" Sol asked when he came out. "Going to stake out the joint?"

"It's a good thing you're not a cop, Sol. With your knowledge of criminal investigation crime would run rampant in the city—"

"It's not doing so bad, even without my help."

"—and we'd all be murdered in our beds. No stake out. I'm going to talk to the girl."

"Now the case gets interesting. Am I allowed to ask what girl?"

"Kid name of Shirl. Really built. She was Big Mike's girl friend, living with him, but she was out of the apartment when he got bumped."

"Do you maybe need an assistant? I'm good at night work."

"Cool off, Sol, you wouldn't know what to do with it if you had it. She plays out of our league. Put some cold water on your wrists and get some sleep."

Using the flashlight, Andy avoided the refuse and other pitfalls of the dark stairwell. Outside, the crowds and the heat were unchanged, timeless, filling the street by day and by night. He wished for a rain that would clear them both away, but the weather report hadn't offered any hope. *Continued no change.*

Charlie opened the door at Chelsea Park with a polite "Good evening, sir." Andy started toward the elevator, then changed his mind and walked on past it to the stairs. He wanted to have a look at the window and the cellar after dark, to see it the way it had been when the burglar came in. *If* he had entered the building that way. Now that he had been assigned to actually try and find the killer he had to go into all the details of the case in greater depth, to try to reconstruct the whole thing. Was it possible to get to the window from outside without being seen? If it wasn't then it might be an inside job and he would have to go through the staff and the tenants of the building.

He stopped, silently, and took out his gun. Through the half-open door of the cellar ahead he saw the flickering beam of a flashlight. This was the room where the jimmied window was. He walked forward slowly, putting his feet down on the gritty concrete floor with care so that they made no noise. When he entered he saw that someone was against the far wall, playing flashlight along the row of windows. A dark figure outlined against the yellow blob of light. The light moved to the next window, hesitated and stopped on the heart that had been traced in the dirt there. The man leaned over and examined the window, so intent in his study that he did not hear Andy cross the floor and come up behind him.

"Just don't move—that's a gun in your back," Andy said as he jabbed the man with his revolver. The flashlight dropped and broke; and Andy cursed and pulled out his own light and squeezed it to life. The beam hit full on an old man's face, his mouth open in terror, his skin suddenly as pale as his long silvery hair. The man sagged against the wall, gasping for air, and Andy put his gun back into the holster, then held the other's arm as he slid slowly down the wall to a sitting position on the floor.

"The shock . . . suddenly . . ." he muttered. "You shouldn't do that . . . who are you?"

"I'm a police officer. What's your name—and what were you doing down here?" Andy frisked him quickly: he wasn't armed.

"I'm a . . . civil officer . . . my identification is here." He struggled to produce his wallet and Andy took it from him and opened it.

"Judge Santini," he said, flashing the light from the identification card to the man's face. "Yes, I've seen you in court. But isn't this a funny place for a judge to be?"

"Please, no impertinence, young man." The first reaction had passed and Santini was in control again. "I consider myself knowledgeable in the laws of this sovereign state, and I cannot recall any that apply to this particular situation. I suggest that you do not exceed your authority. . . ."

"This is a murder investigation and you may have been tampering with evidence, Judge. That's authority enough to run you in."

Santini blinked into the glare of the flashlight and could just make out his captor's legs; they were in tan pants, not a blue uniform. "You are Detective Rusch?" he asked.

"Yes, I am," Andy said, surprised. He lowered the light so that it was no longer shining in the judge's face. "What do you know about this?"

"I shall be happy to tell you, my boy, if you will allow me off the floor and if we could find a more comfortable spot for our chat. Why don't we visit Shirl—you must have made Miss Greene's acquaintance? It will be a bit cooler there, and once arrived I will be happy to tell you all that I know."

"Why don't we do that?" Andy said, helping the old man to his feet. The judge wasn't going to run away—and he might have some official connection with the case. How else had he known that Andy was the detective who had been assigned to the investigation? This looked more like political interest than police interest and he knew enough to tread warily here.

They took the elevator up from the basement and Andy's scowl wiped the curious look from the operator's face. The judge seemed to be feeling better, though he leaned on Andy's arm down the length of the hall.

Shirl opened the door for them. "Judge—is something wrong?" she asked, wide-eyed.

"Nothing, my dear, just a touch of the heat, fatigue. I'm not getting any younger, not at all." He straightened up, concealing well the effort this required, and moved away from Andy to lightly take her arm. "I met Detective Rusch outside, he was good enough to come up with me. Now, if I could be allowed a little closer to the cool breath of that air-conditioner and permitted to rest a moment . . ." They went down the hall and Andy followed.

The girl was really good to look at, dressed like something out of a TV spectacular. Her dress was made of a fabric that shone like woven silver—yet appeared to be soft at the same time. It was sleeveless, cut low in the front and even lower in the back, all the way down to her waist, Andy saw. Her hair was brushed straight to her shoulders in a shining russet wave. The judge looked at her too, out of the corner of his eye, as she guided him to the sofa.

- "We're not disturbing you, are we, Shirl?" he asked. "You're dressed up tonight. Going out?"

"No," she said, "I was just staying home by myself. If you want the truth—I'm just building up my own morale. I've never worn this dress before, it's something new, nylon, I think, with little specks of metal in it." She plumped a pillow and pushed it behind Judge Santini's head. "Can't I get something cool for you to drink? And you too, Mr. Rusch?" It was the first time she had appeared to notice him, and he nodded silently.

"A wonderful suggestion." The judge sighed and settled back. "Something alcoholic if possible."

"Oh, yes—there are all kinds of things in the bar, I don't drink them." When she went to the kitchen Andy sat close to Santini and spoke in a quiet voice.

"You were going to tell me what you were doing in the cellar—and how you know my name."

"Simplicity itself—" Santini glanced toward the kitchen, but Shirl was busy and couldn't hear them. "O'Brien's death him. "I was thinking of something else and I didn't hear been asked to follow the progress being made. Naturally I learned that you had been assigned to the case." He relaxed and folded his hands over his round belly.

"That's an answer to one half of my question," Andy said. "Now, what were you doing in the cellar?"

"It's cool in here, almost chill you might say after being outside. Quite a relief. Did you notice the heart that had been drawn in the dust on the cellar window?"

"Of course. I was the one who found it."

"That is most interesting. Did you ever hear of an individual—you should have, he has a police record—by the name of Cuore?"

"Nick Cuore? The one who has been muscling into the rackets in Newark?"

"The very one. Though 'muscling in' is not quite correct, 'in charge' would be more accurate. He has taken over there, and is such an ambitious man that he is even casting his eyes in the direction of New York."

"What is all this supposed to mean?"

"*Cuore* is a good Italian word. It means heart," Santini said as Shirl came into the room carrying a tray.

Andy took the drink with an automatic thank you, scarcely aware of the other's conversation. He understood now why all the pressure was being brought to bear upon this case. It wasn't a matter of pity, no one seemed to really care that O'Brien was dead, it was the *why* of his killing that really counted. Had the murder been a brutal accident as it appeared to be? Or was it a warning from Cuore that he was expanding into New York City? Or was the killing a power move by one of the local people who was trying to put the blame on Cuore in order to cover himself? Once you entered the maze of speculation the possibilities expanded until the only way the truth could be uncovered was by finding the killer. The interested parties had pulled a few strings and his full-time assignment had been the result. A number of people must be reading his reports and waiting impatiently for an answer.

"I'm sorry," he said, aware that the girl had spoken to him. "I was thinking of something else and I didn't hear you."

"I just asked you if the drink was all right. I can get you something else if you don't like that."

"No, this is fine," he said, realizing that he had been holding his glass all this time, just staring at it. He took a sip, and then a second one. "In fact it's very good. What is it?"

"Whiskey. Whiskey and soda."

"It's the first time I ever tasted it." He tried to remember how much a bottle of whiskey cost. There was almost none being made now because of the grain shortage and each year the stored supplies grew smaller and the price increased. At least two hundred D's a bottle, probably more.

"That was very refreshing, Shirl," Santini said, placing his empty glass against the arm of his chair where it remained, "and you have my most heartfelt thanks for your kind hospitality. I'm sorry I must run along now, Rosa is expecting me, but could I ask you something first?"

"Of course, Judge—what is it?"

Santini took an envelope from his side pocket and opened it, fanning out the handful of photographs that it contained. From where he sat all Andy could see was that they were pictures of different men. Santini handed it over to Shirl.

"It was tragic," he said, "tragic what happened to Mike. All of us want to help the police as much as we can. I know you do too, Shirl, so perhaps you'll take a look at these pictures, see if you recognize any of these people."

She took the first one and looked at it, frowning in

concentration. Andy admired the judge's technique for talking a lot and really saying nothing—yet getting the girl's cooperation.

"No, I can't say I have ever seen him before," she said.

"Was he ever a guest here, or did he meet Mike while you were with him?"

"No, I'm sure of that, he's never been here. I thought you were asking if I had ever seen him on the street or anything."

"What about the other men?"

"I've never seen any of them. I'm sorry I can't be of any more help."

"Negative intelligence is still intelligence, my dear."

He passed the photographs to Andy, who recognized the top one as Nick Cuore. "And the others?" he asked.

"Associates of his," Santini said as he rose slowly from the deep chair.

"I'll keep these awhile," Andy said.

"Of course. You may find them valuable."

"Must you go already?" Shirl protested. Santini smiled and started for the front door.

"Indulge an old man, my dear. Much as I enjoy your company, I must keep sensible hours these days. Good night, Mr. Rusch—and good luck."

"I'm going to make myself a drink," Shirl said after she had shown the judge out. "Can I liven up that one for you? If you're not on duty, that is."

"I'm on duty, and I have been for the last fourteen hours, so I think it is about time that duty and drink mixed. If you won't report me?"

"I'm no ratfink!" She smiled, and when they sat opposite each other he felt better than he had for weeks. The headache was gone, he was cool and the drink tasted better than anything he remembered.

"I thought you were through with the investigation," Shirl said. "That's what you told me."

"I thought so then, but things have changed. There is a lot of interest in getting this case solved. Even people like Judge Santini are concerned."

"All the time I knew Mike I never realized he was so important."

"Alive, I don't think he was. It is his death that is important, and the reasons—if any—for it."

"Did you mean that, what you said this afternoon about the police not wanting anything moved from this apartment?"

"Yes, for the present. I'll have to go through everything, particularly the papers. Why do you ask?"

Shirl kept her eyes on her glass, clutching it tightly with both hands. "Mike's lawyer was here today, and everything is pretty much like his sister said. My clothes, my personal belongings are mine, nothing else. Not that I expected anything more. But the rent has been paid here until the end of August—" she looked up squarely at Andy, "and if the furniture is left here I can stay on until then."

"Do you want to do that?"

"Yes," she said, nothing more.

She's all right, Andy thought. She's not asking any favors, no tears or that kind of thing. Just spreading her cards on the table. Well, why not? It doesn't cost me anything. Why not?

"Consider it done. I'm a very slow apartment searcher, and an apartment this big will take until exactly midnight on the thirty-first of August to search properly. If there are any complaints refer them to Third Grade Detective Andrew Fremont Rusch, Precinct 12-A. I'll tell the parties concerned to get lost."

"That's wonderful!" she said, jumping happily to her feet. "And it deserves another drink. To tell you the truth, I wouldn't feel right about, you know, selling anything from the apartment. That would be stealing. But I don't see anything wrong with finishing off the bottles. That's better than leaving them for that sister of his."

"I agree completely," Andy said, lying back in the soft embrace of the cushions, watching her delicate and attractive wiggle as she took the glasses into the kitchen. This is the life, he thought, and grinned crookedly to himself, the hell with the investigation. At least for tonight. I'm going to drink Big Mike's booze and sit back on his couch and forget everything about police business for just one night.

"No, I come from Lakeland, New Jersey," she said, "we just moved here to the city when I was a kid. The Strategic Air Command was putting in those extra-long runways for the Mach-3 planes and they bought our house and all the other ones nearby and tore them down. It's my father's

favorite story, how they ruined his life, and he has never
voted for a Republican since and swears he would rather die
first."

"I wasn't born here either," he said, and took a sip of the
drink. "We came from California, my father had a ranch
—"

"Then you're a cowboy!"

"Not that kind of a ranch, fruit trees, in the Imperial
Valley, I was just a little kid when he left and I hardly
remember it. All the farming in those valleys was done with
irrigation—canals and pumps. My father's ranch had
pumps and he didn't think it was very important when the
geologists told him he was using fossil water, water that had
been in the ground thousands of years. Old water grows
things just as well as new water, I remember him saying
that. But there must have been little or no new water
filtering down because one day the fossil water was all used
up and the pump went dry. I'll never forget that, the trees
dying and nothing we could do about it. My father lost the
farm and we came to New York, he was a sandhog on the
Moses Tunnel when they were building it.

"I never kept an album," Andy said.

"It's the sort of things girls do." She sat on the couch next
to him, turning the pages. In the front were photographs of
children, ticket stubs, programs, but he was only slightly
aware of them. Her warm bare arm pressed against his and
when she leaned over the album he could smell the perfume
in her hair. He had drunk an awful lot, he realized vaguely,
and he nodded his head and pretended to be looking at the
album. All he was really aware of was her.

"It's after two, I better get going."

"Don't you want some more kofee first?" she asked.

"No thanks." He finished the cup and carefully set it
down. "I'll be around in the morning, if that will be all right
with you." He started toward the door.

"The morning is fine," she said, and put her hand out.
"And thanks for staying here this evening."

"I should be thanking you for the party, remember I
never tasted whiskey before."

He meant to shake hands, that was all, to say good night.
But for some reason he found her in his arms, his face

against her hair and his hands pressed tight to the soft velvet skin of her back. When he kissed her she returned the kiss fiercely and he knew everything would be all right.

Later, lying on the crisp expanse of the bed, he could feel the touch of her warm body at his side and the light stir of her sleeping breath on his cheek. The hum of the air-conditioner seemed to make the night more quiet, covering and masking all the other sounds. He had had too much to drink, he realized now, and smiled up at the darkness. So what? If he had been sober he might never have ended up where he was. He might feel sorry in the morning, but at the present moment this felt like the best thing that had ever happened to him. Even when he tried to feel guilty he couldn't; his hand tightened possessively on her shoulder and she stirred in her sleep. The curtains were parted slightly and through the opening he could see the moon, distant and friendly. This is all right, he said, this is all right, over and over again to himself.

The moon burned in through the open window, a piercing eye in the night, a torch in the breathless heat. Billy Chung had slept a little, earlier, but one of the twins had had a nightmare and wakened him and he had lain there wide awake ever since. If only the man hadn't been in the bathroom. . . . Billy rolled his head back and forth, biting at his lower lip, feeling the sweat beading his face. He hadn't meant to kill him, but now that he was dead Billy didn't care. He was worried about himself. What would happen when they caught him? They would find him, that's what the police were for, they would take the tire iron out of the dead man's head and go over it in their laboratory the way they did and find the man who had sold it to him. . . . His head rolled from side to side on the sweat-dampened pillow and a low, almost voiceless moan was forced between his teeth.

9

"That's not much of a shave you got there, Rusch," Grassioli said in his normal, irritated tone of voice.

"It's no shave at all, lieutenant," Andy said, looking up from the sheaf of reports on the desk. The lieutenant had noticed him while he was passing the detective squadroom on the way to the clerical office; Andy had hoped to sign in and leave the precinct without meeting him. He thought fast. "I'm running down some leads over near Shiptown this afternoon, I didn't want to be too obvious. There probably isn't one razor in that whole neighborhood." That sounded good enough. The truth was he had come in late this morning, direct from Chelsea Park, and never had a chance to shave.

"Yeah. What's the progress on the case?"

Andy knew better than to remind the lieutenant that he had been working on it only since the previous evening.

"I've found out one positive thing that relates to it." He looked around, but there was no one else within earshot, and he continued in a lower voice. "I know why the pressure has been put on the department."

"Why?"

The lieutenant flipped through the pictures of Nick Cuore and his henchmen while Andy explained the significance of the heart on the window and the identity of the men who were interested in the murder.

"All right," Grassioli said when he had finished, "don't write a damn thing about this in any reports, unless you find anything leading to Cuore, but I want you to tell me everything that happens. Now get going, you wasted enough time around here."

It was a record-breaker. Day after day had passed, but the heat stayed the same. The street outside was a tub of hot, foul air, unmoving and so filled with the stench of dirt and sweat and decay that it was almost unbreathable. Yet, for the first time since the heat wave had set in, Andy did not notice it. The previous night was an overwhelming though still unbelievable presence, impossible to put out of his mind. He tried to, he had work to do, but Shirl's face or body would slip around the edges of memory and, despite the heat, he would once again feel the sensation of suffused warmth. This wouldn't do! He smashed his right fist into his open palm and had to smile at the startled looks of the nearby people in the crowd. There was work to do, a lot of it, before he could see her again.

He turned into the alleyway that ran between the locked row of garages behind Chelsea Park and the edge of the moat, leading to the service entrance to the buildings. There was a rumble of wheels behind him and he stepped aside to let a heavy tugtruck pass, a square, boxlike body mounted on old auto wheels, guided by the two men who pulled it. They were bent almost double and aware of nothing except their fatigue. As they plodded by, just a few feet from him, Andy could see how the traces cut into their necks, gouging into the permanent ulcers on their shoulders that stained their shirts wet with pus.

Andy walked slowly behind the tugtruck, stopping while he was still out of sight of the entrance, then leaning over the edge of the moat. Filth and rubbish littered the concrete bottom below, and there were wide gaps between the granite blocks where the cement had fallen away. It would be easy enough to climb down the wall after dark, there were no revealing lights nearby. Even in the daytime an intruder would only be noticed by someone glancing out of the closest windows. No one was watching when Andy let himself over the edge and clambered slowly to the bottom; it was like going into an oven here, with the heat trapped by the high walls. He ignored it as best he could and walked along the inner wall until he found the window with the heart on it, it was very easy to spot and would probably be as easily seen at night as well. There was a ledge just below the row of cellar windows and he found he could lever himself up onto it—and it was wide enough to stand on. Yes, it was very possible to jimmy open the window standing here; the murderer could have broken into the building this way. Sweat dripped from his chin and made dark spots on the concrete of the ledge, the heat was getting to him.

"What do you think you're doing there! You're going to

get your head broken!" The voice shouted down at him and he straightened and looked up at the drawbridge that crossed the moat, at the doorman standing there, shaking his fist. He recognized Andy and his voice changed abruptly. "Sorry—I didn't see it was you, sir. Anything I can do to help?"

"Yes—get me out of here. Do any of those windows open?"

"Just move along a bit, the next one over your head, it's a lobby window." The doorman vanished and a few moments later the window creaked open and his wide face stuck out.

"Give me a lift," Andy said. "I'm half cooked." He took the doorman's hand and scrambled up. The lobby was dim and cool after the sun-blasted heat of the moat. He wiped at his face with his handkerchief. "Is there any place where we can talk—where I can sit down?"

"In the guardroom, sir, just follow me."

There were two men there; the one in building uniform jumped to his feet when they came in. The other was Tab. "Get on the door, Newton," the doorman ordered. "You want to go with him, Tab?"

Tab glanced at the detective. "Sure, Charlie," he said, and followed the guard out.

"We got some water here," the doorman said. "Want a glass?"

"Great," Andy said, dropping into a chair. He took the plastic beaker and drained half of it, then slowly sipped the rest. Facing him was a gray-tinted window that looked out into the lobby; he couldn't remember seeing any window there on the way in. "One-way glass?" he asked.

"That's right. For the residents' protection. It's a mirror on the other side."

"Did you see where I was in the moat?"

"Yes, sir, it looked like you were just outside the cellar window, the one that got jimmied open."

"I was. I came down the other side of the moat, from the back alley, crossed it and climbed up by the window. If it was nighttime do you think you would have seen me there?"

"Well . . ."

"A plain yes or no will do. I'm not trying to trap you into anything."

"The building management, they're already doing something about the security, it's mostly the trouble with the alarm system. No, I don't think I would have seen you at night, sir, not down there in the dark."

"I didn't think so. Then you believe that someone could have entered the building that way, unseen?"

Charlie's small, piggish eyes were half closed, looking around for aid. "I suppose," he admitted finally, "the killer could have got in that way."

"Good. And that particular cellar room is the right one to come in through. Easy to get near the window, a broken alarm on the frame, everything just right. Whoever broke in could have marked the window with that heart so he could find it again from the outside. Which means he had to have been in the building first, probably casing it."

"Maybe," Charlie admitted, and smiled slightly. "And maybe he made the mark there *after* he got in, just to fool you into believing it was an inside job."

Andy nodded. "You're thinking, Charlie. But either way it could have been marked from the inside first, and I have to operate on that principle. I'll want a list of all the present employees, all the new ones and all those who have left here in the last couple of years, a list of tenants and former tenants. Who would have a thing like that?"

"The building manager, sir, he has an office right upstairs. Would you like me to show you where it is?"

"In one minute—I need another glass of water first."

Andy stood facing the inner door of the O'Brien apartment, pretending to be busy with the list of names he had obtained from the building manager. He knew that Shirl might be looking at him in the door TV and he tried to appear preoccupied and busy. When he had left that morning she had been asleep and he had not talked to her since the previous night—not that they had done much talking then, either. It wasn't that he was embarrassed, it was just that the whole thing still had an air of unreality about it. She belonged here and he didn't, and if she pretended that nothing had happened, or didn't mention it—could he? He didn't think he would. She was a long time answering the door, maybe she wasn't home? No, the bodyguard, Tab, was downstairs, which meant she was still in the building. Was something wrong? Had the killer come back? That was a stupid thing to think, yet he hammered loudly on the panel.

"Don't break it down," she said as she opened it. "I was cleaning and I didn't hear the door." Her hair was tied up in a turban and her feet were bare. A lot of her was bare since she was wearing just a pale green halter and shorts. She looked wonderful.

"I'm sorry, I didn't know," he said seriously.

"Well, it's not very important," she laughed, "don't look so sad." She leaned forward and gave him a quick warm kiss on the mouth. Before he could react she had turned away and gone down the hall. The shorts were very short, and very, very round. As the door clicked behind him he realized suddenly that he was quite happy. The air was wonderfully cool.

"I'm almost finished," Shirl said, and there was the sudden whine of a small motor. "It'll just take me a second then I'll clean this mess away." When he came into the living room he saw that she was running a vacuum cleaner over the rug. "Why don't you take a shower?" she called over the sound of the machine. "Mary O'Brien Haggerty will be getting the water bill so you shouldn't care."

A shower! he thought excitedly. "Since I've met Mary Haggerty I'll be glad to send her the bill," he shouted, and they both laughed.

As he went through the bedroom he remembered that this was the room where O'Brien had been killed—he hadn't thought about that at all last night. Poor O'Brien, he must have been a real bastard while he was still alive, since there didn't seem to be a single person who missed him or really felt moved by his death. Including Shirl. What had she thought about him? It didn't matter now. He dropped his clothes on the floor and tested the water with his hand.

There was a razor with a new blade in the cabinet and he hummed happily to himself while he washed the gray whiskers out of it, then lathered his face. For some reason wearing a dead man's shoes didn't bother him in the least. In fact he greatly enjoyed it. The razor slid smoothly over his skin.

All the cleaning apparatus had vanished by the time he had dressed and gone into the living room again, and Shirl had her hair down and what looked like fresh makeup on. Though she was still wearing the shorts and top, for which he breathed a silent thanks. He had never seen a prettier— no, a more beautiful girl in his whole life. He wished he could tell her that, but it wasn't the kind of thing he found it easy to say aloud.

"How about something cold to drink?" she asked.

"I'm supposed to be working—are you trying to corrupt me?"

"You can have a beer, I put some in the fridge. There are almost twenty bottles to finish and I don't really like it." She turned in the doorway and smiled. "Besides, you *are* working. You're interviewing me. Aren't I an important witness?"

The first sip of the cold beer cut a track of pleasure down his throat. Shirl sat down across from him and sipped at a cold kofee. "How is the case going, or is that an official secret?"

"Nothing secret, it goes slow like all cases. You shouldn't let the TV fool you, police work isn't at all like that. It's mostly dull stuff, a lot of walking around, making notes, writing reports—and hoping a stoolie will bring you the answer."

"I know what that is—a *stool pigeon!* There aren't really stool pigeons, are there?"

"If there weren't we would be out of business. Most of our pinches are made on tips from stoolies. Most crooks are stupid and have big mouths and when they start talking there is usually someone around to listen. I hope someone talks this time—because it looks like a next to impossible case if they don't."

"What do you mean?"

He sipped some more beer; it was wonderful stuff. "There are over thirty-five million people in this town, and any one of them could have done it. I'll start running down all the former building employees and questioning them, and I'll try to find out where the tire iron came from, but long before I'm finished the people on top are going to stop worrying about O'Brien and I'll be off the case and that will be that."

"You sound sort of bitter."

"You're right—I am. Wouldn't you be if you had a job you wanted to do, and liked doing, yet you were never allowed to do? We're over our heads with work and have been ever since I came on the force. Nothing is ever finished, no cases are ever followed up, people really do get away with murder every day and no one seems to mind. Unless there is some kind of political reason, like with Big Mike, and then no one really cares about him, it's just their own hides that they are worrying about."

"Couldn't they just hire some more policemen?"

"With what? There's no money in the city budget, almost all of it goes for Welfare. So our pay is low, cops take bribes, and—you don't want to hear a lecture about my troubles!" He drained the rest of the beer from the glass and she jumped to her feet.

"Here, let me get another."

"No, thanks, not on an empty stomach."

"Haven't you eaten at all?"

"Grabbed a piece of weedcracker. I didn't have time for anything more."

"I'll fix us some lunch. How about beefsteak?"

"Shirl, stop it—you'll give me heart failure."

"No, I mean it. I bought a steak for Mike, the other morning of . . . that day. It's still in the freezer."

"I can't remember the last time I had beef—in fact it has been a long time since I have seen a piece of soylent." He stood and took both of her hands. "You're taking very good care of me, you know?"

"I like to," she said, and gave him another of those quick kisses. His hands were on the roundness of her hips when she turned and walked away.

She's a funny girl, he thought to himself, and touched his tongue to the trace of lipstick on his lips.

Shirl wanted to eat in the living room at the big table, but there was a table built into the kitchen, under the window, and Andy could see no reason why they couldn't sit right there. It was a steak all right, a monster piece of meat as big as his hand, and he felt the saliva flow in his mouth when she slid it onto his plate.

"Fifty-fifty," he said, slicing it in half and putting one piece on the other plate.

"I usually just fry some oatmeal in the juices. . . ."

"We'll have that for dessert. This is the start of a new era, equal rights for men and women." She smiled at him and slid into her chair without another word. Damn, he thought, for another look like that I'd give her the whole thing.

There was seacress with it, weedcrackers to sop up the gravy and another bottle of cold beer from which she allowed him to pour her a small glass. The meat was indescribably good and he cut it into very small pieces, savoring each one slowly. He could not remember having eaten as well in his entire life. When he had finished he sat back and sighed with contentment. It was good, yet it was almost too good, and he knew it wouldn't last: he felt a little gnaw of irritation as the words *dead man's shoe*s flicked through his mind.

"I hope you didn't mind, but I was more than a little drunk last night." It sounded crude and he was sorry the instant he had said it.

"I didn't mind at all. I thought you were very sweet."

"Sweet!" He laughed at himself. "I've been called a lot of things, but never that before. I thought you were angry at me ever since I came back."

"I've been busy, that's all, the place was a mess and you were hungry. I think I know what you need."

She moved swiftly around the table and was on his lap, the whole womanly warm length of her and her arms were around his neck. It was a kiss, the kind he remembered, and he discovered that her halter was closed on the front by two buttons which he opened and pressed his face against the smooth fragrance of her skin.

"Let's go inside," she said huskily.

She lay next to him afterward, relaxed and without shame, while his fingers traced the outline of her splendid body. The occasional sounds that pierced the sealed window and closed curtains only emphasized the twilight solitude of the bedroom. When he kissed the corner of her mouth she smiled dreamily, her eyes half closed.

"Shirl . . ." he said, but could not continue. He had no practice in voicing his emotions. The words were there, but he could not say them aloud. Yet the way his hands moved on her skin conveyed his meaning more clearly than words could; her body trembled in response and she moved closer to him. There was a hoarseness in her voice, even though she whispered.

"You're really good in bed, different—do you know that? You make me feel things that I have never felt before." His muscles tightened suddenly and she turned to him. "Are you angry at that? Should I make believe that you are the only man I ever slept with?"

"No, of course not. It's none of my business and doesn't

affect me." The tautness of his body put the lie to his words.

Shirl rolled on her back and looked at the motes of dust glinting in the beam of light that came through the crack between the curtains. "I'm not trying to excuse anything, Andy, just to tell you. I grew up in one of those real strict families, I never went out or did anything and my father watched me all the time. I don't think I minded very much, there was just nothing to do, that's all. Dad liked me, he probably thought he was doing what was right for me. He was retired, they made him retire when he was fifty-five, and he had his pension and the money from the house, so he just sat around and drank. Then, when I was twenty, I entered this beauty contest and won first prize. I remember I gave my prize money to my father to take care of and that's the last time I saw him. There was one of the judges, he had asked me for a date that night, so I went out with him, then I went to live with him."

Just like that? Andy said to himself, but he didn't say it aloud. He smiled at himself: what rights did he have?

"You're not laughing at me?" she said, touching her finger to his lips, a hurt in her voice.

"Good God, no! I was laughing at myself because—if you must know—I was being a little jealous. And I have no right to be."

"You have every right in the world," she said, kissing him slowly and lingeringly. "For me at least, this is very different. I haven't known that many men, and they were all men like Mike. I was just sort of there, I felt. . . ."

"Shut up," he said. "I don't care." He meant it. "I just care about you here and now and not another thing in the world."

10

Andy was almost to the bottom of his list, and his feet hurt Ninth Avenue simmered in the afternoon sun and every patch of shadow was filled with sprawled figures, old people, nursing mothers, teen-agers with their heads close together, laughing with their arms about one another. People of all ages on every side, bare and dusty limbs projecting, scattered about like corpses in the aftermath of a battle. Only the children played in the sun, but they moved about slowly and their shouts were subdued. There was a fit of screaming and sudden movement as they eddied about two boys coming from the direction of the docks, whose arms were spotted with bites and streaks of uncongealed blood. On the end of a string they carried their prize, a large gray dead rat. They would eat well tonight. In the center of the crowded street the tugtruck traffic moved at a snail's pace, the human draught animals leaning exhaustedly into their traces, mouths gaping for air. Andy pushed through between them, looking for the Western Union office.

It would be impossible to check every person who had gone in or out O'Brien's apartment during the previous week, but he had to at least try the most obvious leads. Any visitor to the building could have discovered the disconnected burglar alarm in the cellar, but only someone who had been in the apartment could have seen that this alarm had been cut off as well. There had been a short circuit eight days before the murder, and the alarm on the door had been disconnected until it could be fixed. The killer, or some informant, could easily have seen this if he had been in the apartment. Andy had made a list of possibilities and was checking them out. They were all negative. No meter readers had visited the apartment, and all the deliveries had been made by men who had been coming there for years. Negative, all the way down the line.

Western Union was another long shot. There had been plenty of telegrams delivered to the building during that week, and the doorman was sure that some of them had been to O'Brien. He and the elevator boy had both remembered a telegram coming the night before the murder, it had been brought by a new messenger, a Chinese boy they had said. The chances were a thousand to one that it didn't mean anything—but it still had to be checked out. Any lead at all, no matter how slight would have to be investigated. Whatever happened it would at least be something to report to the lieutenant, to keep him off Andy's neck for a while. The yellow and blue sign hung out over the sidewalk and he turned in under it.

A long counter divided the office and at the far end of it

was a bench on which three boys were sitting. A fourth boy stood at the counter talking to the dispatcher. None of them was Chinese. The boy at the counter took a message board from the man there and went out. Andy walked over, but before he could say anything the man shook his head angrily.

"Not here," he snapped. "Front counter for telegrams, can't you see I'm the dispatcher?"

Andy looked at the sullen fatigue and the deep lines cut into the man's face by the perpetually pulled-down corners of his mouth, and at the clutter of boards and chalk and washable teletype tape on the desk before him, the peeling gold paint on the little sign that said *Mr. Burgger*. All the years of bitterness were clear to see in the clutter of the desk and the hatred in his eyes. It would take patience to get any cooperation from this man. Andy flashed his badge.

"Police business," he said. "You're the man I want to talk to, Mr. Burgger."

"I haven't done anything, there's nothing for you to talk to me about."

"No one's accusing you. It's information I need to aid an investigation. . . ."

"I can't help you. I don't have any police information."

"Let me decide that. Is Twenty-eighth Street inside your delivery area?"

Burgger hesitated, then nodded slowly and reluctantly as though he were being forced to reveal a state secret.

"Do you have any Chinese messenger boys?"

"No."

"But you have had at least one Chinese boy working for you?"

"No." He scratched on a board, ignoring Andy. Perspiration beaded the top of his bald head and collected in droplets on the strands of gray hair. Andy didn't enjoy putting on pressure, but he could do it when he had to.

"We have laws in this state, Burgger," he said in a low, toneless voice. "I can drag you out of here right now and take you over to the station and throw you into the can for thirty days for interfering with an officer. Do you want me to do that?"

"I haven't done anything!"

"Yes you have. You've lied to me. You said you never had a Chinese kid working here."

Burgger squirmed in his seat, pulled two ways by the conflict between his fear and his desire to remain uncommitted. Fear won.

"There was a Chinese kid, worked just one day, never came back."

"What day was that?"

The answer came reluctantly. "Monday of this week."

"Did he deliver any telegrams?"

"How the hell should I know?"

"Because that's your job," Andy said, putting a snap into his words again. "What telegrams did he deliver?"

"He sat around all day, I didn't need him. It was his first day, I never send a new kid out the first day, let them get used to the bench first so they don't get ideas. But we had a rush that night. I had to use him. Just once."

"Where to?"

"Look, mister, I can't remember every telegram I send out. This is a busy office and besides, we don't keep records. A telegram is received, delivered, accepted, that's the end of it."

"I know all that, but this telegram is important. I want you to try and remember where it went. Was it to Seventh Avenue? Or Twenty-third Street? Chelsea Park . . . ?"

"Wait, I think that was it. I remember I didn't want the kid to go to Chelsea Park, they don't like new kids there, just the regulars, but there was no one else in, so I had to use him."

"Now we're getting someplace," Andy said, taking out his notepad. "What's the kid's name?"

"Some Chink name, I forget now. He was only here that one day and never came back."

"What did he look like, then?"

"Like a Chink kid. It's not my job remembering what kids look like." He was sinking back into his sullen hatred.

"Where did he live?"

"Who knows? Kid comes in and puts up his board money, that's all I know. Not my job—"

"Nothing seems to be your job, Burgger. I'll be seeing you again. Meanwhile try to remember what the kid looked like, I'll want some more answers from you."

The boys stirred on the bench when Andy went out and Burgger flashed them a look of pure hatred.

It was a thin lead, but Andy was cheerful; at least he had something to talk to Grassy about. Steve Kulozik was also in the lieutenant's office when he went in, and they nodded to each other.

"How's the case?" Steve asked.

"You can do your gossiping on your own time," Grassioli broke in; the tic in his eye was going fine today. "You better have come up with something by now, Rusch, this is a case, not a holiday and a lot of brass up and down the line are getting peed off."

Andy explained about the disconnected burglar alarm and the timing necessary for anyone to have visited the apartment. He quickly ran through the unproductive interviews he had had until he came to the Western Union boy: this he told in detail.

"So what does it add up to?" the lieutenant asked, both hands clasped on his stomach, over the spot where the ulcer was.

"The kid might have been working for someone. Messenger boys have to put up ten D's board money—and how many kids have that kind of loot? The kid could have been brought in, maybe from Chinatown, and paid to snoop the apartments he brought telegrams to. He hit the jackpot first time out when he saw the disconnected alarm on Big Mike's door. Then, whoever hired him pulled the job and the killing, after which they both faded."

"Sounds pretty slim, but it's about the only lead you've managed to come up with. What's the kid's name?"

"No one knows."

"Well, what the hell!" Grassioli shouted. "You come up with this fancy damned complicated theory and where does it go if you can't find the kid? There are millions of kids in this city—so how do we find the right one?"

Andy knew when to be silent. Steve Kulozik had been leaning his bulk against the wall, listening while Andy explained. "Could I say something, lieutenant?" he asked.

"What do you want?"

"Let's just for a minute think of this whole case as being inside this precinct. The kid could have come from Chinatown or from anywheres, but let's forget about that. Say he came from Shiptown, right here, and you know how those people are about sticking together, so maybe there's another Chink who was using the kid. Just suppose."

"What are you trying to say, Kulozik? Get to the god-damn point."

"I was just about to, lieutenant," Steve said imper-turbably. "Let's say the kid or his boss comes from Ship-town. If they do we may have fingerprints on them. It was before my time, but you were here in seventy-two, weren't you, lieutenant, when they brought all the Formosa refugees in after General Kung's invasion got its ass blown off on the mainland?"

"I was here. I was a rookie then."

"Didn't they fingerprint everybody, kids and all? Just in case some Commie agent slipped in with them before the airlift?"

"It's a long shot," the lieutenant said. "They were all fingerprinted and so were all the kids for a couple of years after that just in case they might defect. Those cards are all down in the cellar here. That's what you were thinking about, wasn't it?"

"That's right, sir. Go through them and see if the prints from the murder weapon can be matched up with one of the cards. It's a long shot, but it doesn't hurt to try."

"You heard him, Rusch," Grassioli said, pulling over a stack of reports. "Get the weapon prints and get down there and see if you can find anything."

"Yes, sir," Andy answered, and he and Steve went out together. "Big buddy you are," he told Steve as soon as the door had closed. "I should be knocking off soon and instead you got me buried in the cellar, and I'll probably be there all night."

"It's not that bad," Steve said complacently. "I had to use the file once, all the prints are coded so you can get to the ones you want fast. I'd help you except my brother-in-law is coming to dinner tonight."

"The one you hate so much?"

"That's the one. But he's working on one of the fishing trawlers now, and he's going to bring a fish he stole. Fresh fish. Doesn't your mouth water?"

"Just for a bite out of your hide, you ratfink. I hope you get a bone stuck in your throat."

The fingerprint files were not in quite the same condition that Steve had described. Others had used them since and whole groups of cards were filed out of sequence and one entire boxful had been spilled and afterward had just been jammed back in at random. Though the basement was cooler than the rest of the building the air was filled with dust and felt almost too thick to breathe. Andy worked until nine o'clock before his head started to pound and his eyes burned. He went upstairs and put some water on his face and breathed in some fresh air. For a few moments he wavered between finishing the job or waiting until morning, but he had some idea of what Grassy would have to say about that, so he went back downstairs.

It was going on eleven o'clock when he found the card. He almost put it aside because the prints were so small, an infant's, then he realized that children grew up and had a closer look at it through the scratched plastic magnifying lens.

There was no doubt at all. These prints were the same as the ones that had been found on the window and on the tire iron.

" 'Chung, William,' " he read. " 'Born 1982, Shiptown Infirmary . . .' "

He stood up so fast that he knocked the chair over. The lieutenant would be home by now, maybe in bed, and would be in a filthy humor if he was wakened. That didn't matter.

This was it.

11

Far out in the river a boat whistle blew, two times, then two times again, and the sound echoed from the steel flanks of the ships until it had no source or direction and became a mournful wail that filled the hot night. Billy Chung rolled back and forth on his lumpy mattress, wide awake after hours of lying there staring into the darkness. Against the far wall the twins breathed hoarsely in their sleep. The whistle sounded again, beating at his ears. Why hadn't he just grabbed the stuff and got out of the apartment? He could have done it faster. Why did the big bastard have to

come in just then? It was right he should have been killed,
anyone as stupid as that. It had been self-defense, hadn't it?
He had been attacked first. The same memory repeated
itself again like an endless circle of film in a projector: the
iron bar swinging up, the look on the fat red face. The sight
of the iron sticking out of his head and the thin trickle of
blood. Billy writhed, tossing his head from one side to the
other, his fingers pulling at the damp skin on his chest.

Was every night going to be like this? With the heat and
the sweat and the memories, over and over again? If he
hadn't come into the bedroom just then. . . . Billy groaned,
then cut off the sound before it left his throat. He sat up and
put his palms to his eyes, pressing hard until the jagged
redness of their pressure filled the darkness before him.
What about the dirt, should he use it now? He had bought it
for a time like this, it had cost two D's, maybe now was the
right time. They said you couldn't get hooked on it, but
everybody lied.

Feeling his way in the darkness, he ran his hand up the
armored cable on the steel wall to the disused junction box.
The dirt was still there; his fingers pressed against the scrap
of polythene it was wrapped in. Should he use it now? The
whistle throbbed through the heat again and he found that
he had dug his fingernails into the sides of his legs. His
shorts were against the wall where he had thrown them and
he pulled them on and reached down the little packet and
went and opened the passageway door as quietly as he
could. His bare feet were silent on the warm metal deck.

All of the portholes and windows were open, blind black
eyes in the rust-streaked walls. People were sleeping there,
on all sides, in every cabin and compartment. Billy climbed
to the top deck and the blind eyes still gaped at him. The last
ladder led up to the bridge, once sealed and inviolate before
two generations of children had patiently picked away at the
covers and shattered the locks. Now the door was gone, the
frames and glass long vanished from the windows. During
the day this was a favorite playground for the swarming
children of the *Columbia Victory,* but it was deserted and
silent now, the only reminder of their presence the sharp
smell of urine in the corners. Billy went in.

Only the most solid of the nautical fittings remained: a
steel chart table welded to one wall, the ship's telegraph, the
steering wheel with half of its spokes missing. Billy carefully

opened the packet of dirt on the chart table and poked his finger into the gray dust that was barely visible in the starlight. What did they call it? LSD? It was cut anyway, whatever it was, that's why they called it dirt. They mixed dirt or something with it to stretch it. You had to take all of it, dirt and all, to get enough LSD into you so you could feel it. He had watched Sam-Sam and some of the other Tigers sniff it, but he had never done it himself. How had they done it? He lifted the crumpled plastic and held it to his nose, sealing one nostril with his thumb, then inhaled strongly. The only sensation was an outrageous tickling and he pinched his nose shut tightly so he wouldn't sneeze all the stuff away. When the irritation died down he snuffed the remaining powder into his other nostril and threw the scrap of thin plastic to the floor.

There was no sensation, nothing at all, the world was the same and Billy knew that he had been cheated. Two D's shot, gone for nothing. He leaned out of the glassless, frameless window and tears mixed with the perspiration on his face. He cried and thought about that for a while and thought how glad he was it was dark and no one could see him crying, not him, eighteen years old. Under his fingers the rough metal of the window opening had the feel of miniature mountain peaks and valleys. Jagged, smooth, soft, hard. He leaned close and stroked with his fingertips and the pleasure of the touch sent shivers of love running the length of his spine. Why had he never noticed this before? Bending, he put out his tongue and the sweet-sour-iron-dirt taste was so wonderful, and when he let the sharp front edges of his teeth touch the metal it felt as though he had bitten off a piece of steel half as big as the bridge.

A ship's whistle filled the world with its sound, somewhere out on the river or close by, and he knew that it was more than a whistle, it was music, high, low and all around him and he opened his mouth wide so that he could taste it better. Was it his ship that had sounded the whistle? The dark outlines of spars, masts, wires, funnels, aerials, guys, stays, boats, moved on all sides of him, dancing black patterns against the other blackness of the sky. They were all sailing, of course, he had always known they would and this was the time. He signaled the engine room and grabbed the wheel—the wood of the handles so filling and round as tumescent organs, one for each hand!—turning and steering and sending the ship through the heaving forest of black skeletons.

And the crew worked too, good crew. He whispered orders to them because they were so good they could hear his orders even if he only thought them, not said them, and he wiped at his streaming nose. They were down below on the decks doing all the good things a good crew did while he guided the ship up here for all of them. They whispered as they toiled and two of them just below the bridge leaned together and he heard one ask "Everyone in position?" which was good to hear, and another said "Yes, sir," which was good to hear and he could see some of his men moving on the decks and others at the gangplanks and others going below. In his hands the wheel felt strong and big and he kept it turning slowly back and forth guiding his ship through the other ships.

Lights. Voices. Below. People. On deck.

"He's not in the apartment, lieutenant."

"The bastard got away when he heard you coming."

"Maybe, sir, but we had men at all the hatchways and stairs. And on the connections to the other ships. He must still be on board. His mother said he went to bed same time as everyone else."

"We'll find him. You got half the damned force to catch one kid. So catch him."

"Yes, sir."

Catch him. Catch who? Why, catch *him,* of course. He knew who the people were down there, police, and they wanted him. They had found him the way he knew they would. But he didn't want to go with them. Not when he was feeling like this. Did the dirt make him feel like this? Wonderful dirt. He would have to get more dirt. He didn't know a lot of things, he knew a lot of things, one thing he knew the cops didn't have dirt or give you dirt. No dirt?

The handrail creaked and heavy feet clanged up the stair to the bridge. Billy climbed onto the steel table and out through the side window on the other side, reached up and grabbed and pulled himself up and out. It was easy. And it felt good too.

"What a stink," a voice said, then louder out of the window below, "He's not up here, lieutenant."

"Keep looking. Cover the ship, he has to be here someplace."

The night air was warm enough and when he ran it felt solid enough to hold him up and he thought of walking over to the next ship, then he came to the funnel and this looked better. Bolted-on, curved steel rods rose up the side of the funnel making a ladder, and he climbed them.

"Did you hear something up there?"

One last rod and there was the top and the shouting black oval mouth of the smokestack black against the blackness beyond. He could go no farther, except inside, and he waved his arm over the nothingness and his foot slipped and for an instant he tottered and began to swim down the long black tunnel, then his hand struck against a bar inside: rough, rusted, coated with crumbling greasy darkness. Up and over he climbed until he half crouched on the bar and held the edge of the metal that formed the smokestack and looked up at the stars. He could notice them now that the voices were only a murmur far away like waves, and he had never seen stars like these before. Were there new stars? They were all different colors, colors he couldn't remember ever having seen before.

His legs were cramped and his fingers stiff where they held the metal and he could no longer hear voices. At first he could not stand and he thought he might drop down the endless dark tunnel below him, and now it didn't seem as good an idea as it had seemed before. By forcing, he finally straightened his legs and crawled over the metal of the top and found the rungs that climbed the smoothness of the painted metal.

When you are born on the ships and live on the ships, they are as normal a world as streets, or any other. Billy knew that if you climbed out to the tip of the bow and hung and jumped you could land on the stern of the next ship along. And there were other ways of getting from ship to ship that avoided the gangways and walkways and he used them, even in the dark, without conscious thought, working his way toward shore. He was almost there when he became aware of the pain in his bare feet where he had walked along a rusted steel hawser and filled the soles with the sharp, rusty needles of wire ends. He sat and tried to get some of them out by touch. While he was sitting there, leaning against the rail, he began to shiver.

Memory was clear. He knew what he had heard and done, but only now was the true import beginning to penetrate. The police had found him and tracked him down, and it was only an accident that he had been topside and avoided them.

They were looking for him and they knew who he was!

The sky was gray behind the dark silhouette of the city when he reached the waterfront, far uptown toward the end of the row of ships. There seemed to be people near Twenty-third Street, but it was too dark to be sure.

He jumped to the dock and ran toward the row of sheds, a small soot-smeared figure, bare-footed and afraid. The shadows swallowed him up.

12

The heat wave had gripped the city for such a long time that it was not mentioned any more, just endured. When Andy rode up in the elevator the operator, a thin, tired-looking boy, leaned against the wall with his mouth open, sweating into his already sodden uniform. It was just a few minutes past seven in the morning when Andy opened the door of apartment 41-E. When the outer door had closed behind him he knocked on the inner one, then made an exaggerated bow in the direction of the TV pickup. The lock rattled open and Shirl stood in the doorway, her hair still tangled from the bed, wearing only a sheer peignoir.

"It's been days—" she said and came willingly into his arms while he kissed her. He forgot the plastic bundle under his arm and it dropped to the floor. "What's that?" she asked, drawing him inside.

"Raincoat, I have to take it on duty in an hour, it's supposed to rain today."

"You can't stay now?"

"Don't I wish I could!" He kissed her soundly again and groaned, only half in humor. "A lot has been happening since I saw you last."

"I'll make some kofee, that won't take long. Come and tell me in the kitchen."

Andy sat and looked out of the window while she put the

water up. Dark clouds filled the sky from horizon to horizon, so heavy that they seemed to be just above the rooftops of the buildings. "You can't feel it here in the apartment," he said, "but it's even worse out today. The humidity I guess, it must be up around ninety-nine."

"Have you found the Chung boy?" she asked.

"No. He might be at the bottom of the river for all we know. It's been over two weeks since he got away from us on the ship, and we haven't found a trace of him since. We even got a paper priority and had indentikit pictures printed with his fingerprints and description, then sent them around to all the precincts. I brought copies to Chinatown and all the nearby ones myself, and talked to the detectives there. At first we had a stakeout on the kid's apartment, but we pulled that off and instead have a couple of stoolies who live on the ship—they'll keep their eyes open and let us know if he shows, they're not paid unless they see him. That's about all we can do now."

"Do you think you'll catch him?"

Andy shrugged and blew on the cup of kofee she handed him. "There's no way to tell. If he can stay out of trouble, or get out of town, we'll never see him again. It'll just be a matter of luck now, one way or the other. I wish we could convince City Hall of that."

"Then—you're still on the case?"

"Half and half, worse luck. The pressure is still on to find the kid, but Grassy managed to convince them that I could do just as well part time, running down whatever leads there are, and they agreed. So I'm supposed to be half time on this case and half time on squad duty. Which, if you know Grassy, means I'm full time on squad duty and the rest of the time I'm looking for Billy Chung. I'm getting to hate that kid. I wish he had been drowned and I could prove it."

Shirl sat down across from him and sipped her kofee. "So that's where you have been the past days."

"That's where I've been. On duty and up at Kensico Reservoir for two days, with no time to stop by here or even send you a message. I'm on day duty now and have to sign in by eight, but I had to see you first. Today's the thirtieth. What are you going to do, Shirl?"

She just shook her head in silence and stared down at the table, the look of unhappiness sweeping across her face as soon as he had spoken. He reached over and took her hand but she did not notice, nor did she try to pull it away.

"I don't like talking about it either," he said. "These past weeks have been, well . . ." He switched the subject, he could not express all that he felt, not at this time, so suddenly. "Has O'Brien's sister bothered you again?"

"She came back but they wouldn't let her in the building. I said I didn't want to see her and she caused a scene. Tab told me all the building staff enjoyed it very much. She wrote a note, said she would be here tomorrow since it is the last day of the month, to take everything away. I guess she can do that. Wednesday is the first, so the lease is up at midnight."

"Do you have any plans about where . . . what you are going to do?" It sounded stiff and unnatural the way he said it, but he could not do any better.

Shirl hesitated, then shook her head no. "I haven't been thinking about it at all," she said. "With you here it was like a holiday and I just kept putting off worrying about it from one day to the next."

"It was a holiday, all right! I hope we don't leave any beer or liquor for the Dragon Lady?"

"Not a spoonful!"

They laughed together. "We must have drunk a fortune in booze," Andy said. "But I don't regret a drop of it. What about the food?"

"Just some weedcrackers left—plus enough other things to make one big meal. I have tilapia in the freezer. I was hoping that we could eat it together, sort of a finishing-off party or a house-cooling party, instead of a housewarming party."

"I can do it if you don't mind eating late. It could even be midnight."

"That's fine by me, it might be more fun that way."

When Shirl was happy every inch of her showed it. He had to smile when she did. New highlights seemed to glisten in her hair and it was as though happiness were a substance that flowed through her and radiated in all directions. Andy felt it and was buoyed up by it, and he knew if he didn't ask her now he never would be able to.

"Listen, Shirl——" He took both her hands in his and the warmth of her touch helped a good deal. "Will you come with me? You can stay at my place. There's not much room, but I'm not home much to get in the way. It's all yours for as long as you like." She started to say something but he hushed her with his finger to her lips. "Wait a second before you answer. There are no strings attached. This is temporary—for as long as you want it. It's nothing like Chelsea Park, but a crummy walk-up, half a single room, and . . ."

"Will you be quiet!" she laughed. "I've been trying to say yes for hours now and you seem to be trying to talk me out of it."

"What . . . ?"

"I don't want anything in this world except to be happy, and I've been happier these weeks with you than I ever was at any time in my life before. And you can't frighten me with your apartment, you should see where my father lives, and I was there until I was nineteen."

Andy managed to get around the table without knocking it over and was hugging her to him. "And I have to be in the precinct in fifteen minutes," he complained. "But wait for me here, it could be any time after six, but it's sure to be late. We'll have the party, and afterward we'll move your stuff. Do you have very much?"

"It'll all fit in three suitcases."

"Perfect. We'll carry it, or we can use a cab. I have to get going." His voice changed, became almost a whisper. "Give me a kiss." She did, warmly, sharing his feelings.

It took a heroic effort to leave, and before he went he ran through all the possible excuses he might give for being late, but he knew that none of them would satisfy the lieutenant. When he came into the lobby he was aware for the first time of a thundering, drumming noise and saw the doorman, Tab, and four of the guards crowded around the front door, looking out. They made way for him when he came over.

"Now just look at that," Charlie said. "That should change things."

The far side of the street was almost invisible, cut off by a falling curtain of water. It poured down on the roofs and sidewalks, and the gutters were already filled with a rushing, debris-laden torrent. Adults huddled in the doorways and halls for protection, but the children saw this as a holiday and were running and screaming, sitting on the curb and kicking their legs in the filthy stream.

"Soon as the storm sewers block up, that water'll be a couple of feet deep. Drown a few of those kids," Charlie said.

"Happens every time," Newton, the building guard, agreed, nodding with morbid satisfaction. "The little ones get knocked down and no one even knows about it until after the rain."

"Could I see you a moment, please?" Tab said, tapping Andy on the arm and walking off to one side. Andy followed him, shrugging into the sticking folds of his raincoat.

"Tomorrow's the thirty-first," Tab said. He reached out and held the coat while Andy struggled his hand into the sealed-together arm of the coat.

"I guess you'll be looking for another job then," Andy said, thinking about Shirl and the hammering rain outside.

"That's not what I meant," Tab said, and as he talked he turned away to look out of the window. "It's Shirl, she'll be leaving the apartment tomorrow, she'll have to. I heard that the old bat sister of Mr. O'Brien's has hired a tugtruck, she's moving all the furniture out first thing in the morning. I wish I knew what Shirl was going to do." His arms were folded across his chest and he brooded out at the falling rain with the solidity of a carved statue.

It's none of his business, Andy thought. But he has known her a lot longer than I have.

"Are you married, Tab?" he asked.

Tab glanced at him out of the corners of his eyes and snorted. "Married man, happily married and three kids and I wouldn't change if you offered me one of those TV queens with the knockers big as fire hydrants." He looked closely at Andy, then smiled. "Nothing there for you to worry about. I just like the kid. She's just a nice kid, that's all. I'm worried what's going to happen to her."

There's no secret, Andy thought, realizing this wasn't the first time the question would be asked. "She's going to be staying with me," he said. "I'm coming over later tonight to help her move." He glanced at Tab, who nodded seriously.

"That's very good news. I'm glad to hear that. I hope things work out okay, I really do."

He turned back to look at the rain and Andy looked at his watch and saw that it was almost eight and hurried out. The air was cool, cooler than the lobby, the temperature must have dropped ten degrees since the rain had begun. Maybe this was the end of the heat wave; it had certainly lasted long enough. There were already a few inches of water in the moat and the surface was dimpled and ringed by the falling drops. Before he had crossed the drawbridge to the street he felt the water run into his shoes; his pants legs were sopping and his wet hair was plastered to his head. But it was cool and he didn't mind, and even the thought of the perpetually annoyed Grassioli didn't seem to bother him too much.

It rained the rest of the day, which, in every other way, was like any other day. Grassioli chewed him out twice personally, and included him in a general berating of the entire squad. He investigated two holdups, and another that was combined with felonious assault that would soon be changed to manslaughter or murder, since the victim was rapidly dying from a knife wound in his chest. There was more work piled up than the squad could get through in a month, and new cases coming in all the time while they plodded away at the backlog. As he had expected he didn't leave at six, but a phone call took the lieutenant away at nine o'clock and all of the day squad still on duty—in spite of Grassioli's parting threats and warnings—had vanished ten minutes later. The rain was still falling, though not so heavily as before, and the air felt cool after the weeks of continuous heat. As he walked along Seventh Avenue, Andy realized that the streets were almost empty, for the first time this summer. A few people were out in the rain and there were dark forms huddled in every doorway, but the sidewalks and streets were strangely vacant. Climbing the stairs in his building was worse than usual, the people who normally crowded the stoop and curb were sitting here, some of them even lying asleep across the steps. He pushed by them and stepped over the recumbent ones, ignoring their mumbled curses. This was an indication of what it would be like in the fall unless the building owner hired bodyguards to drive the squatters out. It was scarcely worth it any more, there were so many of them, and they just came right back when the guards left.

"You'll ruin your eyes looking at that thing all the time," he told Sol when he came in. The old man lay on the bed propped up by pillows, watching a war film on TV. Cannon fire thundered scratchily from the speaker.

"My eyes were ruined before you were born, Mr.

Wiseguy, and I can still see better than ninety-nine per cent
of the fogies my age. Still working union hours, I see."

"Find me a better job and I'll quit," Andy said, turning
on the light in his room and digging through the bottom
drawer. Sol came in and sat on the edge of the bed.

"If you're looking for your flashlight," he said, "you left
it on the table the other day. I meant to tell you, I put it in
your top drawer there, under the shirts."

"You're better than a mother to me."

"Yeah, well, don't try to borrow no money, son."

Andy put the flash in his pocket and knew that he would
have to tell Sol now. He had been putting it off and he
wondered why it bothered him. After all, this room was all
his, they shared food rations and meals because it made
things easier, that was all. It was just a working arrangement.

"I've got someone coming to stay with me for a while,
Sol. I'm not sure how long."

"It's your room, buddy-boy. Do I know the guy?"

"Not exactly. Anyway it's not a guy—"

"Hoo-ha! That explains it all." He snapped his fingers.
"Not the chick, Big Mike's girl, the one you been seeing?"

"Yes, that's the girl. Her name's Shirl."

"A fancy name, a fancy girl," Sol said, heaving to his feet
and going toward the door. "Very fancy. Watch out you
don't get your fingers burned, buddy-boy."

Andy started to say something but Sol was out of the
room and closing the door behind himself. A little harder
than necessary. He was looking at the TV again when Andy
left and did not glance away from it or say anything.

It had been a long day and Andy's feet hurt and his neck
hurt and his eyes burned; he wondered why Sol was being
sore. He had never met Shirl—so what did he have to
complain about? Tramping crosstown through the slowly
falling rain, he thought about Shirl and, without realizing it,
began to whistle. He was hungry and he was tired and he
wanted to see her very much. The turrets and spires of
Chelsea Park rose before him through the rain and the
doorman nodded and touched his cap to Andy as he hurried
across the drawbridge.

Shirl opened the door for him and she was wearing the
silver dress, the same one that she had been wearing that
first night, with a tiny white apron tied over it. There was a

silver clip holding her copper hair in place and a matching silver bracelet on her right arm, and rings on both her hands.

"Don't get me wet," she said, leaning over to kiss him. "I've got all my good things on for the party."

"And I look like a bum," he said, peeling off the dripping raincoat.

"Nonsense. You look like you've had a hard day in the office or whatever you call that place where you work. You need a party. Hang that thing in the shower and dry your hair before you catch a cold, then come into the living room. I have a surprise."

"What is it?" he called after her receding back.

"If I told you it wouldn't be a surprise," she said with devastating female logic.

Shirl had the apron off and was waiting for him in the living room, standing proudly by the dining table. Two tall candles reflected highlights from the silverware, china plates and crystal glasses. A white tablecloth hung in thick folds. "And that's not all," Shirl said, pointing to the end table where the neck of a bottle projected from a silver bucket.

Andy saw that the bottle had wires over the top and around the neck, and that the bucket was full of ice cubes and water. He took out the bottle and held the label to the light so that he could read it aloud.

" 'Frenchwine Champagne—a rare, selected, effervescent beverage of great vintage. Artificially colored, flavored, sweetened and carbonated.' " He placed it carefully back into the bucket. "We used to have wine in California when I was a kid and my father let me taste it, but I don't remember it at all. You're going to spoil me, Shirl, with this kind of stuff. And you were kidding me—you said that we had finished all the drink in the house—and all the time you had this tucked away."

"I did not! I bought that today, special for this party. Mike's liquor man came around, he's from Jersey and didn't even know what had happened to Mike."

"It must have cost a fortune—"

"Not as bad as you think. I sold him back all the empty bottles and he gave me a special price. Now open it, for goodness' sake, and let's try it."

Andy wrestled with the wire over the cork. He had seen

them open bottles like this on TV, but it looked a lot easier than it really was. He worked it off finally and there was a satisfactory bang that shot the cork across the room, while Shirl caught the foaming wine in the glass that she held ready, just as the liquor man had instructed her.

"Here's to us," she said, and they raised their glasses.

"This is very good, I've never tasted anything like it before."

"You've never tasted anything like this dinner before, either." she said and hurried to the kitchen. "Now sit down and sip your wine and look at TV, it'll only be a few minutes more."

The first course was lentil soup, but with a richer and better flavor than usual. Meat stock, Shirl explained, she had saved it from the steak. There was a white sauce on the broiled tilapia, which were scattered with green flecks of cress and served with dumplings of weedcracker meal and a seacress salad. The wine went with everything and Andy was sighing with contentment and a pleasurable sense of unaccustomed fullness when Shirl brought in kofee and dessert, a flavored agar-agar gelatine with soymilk on it. He groaned, but he had no trouble eating it.

"Do you smoke tobacco?" she asked as she cleared the table.

He leaned back in the chair, eyes half closed and utterly relaxed. "Not on a cop's salary, I don't. Shirl, you are an absolute genius in the kitchen. I'll be spoiled if I eat too much of your cooking."

"Men should be spoiled, it makes them easier to live with. It's too bad you don't smoke, because I found two cigars left in a box that Mike had hidden away, he saved them for special guests."

"Take them to the flea market, you'll get a good price."

"No, I couldn't do that, it doesn't seem right."

Andy sat up. "If you want to do something, I know that Sol used to smoke, he's the guy I told you about, who lives in the adjoining room. It might cheer him up. He's a pretty good friend of mine."

"That's a wonderful idea," she said, sensing the edge of concern in Andy's words. Whoever this Sol was, she wanted him to like her, living right in the next room like that. "I'll put them into my suitcase." She carried the loaded tray into the kitchen.

When the dishes were cleaned she went to finish her packing in the bedroom, and called Andy in to help her get the last case down from the top shelf. She had to change for the street and he helped her with the zipper on her dress and this had just the effect she hoped it would have.

It was after midnight when the last bag was packed and she had put on her gray street dress and was ready to leave.

"Did you forget anything?" Andy asked.

"I don't think so, but I'll have a last look around."

"Shirl, when you came here, moved in, I mean, did you bring any towels or bed linen or anything like that with you?" He pointed toward the rumpled bed and seemed uncomfortable about something.

"No, nothing like that, I just had a bag with some clothes in it."

"I was just hoping that you owned some of these sheets. You see—well, I only have one, and it's getting old, and they cost a fortune these days, even used ones."

She laughed. "You sound like you're planning to spend a lot of time in bed. Now that you remind me, I remember, two of these sheets are mine." She opened her bag and began swiftly to fold and pack them away. "He owed me at least this much."

Andy carried the suitcases into the hall and rang for the elevator. Shirl stood for a moment, watching as the apartment door closed, then hurried after him.

"Doesn't he ever sleep?" Andy asked as they crossed the lobby toward Charlie, who stood at his post by the front door.

"I'm not sure," Shirl said. "He always seems to be around when something is happening."

"Hate to see you leaving, Miss Greene," Charlie said as they came up. "I can take the keys to the apartment now, if you want me to."

"You better give her a receipt," Andy said as she handed the keys over.

"Be happy to," Charlie said imperturbably, "if I had anything to write on."

"Here, put it in my notepad," Andy said. He looked over the doorman's shoulder and saw Tab coming out of the guardroom.

"Tab—what are you doing here at this time of night?" Shirl asked.

"Waiting for you. I heard you were leaving and I thought I'd give you a hand with your bags."

"But it's so late."

"Last day of the job. Got to finish it off right. And you don't want to be seen walking around this time of night with suitcases. Plenty of people will cut your throat for less." He picked up two of the bags and Andy took the third.

"Hope someone does bother me," she said. "A high-priced bodyguard and a city detective—just to walk me a couple of blocks."

"We'd wipe the street with them," Andy said, taking back his notebook and leading the way through the door Charlie held open.

When they went out the rain had stopped and stars could be seen through holes in the clouds. It was wonderfully cool. She took each of the men by an arm and led the way down the street, out of the pool of light in front of Chelsea Park and into the darkness.

13

It had been strange climbing the stairway in the dark, sweeping the light over the sleeping figures on the stairs while Andy carried the bags up behind her. His friend Sol had been asleep, and they had gone quietly through his room into Andy's. The bed was just big enough for both of them and she had been tired and curled up with her head on his shoulder and slept so soundly that she didn't even know it when he had gotten up, dressed and left. She awoke to see the sun streaming through the window onto the foot of the bed and, when she kneeled with her elbows on the windowsill, she smelt the clean, fresh-washed air; the only time the city was ever like this was after a rainstorm. With all the dust and soot washed away it was wonderfully clear, and she could see the sharp-edged buildings of Bellevue rising above the lower jumble of tar-black roofs and stained brick walls. And the heat was gone, vanished with the rain, that was the best part. She yawned pleasurably and turned back to look at the room.

Just what you would expect from a bachelor, neat enough—but as empty of charm as an old shoe. There was a thin patina of dust on everything, but that was probably her fault since Andy certainly had not been spending much time here of late. If she could get some paint somewhere, a coat of it wouldn't do that dresser any harm. It couldn't have been more gouged and nicked if it had been in a landslide. At least there was a full-length mirror, cracked but still good, and a wardrobe to hang her things in. There was nothing to complain about, really, a little brightening up and the room would be nice. And get rid of those million spider webs on the ceiling.

A water tank with a faucet was on the partition wall next to the door, and when she turned it on, a thin brownish stream tinkled into the basin that was fixed on brackets beneath it. It had the sharp chemical smell that she had almost forgotten, since all the water in Chelsea Park was run through expensive filters. There didn't seem to be any soap here but she splashed water on her face and rinsed her hands, and was drying them on the tattered towel that hung next to the tank when a clanking, squealing sound came through the partition in front of her. She couldn't imagine what it possibly could be, though it was obviously coming from the room next door where Sol lived. Something of his was making the noise, and it hadn't started until after he heard her moving around and running the water, which was nice of him. It also meant that, as far as sound went, this room had as much privacy as a birdcage. Well, that couldn't be helped. She brushed her hair, put on the same dress she had worn the night before, then added just a touch of makeup. When she was ready she took a deep breath and opened the door.

"Good morning—" she said, and could think of nothing else to say, but just stood there in the doorway, trying not to gape. Sol was sitting on a wheelless bicycle, going no-where—but going at a tremendous rate, his gray hair flying in all directions and his beard bobbing up and down on his chest as he pedaled. His single garment was a pair of ancient and much-patched shorts. The squealing sound came from a black object at the rear of the bicycle. "Good morning!" she called again, louder this time, and he glanced up at her and his pedaling slowed to a stop. "I'm Shirl Greene," she said.

"And who else could you be," Sol said coldly, climbing down from the bike and wiping the sweat from his face with his forearm.

"I've never seen a bicycle like that before. Does it do something?" She wasn't going to fight with him, no matter how much he wanted to.

"Yeah. It makes ice." He went to put his shirt on.

At first she thought it was one of these deep jokes, the kind she never understood, then she saw that wires led from the black motorlike thing behind the bike to a lot of big batteries on top of the refrigerator.

"I know," she said, happy at her discovery. "You're making the fridge go with the bike. I think that's wonderful." His only answer was a grunt this time, no remarks, so she knew she was making headway. "Do you like kofee?"

"I wouldn't know. It's been so long since I tasted any."

"I've got a half a can in my bag. If we had some hot water we could make some." She didn't wait for an answer but went into the other room and got the can. He looked at the brown container for a moment, then shrugged and went to fill a pot with water.

"I bet it tastes like poison," he said as he put the pot on the stove. First he turned on the hanging light in the middle of the room and studied the glowing filament in the bulb, then nodded begrudgingly. "Just for a change we got some juice today, so let's hope it lasts long enough to boil a half inch of water." He switched on the electric heating element of the stove.

"I've only been drinking kofee the last couple of years," Shirl said, sitting in the chair by the window. "They tell me it doesn't taste a thing like real coffee, but I wouldn't know."

"I can tell you. It don't."

"Have you ever tasted *real* coffee? More than once?" She had never met a man yet who didn't enjoy telling about his experiences.

"Taste it? Honeybunch, I used to live on it. You're a kid, you've got no idea how things used to be in the old days. You drank three, four cups, maybe even a whole pot of coffee and never even thought about it. I was even coffee poisoned once, my skin turned brown and everything, because I used to drink up to twenty cartons a day. A champion coffee drinker, I could of won medals."

Shirl could only shake her head in admiration, then sipped at the kofee. It was still too hot. "I just remembered," she said, jumping up from the chair and going into the other room. She was back in a moment and gave the two cigars to Sol. "Andy said I should give these to you, that you used to smoke them."

Sol's air of masculine superiority fell away and he almost gaped. "Cigars?" was all he could say.

"Yes, Mike had a box of them, but there were just these two left. I don't know if they are any good or not."

Sol groped for memory of the cigar ritual that had once controlled a judgment of this kind. He sniffed suspiciously at the end of one. "Smells like tobacco at least." When he held it to his ear and pinched the smaller end there was a decided crackling sound. "Aha! Too dry. I might have known. You got to take care of cigars, keep them in the right climate. These are all dried out. They should be in a humidor. They can't be smoked this way."

"Do you mean they're no good? We'll have to throw them away?" It was a terrible thought.

"Nothing like that, relax. I'll just take a box, put a wet sponge in it along with these stogies and wait three, four days. One thing about cigars, if they dry out you can bring them back to life just like Lazarus, or better maybe, he couldn't have been smelling too good after being buried four days. I'll show you how to take care of these."

Shirl sipped her kofee and smiled. It was going to be all right. Sol just hadn't liked the idea of someone coming to stay with Andy, it must have upset him. But he was a nice guy and had some funny stories and a funny, sort of old-fashioned way of talking, and she knew that they were going to get along.

"This stuff doesn't taste too bad," Sol said, "if you can forget what real coffee tastes like. Or Virginia ham, or roast beef, or turkey. Boy, could I tell you about turkey. It was during the war and I was stationed at the ass-end of Texas and all the food was sent out of St. Louis and we were right on the end of the supply line. What reached us was so bad I saw mess sergeants shudder when they opened the GI cans the stuff was shipped in. But once, just once it worked the other way around. These Texans raise billions of turkeys down there on ranches, then ship them north for Christmas and Thanksgiving, you know." She nodded, but she didn't know. "Well, the war was on and there was no way to ship all these turkeys out, so the Air Corps bought them for next to nothing and that's what we had to eat for about a month. I tell you! We had roast turkey, fried turkey, turkey soup, turkey burgers, turkey hash, turkey croquettes. . . ."

There was the sound of running footsteps in the hall and someone rattled the knob so loudly that the door shook. Sol quietly slipped open the table drawer and took out a large meat cleaver.

"Sol, are you there?" Andy called from the hall, shaking the handle again. "Open up."

Sol threw the cleaver onto the table and hurried over to unlock the door. Andy pushed in, sweating and breathing hard, closing the door behind him and talking in a low voice despite his urgency.

"Listen, fill the water tanks and all the jerry cans. And fill whatever else we have that will hold water. Maybe you can plug the sink, then you can put water in that too. Fill as many jerry cans as you can at our water point, but if they begin to notice you coming back too often, go to the other one on Twenty-eighth Street. But get going. Sol—Shirl will help you."

"What's it all about?"

"Christ, don't ask questions, just do it! I shouldn't be telling you this much—and don't let on I did or we'll all be in trouble. I have to get back before they find me missing." He went out as fast as he came in, the slammed door an echo to his receding footsteps.

"What was all that about?" Shirl asked.

"We'll find out later," Sol said, kicking into his sandals. "Right now we get moving. This is the first time Andy has ever pulled anything like this and I'm an old man—I scare easy. There's another jerry can in your room."

They were the only ones who appeared concerned in any way and Shirl wondered what Andy could have possibly meant. There were only two women waiting in line at the corner water point, and one of them only wanted to fill a quart bottle. Sol helped to carry the filled jerry cans, but Shirl insisted on taking them up the stairs. "Work some of the fat off my hips," she said. "I'll bring down the empties and you can get back in line while I pour out the others."

The line was a little longer now, but there was nothing

unusual about it, this was the time when most people started
to show up to make sure they had their water before the
point closed at noon.

"You must be thirsty, Pop," the patrolman on duty said
when they reached the head of the line again. "Ain't you
been around before?"

"So what's your trouble?" Sol snapped, pointing his
beard at the cop. "All of a sudden you're being paid to count
the house? Maybe I like to take a bath once in a while so I
don't stink like some people I could mention, but I won't.
. . ."

"Take it easy, grandpa."

". . . I'm not your grandpa, *shmok,* since I haven't committed suicide yet, which I would if I was. All of a sudden
cops got to count how much water people need?"

The policeman retreated a yard and half turned his back.
Sol filled the containers, still grumbling, and Shirl helped
carry them to one side to screw the lids back on. They had
just finished when a police sergeant pulled up on a sput-
tering motorbike.

"Lock this point up," he said. "It's closed for the day."

The women who were waiting to fill their containers
screamed at him and pushed forward around the spigot, getting in each other's way and trying to get some water before
it was closed down. The patrolman fought his way through
the shouting crowd to turn the valve handle. Even before he
touched it the water hiccoughed, died to a thin trickle, then
stopped. He glanced at the sergeant.

"Yeah, that's the trouble," the sergeant said. "There's a
. . . broken pipe, they had to shut down. It'll be all right
tomorrow. Now break this up."

Sol looked wordlessly at Shirl as they picked up the jerry
cans, then turned away. Neither of them had missed the
hesitancy in the sergeant's voice. This was something more
than a broken pipe. They carried the containers slowly up
the stairs, careful not to spill a drop.

14

Even though the cops knew who he was and were after him, luck was on his side, that's what Billy Chung kept telling himself. Sometimes he would forget it for a while and the shakes would come back and he would have to start thinking all about the luck again. Hadn't the cops come when he was out of the apartment—wasn't that luck? And he had gotten away without being seen, that was luck too. What if he had to leave everything behind? He had put his shorts on, and just the day before he had sewed all his money into them because he was afraid of losing it out of his shoe. So he had the loot, and loot was all you really needed. He had run, but he had run smart, going to the flea market in Madison Square first and waking up one of the guys who slept under his stall and buying sandals. Then he headed downtown, out of the district, keeping moving. When the water points opened he had washed up, then bought an old shirt from another stall, and some weedcrackers, and ate them while he walked. It was still early when he got to Chinatown, but the streets were already filling up, and all he had to do was find a clear spot against the wall, curl up and go to sleep.

When he woke up he knew that he couldn't stay here, this would be the first place that the cops would try, he had to move on. Some of the locals who lived in the street were already beginning to give him funny looks and he knew if his description was out they'd finger him in a minute for a couple of D's. He had heard once that there were some Chinese over on the East Side and he headed that way. If he stayed anywhere too long he would be noticed, and as long as it was this hot it didn't matter where he slept. It hadn't been a conscious plan in the beginning but in a few days he discovered that if he moved around while the streets were crowded no one paid any attention to him, and he could even sleep during the day, and some at night too if he could find a quiet spot. No one ever noticed him as long as he stopped some place where there were other Chinese in the area. He kept moving and it kept him busy, this way he didn't worry too much about what was going to happen to him. It would be all right as long as his money lasted. And then . . . He didn't like to think about what would happen then, so he didn't.

It was the rainstorm that made him decide that he had to find a place to hole up. He had been caught in it and got soaked and at first it wasn't bad at all, but just at first. Along with thousands more of the homeless he had sought shelter under the high, soaring roadways of the Williamsburg Bridge, and even here it wasn't very dry with every change in the wind blowing in sheets of rain. He was wet and cold the whole night, he didn't sleep at all, and in the morning he climbed the stairway to the bridge to get into the sun. Ahead of him the walkway stretched out over the river and he walked along it to keep warm, into the face of the rising sun. He had never been this high before and it was completely new, looking down on the river and the city like this. A gray nuclear freighter was moving slowly upstream and all the rush of sail and rowboat traffic scurried away before it. When he looked down he had to hold tight to the railing.

Halfway across he realized that he was out of Manhattan—for the first time in his life—and all he had to do was keep going and the police would never find him. Brooklyn lay ahead of him, a jagged wall of strange outlines against the sky, a wholly new and frightening place. He didn't know anything about it—but he could find out. The police would never think of looking for him this far away, never in a hundred years.

Once he was off the bridge the fear ebbed slowly away—this was just like Manhattan only with different people, different streets. His clothes were dry now and he felt all right, except that he was tired and very sleepy. The streets went on and on, crowded and noisy with people, and he followed them at random until he came to a high wall that stretched all along one side of the road and seemed to be endless. He followed it, wondering what was on the other side, until he reached a sealed, iron gate with rusty barbed wire strung over the top of it so you couldn't climb over. BROOKLYN NAVY YARD—KEEP OUT a weathered sign read. Through the bars of the gate Billy could see a wasteland of sealed buildings, empty sheds, rusting moun-

tains of scrap, pieces of ships, broken hills of concrete and
rubble. A potbellied guard in a gray uniform walked by
inside, he carried a heavy night stick, almost a club, and he
looked suspiciously at Billy, who let go of the gate and
walked on.

Now that was something. Looked like a hundred miles of
land in there and no people at all, closed up and forgotten.
If he could get in there without the cop seeing him he could
hide forever in a place like that. If there was a way to get in.
He kept walking along the wall, until the solid stone and
concrete gave way to a chain-link fence, rusty and drooping.
More barbed wire topped it, but it was clumped rustily
together and torn away in spots. This was a piece of street
where there weren't too many people, either, just blank
walls of old warehouses. It wouldn't be hard getting over the
fence here.

That he wasn't the first person with this kind of idea was
proven a minute later, while he was studying the fence.
There was a stirring of motion on the other side and a man,
not much older than he was, ran into sight. He stopped a
minute, looking up and down the street outside to be sure no
one was too close, then bent to the bottom of the wire fence
and pushed a jagged boulder of broken concrete under it.
Then, in a practiced, wriggling motion, he crawled under
the fence, pushed away the supporting chunk of concrete so
that the fence dropped down again, rose to his feet and
walked off down the street.

Billy waited until he was out of sight, then went over to
the spot. A shallow impression had been scratched into the
ground at this point, not deep enough to draw attention, but
deep enough to crawl through when the bottom of the
fence was propped up. He pulled the concrete into place as
the other had done, looked around—no one in sight was
paying any attention to him—and then slipped under. There
was nothing to it. He kicked the concrete away so that the
fence fell, then ran quickly to the shelter of the nearest
building.

There was something frightening about these acres of
empty silence; he had never been this alone before, without
others somewhere close by. He walked slowly now, pressed
against the sun-warmed bricks of the building, pausing and
peering out cautiously when he came to the corner. Ahead
was a wide, wreckage-strewn avenue of emptiness. Just as

he started across there was a movement far down the street and he fell back to the wall as a gray-uniformed guard passed slowly across. When he was gone, Billy hurried in the opposite direction, taking shelter in the shadows of the rusted steel beams of a floating dry dock.

From wreckage to ruin he went on, looking for some shelter he could crawl into, to hide and sleep. There were other guards about but they were easy to spot; they stayed on the wider avenues and never came near the buildings. If he could find a way inside one of the locked structures he would be safe enough from discovery. One of them looked promising, a long, low building with a collapsed roof and glassless windows. It was sided with slabs of asbestos sheeting and many of the panels were cracked and one of them had been almost completely torn away. He came close and looked in and could see only darkness. The fallen roof was only a few feet above the floor, making a dark and silent cavern. This was just what he needed. He yawned and crawled through the opening. The big chunk of iron caught him in the side and he screamed in agony.

The darkness filled with red tongues of pain as he scrambled backward out of the opening, hurling himself to one side. Something heavy rushed through the air next to his head and crashed into the wall, cracking and splintering it. Billy stumbled to his feet, away from the entrance, but no one tried to follow him. There was only silence within the dark opening as he hobbled away as fast as he could, favoring his side, glancing back fearfully at the building. When he turned a corner and it was out of sight he stopped and pulled up his shirt, looking at the scratched rawness just below his ribs that was already starting to turn black-and-blue. It didn't seem to be more than a bad bruise, but how it hurt.

Something to fight with, that's what he needed. Not that he was going back to that building—never!—he was just going to need a weapon of some kind in this place. There were shattered chunks of concrete around and he picked up one that fitted into his hand, and even had a broken stub of rusty reinforcing rod sticking out of it. Lots of other people must have had the idea to hide in here, he should have known that when he saw the guy who came out under the fence. They stayed out of sight of the guards, that seemed easy enough to do. Then they found a place and took it over,

keeping anyone else out, that's how it would be. There
might be a way into every one of these buildings, and there
might be someone hiding in each one. He shivered as he
thought of this and pressed his hand to his sore side and
moved away from the shelter of the building. Maybe he
should get out of here while he was still in one piece? But
this was too good a spot to leave. If he did find a place to
hole up it would be perfect, just what he needed. He should
look around some more before he got out. And find
something better than this lump of concrete to fight with. He
searched as he walked and realized that, in spite of the
ruined and crumbled landscape, there was nothing lying
about that was small and handy enough to use for a weapon.
It was as if many others had been through here before him,
bent on the same mission. Clutching the concrete tighter, he
limped on.

A little later, he wanted to escape this collapsing and
rusted jungle, but he had lost his way and could not get out.
The sun was hot on the top of his head, bouncing up from
the cracked pavement around him. He walked along the
brink of a vast and silent dry dock, empty and forgotten, a
canyon of scrap-littered silence, feeling like an insect
crawling along the edge of the world. Beyond was the oily
rush of the East River cutting him off from the distant
towers of Manhattan; his side hurt when he breathed and
loneliness was a weight pressing down on his shoulders.

A dismantled ship rested on blocks at the edge of the
water from which it had been reluctantly pulled, its skin
peeled off by the wreckers and its rusting ribs standing like
the skeleton of a dead sea monster. The work had never
been finished; the after part of the ship was almost intact,
while some of the deckhouse and the stern were still
untouched. There were no openings at ground level, the ship
had been a tanker and the transverse bulkhead was still in
place, but high above were portholes and a doorway. It
wouldn't be hard to climb the framework and Billy
wondered if anyone had been there before him. They might,
they might not, there was no way to tell. He had to rest and
the ship made him think of home. He had to try some place.
Carrying the chunk of concrete made climbing difficult, but
he still took it with him.

In front of the deckhouse door there remained only a
jagged-edged piece of deck, just a few feet wide. Billy pulled

himself up onto this and faced the doorless opening to the cabin, holding the concrete ready.

"Is anyone there?" he called softly. The circular openings that had once contained portholes threw beams of light into the interior, bright spots on the deck that made the surrounding darkness more intense. "Hello," Billy called again, but there was only silence.

Reluctantly he advanced through the doorway and into the blackness of the room. No one struck at him this time. Nothing moved and he blinked his eyes, dimmed by the bright sunlight outside, at a dark shape, but it was only a pile of rubbish. There was another pile in the far corner, and he had to look at it twice before he realized that it was a man, squatting against the wall with his legs pulled up before him, looking intently at Billy.

"Put that thing down, the thing in your hand," the man said in a hushed voice, almost a whisper. He reached out a long arm and clanged a twisted length of pipe against the decking. Billy stared at it wide-eyed, and his side ached. He dropped the concrete.

"That's very wise," the man said, "very wise." He stood up jerkily, unfolding like a carpenter's rule, a tall man with spiderlike arms, thin to the point of emaciation. When he walked into a beam of sunlight Billy saw that the skin was stretched tight across his cheekbones and almost hairless skull, while his lips were drawn back to reveal long yellow teeth. His eyes were round as a child's and of such a watery blue that they seemed almost transparent. Not empty, but more like windows to look through—with nothing to be seen on the other side. And he kept staring at Billy, swinging the pipe slowly, saying nothing, his lips pulled away from his teeth in an expression that might have been a grin, but also might be something else, very different.

When Billy took a slow step back toward the doorway the end of the pipe twitched out and stopped him. "What do you want here?" the whisper asked.

"I don't want anything, I'm going—"

"What do you want?"

"I was just looking for a place to lie down, I'm tired, I don't want any trouble."

"What is your name?" the voice whispered, the eyes never blinked or moved.

"Billy . . ." Why had he answered so fast! He bit his lip:
why had he given his right name?

"Do you have anything to eat, Billy?"

He started to lie, then thought better of it. He reached
inside his shirt. "Here, I got some weedcrackers. You want
some? They're a little broken."

The pipe dropped to the deck and rolled away while the
man stepped forward with both hands cupped before him,
towering over Billy. " 'Cast thy bread upon the waters: for
thou shalt find it after many days.' Do you know where that
comes from?" he asked.

"No—no, I don't," Billy said uneasily, dropping the
crackers into the outstretched hands.

"I didn't think you would," the man complained, then sat
down with his back to the wall at the same spot as before.
He began to eat with a steady, automatic motion. "You're a
heathen, I imagine, a yellow heathen, though that doesn't
matter. It will to you as to the rest of His creatures. You
wish to sleep, sleep. This place is large enough for two."

"I can get out, you were here first."

"You are afraid of me, aren't you?" Billy turned away
from the unchanging stare, and the man nodded. "You
should not be, because we are coming very near the end of
fear. Do you know what that means? Do you know the
significance of this year, do you?"

Billy sat silent. He did not know what to answer. The
man finished the last of the crumbs, wiped his hands on his
filthy pants and sighed heavily. "You could not know. Go to
sleep, there is nothing to worry about here. No one will
come near to bother you, we have strict rules of property in
our community. Usually it is only strangers, like you, who
trespass, though the others will do it if they think it
worthwhile. But they won't come here, they know I have
nothing for them to covet. You may sleep undisturbed."

It seemed impossible to even consider sleeping, no matter
how tired he felt, not with this strange man watching him.
Billy lay against the wall in the far corner, eyes open and
alert, wondering what he should do next. The man mumbled
to himself and scratched at his ribs inside his thin shirt. A
high-pitched hum whined in Billy's ear and he slapped at the
mosquito. Another bit him on the leg and he scratched the
spot. There seemed to be an awful lot of mosquitoes here.
What should he do? Should he try to leave?

With a sudden start he realized that he had been asleep and that the sun was low in the west, coming almost directly in through the open doorway. He sat up in a scramble and looked around, but the cabin was empty. His side ached terribly.

The clattering, metallic sound came again, and he realized that this was what had wakened him. It came from outside. He went as quietly as he could to the doorway and looked down. The man was climbing toward him, and the length of pipe he carried was scratching on the metal making the noise that had disturbed him. Billy shrank back as the man threw the pipe up ahead of him, then hauled himself over the edge and onto the strip of deck.

"The water points did not open today," he said, and held out an ancient and dented paint can that he had brought up with him. "But I found a place where there was still water from the rain yesterday. Would you like some?" Billy nodded, aware suddenly of his dry throat, and took the extended can. It was filled halfway with clear water through which the caked green paint could be seen. The water was very sweet. "Take more," the man said. "I drank my fill when I was there."

"What is your name?" he asked as he took the can back.

Was it a trap? This man must remember his name, he didn't dare give him a different one. "Billy," he said.

"You may call me Peter. You can stay here if you like." He went inside with the can and seemed to have forgotten the piece of pipe. Billy looked at it suspiciously, not sure of his ground.

"You left your pipe here," he called out.

"Bring it, if you please. I shouldn't leave it lying around. Just put it there," he said when Billy brought it in. "I think I have another piece like that around here someplace, you can take it with you when you leave these quarters. Some of our neighbors can be dangerous."

"The guards?"

"No, they are of no importance. Their work is a sinecure, and they have no more wish to bother us than we have to bother them. As long as they do not see us we are not here, so just stay away from them. You'll find that they don't look very hard, they can collect their money without putting themselves in any danger—so why should they? Sensible men. Anything worth stealing or removing vanished years ago. The guards remain only because no one has ever decided what to do with this place and the easiest solution is just to forget about it. They are living symbols of the state of decay of our culture, just as this wasteland is a vastly more important symbol, that is why I am here." He laced his hands about his shins and leaned forward, resting his bony chin on his knees. "Do you know how many entrances there are to this place?" Billy shook his head no, wondering what Peter was talking about.

"Then I will tell you. There are *eight*—and only one is unlocked and in use by the guards. The others are closed and sealed, seven seals. Does that mean something to you? Seven seals? No, I can see it does not. But there are other signs, some hidden, some clear for any eye to see. And more will come and be revealed to us one by one. Some have been written for centuries, such as the great harlot named Babylon which never was Rome as many falsely believed. Do you know the name of the city out there?"

"Here? You mean New York?"

"Yes, that is one name, but there is another that it is called and has been called and no one protests its use, that is Babylon-on-Hudson. So you see that this is the great harlot and Armageddon will be here, that is why I have come. I was a priest once, would you believe that?"

"Yes, sure," Billy said and he yawned, looking around the walls and out the doorway.

"A priest of the Church should speak the truth and I did and they cast me out for it, and they are the same ones who tempt the Antichrist into their chambers. The college of cardinals has advised the Holy Father to withdraw his ban on the destruction of infant life, and he considers it, when the truth of God's law is all about us. He said be fruitful and multiply and we have, and He gave us the intelligence to make the sick well and the weak strong, and that is where the truth lies. The millennium is here, now, upon us, a populous world of souls awaiting His call. *This* is the true millennium. False prophets said it was the year one thousand, but there are more people here in this single city than there were in the entire world at that time. *Now* is the hour, we can see it nearing, we can read the signs. The world can hold no more, it will crack asunder under the weight of the masses of people—but it will *not* crack until the seven

trumpets blast, this New Year, Century Day. Then we will
have the reckoning."

When he stopped, the thin whine of mosquitoes was loud
in the still air and Billy swatted his leg, killing one and
leaving a thick splotch of blood that he brushed away with
the heel of his hand. Peter's arm was in the sun and Billy
could see the welts and scabs of old bites that covered it.

"I've never seen so many mosquitoes as you got around
here," Billy said. "And in the daytime. I never got bitten in
the daytime before." He stood up and prowled about the
refuse-filled chamber, walking to get away from the droning
insects, kicking at dirt-stiffened rags and pieces of crumbling wood. In the center of the rear bulkhead was a heavy
steel door, standing open a few inches. "What's in here?" he
asked.

Peter did not hear, or pretended not to hear, and Billy
pushed against the door, but the hinges were rusted into
position and it would not move. "Don't you know what's in
here?" he asked again in a louder voice, and Peter stirred
and turned. "No," he said, "I have never looked."

"It's been closed a long time, there might be stuff in there
we could use, you never can tell. Let's see if we can open it."

Pushing together, and using the length of steel pipe as a
lever, they managed to move it a few inches more until the
opening was wide enough to slip through. Billy went first
and his foot rattled against something on the deck; he
picked it up.

"Look at that, I said we would find something. I can sell
it or just hold on to it for a while." It was a steel crowbar,
over a yard long, abandoned here by some workman years
before. It was coated with rust on the surface, but was still
sound. He put the curved and sharpened end into the
opening of the door next to the hinges and threw his weight
onto the other end; the rusty hinges squealed and the door
opened all the way. There was a small platform on the other
side with metal steps falling away from it into the darkness.
Billy started down slowly, holding the crowbar tightly in
one hand, the railing in the other, and on the fifth step went
up to his ankle in water. "It's not just dark down there—it's
full of water," he said.

Peter stepped in and looked, then pointed up at two
bright patches above them. "Apparently the top deck

catches the rain and it drains inside through those holes
there. It must have been collecting for years down here."

"That's where your mosquitoes are coming from too."
The enclosed space was filled with their humming. "We can
close that door and keep them out."

"Very practical," Peter agreed and looked at the dark
surface below them. "It will also save our going to the water
point on the other side of the fence. There is all the water we
could possibly need here, more than we can ever use."

15

"Hello, stranger," Sol said.

Shirl could hear his voice clearly through the partition
that divided the two rooms. She was sitting at the window
doing her nails; she dropped her manicure set on the bed
and ran to the door.

"Andy—is that you?" she called out and when she
opened the door she saw him standing there, swaying a little
with fatigue. She ran to him and kissed him, and he gave her
a brief kiss in return, then released her and dropped into the
car seat by the table.

"I'm wiped out," he said. "No sleep since—when was
it?—night before last. Did you get the water?"

"Filled both the tanks," Sol said, "and got the jerry cans
filled again before it got shut off. What's going on with the
water? I heard some fancy stories on the TV, but it was so
much bushwa. What aren't they telling?"

"You're hurt!" Shirl called out, noticing for the first time
the torn sleeve of his shirt with an edge of bandage showing
below it.

"It's not much, just a scratch," Andy said and smiled.
"Wounded in the line of duty—and by a pitchfork too."

"Chasing the farmer's daughter, probably. Some story,"
Sol snorted. "You want a drink?"

"If any of the alky is left you can cut it a bit with water. I
could use it." He sipped at the drink and sat back in the

chair, some of the strain went out of his face but his eyes were red with fatigue and squinted almost shut. They sat down across from him. "Don't tell anyone until the official word goes out, but there is a lot of trouble over the water—and there's bigger trouble on the way."

"Is that why you warned us?" Shirl asked.

"Yes, I heard part of it at the station on my lunch break. The trouble started with the artesian wells and pumps on Long Island, all the Brooklyn and Queens pumping stations. You know, there's a water table under the Island, and if too much water is pumped out too fast the sea water comes in, then salt water instead of fresh starts coming out of the pumps. It's been brackish for a long time, you can taste it when it's not mixed with upstate water, but they were supposed to have figured out just how much to pump so it wouldn't get worse. There must have been a mistake or the stations have been pumping more than their quota, whatever happened it's coming out pure salt now all over Brooklyn. All the stations there have shut down and the quota coming from Croton and upstate had to be enlarged."

"The farmers been bitching away about the dry summer, I bet they loved this."

"No bets. They must have had it planned for a long time because they jumped the guards on the aqueduct, they had plenty of guns and explosives, the lot that was stolen from the Albany armory last year. There are at least ten cops dead, I don't know how many injured. They blew up at least a mile of pipe before we got through. Every hayseed in the state must have been out there trying to stop us. Not many had guns, but they were doing fine with pitchforks and axes. The riot gas cleared them out, finally."

"Then—there's no water at all for the city?" Shirl asked.

"We'll bring water in, but it's going to be very thirsty around here for a while. Go easy on the water we have, make it last. Use it for drinking or cooking, nothing else."

"But we have to wash," Shirl said.

"No, we don't." Andy rubbed at his sore eyes with the heel of his hand. "The plates can be wiped off with a rag. And as for ourselves—we just stink."

"Andy!"

"I'm sorry, Shirl. I'm being awful and I know it. But you have to realize that things are just that serious. We can go without washing for a while, it won't kill us, and when the

water is connected up again we can all have a good scrub.
It's something to look forward to."

"How long do you think it will be?"

"There's no way to tell yet. The repairs will take a lot of
concrete and reinforcing rods, these are both on top
priority, mixing machines, things like that. Meanwhile most
of the water will have to come in by railroad tank cars, tank
trucks and barges. There is going to be one hell of a problem
with distribution and rationing, you can count on things getting worse before they get better." He dragged himself to his
feet and yawned deeply. "I'm going to sack out for two
hours, Shirl. Will you wake me up by four at the latest? I
have to shave before I leave."

"Two hours! That's not enough sleep," she protested.

"I don't think so either—but it's all I'm getting. Someone
upstairs is still pushing on the O'Brien killing. An informer
in Chinatown has a lead and I have to see him today, instead
of sleeping before I go on precinct patrol tonight. I am
slowly developing a big hate for Billy Chung, wherever he is
hiding." He went into the other room and dropped onto the
bed.

"Can I stay out here while he's sleeping, Sol?" she asked.
"I don't want to bother him—but I don't want to bother you
either—"

"Bother! Since when has a good-looking *chachka* been a
bother? Let me tell you, I may look old but that's just
because of my age. Not that I'm saying you ain't safe
around me, the years for action have passed. I get my kicks
now just thinking about it, which is cheaper anyway and you
don't have to worry about getting a dose. Bring out your
knitting and I'll tell you about the time I was stationed in
Laredo, and I and Luke took a weekend pass and stayed in
Boys Town in Nuevo Laredo, though on second thought
maybe I better not tell you that one."

When Shirl went in Andy was sound asleep, sprawled
across the bed fully dressed; he hadn't even taken his shoes
off. She pulled down the curtain and darkened the room,
then took her manicure set off the foot of the bed. There was
a hole worn in the sole of his right shoe and it stared at
her like a mournful dusty eye. If she tried to take his shoes
off she knew it would only disturb him, so she went out
quietly and closed the door.

"Batteries need charging," Sol said, holding the hydrometer up to the light and squinting at the float through the glass barrel. "Has Andy corked off yet?"

"He's sound asleep."

"Wait until you try to wake him up. When he goes off like that you could drop a bomb and if it didn't kill him he wouldn't hear it. I'll run the batteries up, he'll never know it."

"It's not fair," Shirl burst out suddenly. "Why should Andy have to do two jobs at the same time and be the one to get hurt, fighting for the water for the people in the city? What are all these people doing here? Why don't they go somewhere else if there isn't enough water?"

"For that there is a simple answer—there's no place to go. This whole country is one big farm and one big appetite. There's just as many people down South as there is up North and, since there is no public transportation, anyone who tried to walk to the land of sunshine would starve to death long before he got there. People stay put because the country is organized to take care of them where they are. They don't eat well, but at least they eat. It needs a big catastrophe like the water failures in the California valleys to move people out, or the Dust Bowl—which I hear has now become international and crossed the Canadian border."

"Well, other countries then. Everyone came to America from Europe and places. Why don't some of them go back?"

"Because if you think you got problems you should see the other guy. All of England is just one big city and I saw on TV where the last Tory got shot defending the last grouse woods when they came to plow it up. Or you want to go to Russia maybe? Or China? They been having a border war for fifteen years now, which is one way of keeping the population down—but you're draft age and they draft girls there so you wouldn't like that. Denmark maybe. Life is great there if you can get in, at least they eat regular, but they got a concrete wall right across Jutland and beach guards who shoot on sight because so many starving people keep trying to break into the promised land. No, maybe we got no paradise here, but it's at least livable. I got to run up the batteries."

"It's not fair, I still say that."

"What's fair?" Sol smiled at her. "Relax. You got your

youth, you got your looks, you're eating and drinking
regular. So what's your complaint?"

"Nothing, really." She smiled back at him. "It's just that I
get so angry seeing Andy working all the time, taking care of
people and they don't even know it or care."

"Gratitude you can't expect, a salary you can. It's a job."

Sol dragged out the wheelless bicycle and hooked up the
wires from the generator to the ranked batteries on top of
the refrigerator. Shirl pulled a chair over to the window and
opened her manicure set on the sill. Behind her the creaking
moan of the generator rose to a high-pitched whine. She
pushed at her cuticle with the orange stick. It was a nice day,
sunny but not hot, and it promised to be a nice fall. There
was the trouble with the water, but that would straighten
out. She frowned a little as she looked out across the roofs
and high buildings, only half aware of the endless background roar of the city, cut through by the nearby shrieks of
children.

Outside of this business with the water, everything was all
right. But it was funny: even though she knew that things
were all right, she still had this little knot of tension, a
nagging feeling of worry that just wouldn't go away.

PART TWO

1

"Everyone says this is the coldest October ever, I never seen a colder one. And the rain too, never hard enough to fill the reservoy or anything, but just enough to make you wet so you feel colder. Ain't that right?"

Shirl nodded, hardly listening to the words, but aware by the rising intonation of the woman's voice that a question had been asked. The line moved forward and she shuffled a few steps behind the woman who had been speaking—a shapeless bundle of heavy clothing covered with a torn plastic raincoat, with a cord tied about her middle so that she resembled a lumpy sack. Not that I look much better, Shirl thought, tugging the fold of blanket farther over her head to keep out the persistent drizzle. It wouldn't be much longer now, there were only a few dozen people ahead, but it had taken a lot more time than she thought it would; it was almost dark. A light came on over the tank car, glinting off its black sides and lighting up the slowly falling curtain of rain. The line moved again and the woman ahead of Shirl waddled forward, pulling the child after her, a bundle as wrapped and shapeless as its mother, its face hidden by a knotted scarf, that produced an almost constant whimpering.

"Stop that," the woman said. She turned to Shirl, her puffy face a red lumpiness around the dark opening of her almost toothless mouth. "He's crying because he's been to see the doc, thinks he's sick but it's only the kwash." She held up the child's swollen, ballooning hand. "You can tell when they swell up and get the black spots on the knees. Had to sit two weeks in the Bellevue clinic to see a doc who told me what I knew already. But that's the only way you get him to sign the slip. Got a peanut-butter ration that way. My old man loves the stuff. You live on my block, don't you? I think I seen you there?"

"Twenty-sixth Street," Shirl said, taking the cap off the jerry can and putting it into her coat pocket. She felt chilled through and was sure she was catching a cold.

"That's right, I knew it was you. Stick around and wait for me, we'll walk back together. It's getting late and plenty of punks would like to grab the water, they can always sell it. Mrs. Ramirez in my building, she's a spic but she's all right, you know, her family been in the building since the World War Two, she got a black eye so swole up she can't see through it and two teeth knocked out. Some punk got her with a club and took her water away."

"Yes, I'll wait for you, that's a good idea," Shirl said, suddenly feeling very alone.

"Cards," the patrolman said and she handed him the three Welfare cards, hers, Andy's and Sol's. He held them to the light, then handed them back to her. "Six quarts," he called out to the valve man.

"That's not right," Shirl said.

"Reduced ration today, lady, keep moving, there's a lot of people waiting."

She held out the jerry can and the valve man slipped the end of a large funnel into it and ran in the water. "Next," he called out.

The jerry can gurgled when she walked and was tragically light. She went and stood near the policeman until the woman came up, pulling the child with one hand and in the other carrying a five-gallon kerosene can that seemed almost full. She must have a big family.

"Let's go," the woman said and the child trailed, mewling faintly, at the end of her arm.

As they left the Twelfth Avenue railroad siding it grew darker, the rain soaking up all the failing light. The buildings here were mostly old warehouses and factories with blank solid walls concealing the tenants hidden away inside, the sidewalks wet and empty. The nearest streetlight was a block away. "My husband will give me hell coming home this late," the woman said as they turned the corner. Two figures blocked the sidewalk in front of them.

"Let's have the water," the nearest one said, and the distant light reflected from the knife he held before him.

"No, don't! Please don't!" the woman begged and swung her can of water out behind her, away from them. Shirl huddled against the wall and saw, when they walked forward, that they were just young boys, teen-agers. But they still had a knife.

"The water!" the first one said, jabbing his knife at the woman.

"Take it," she screeched, swinging the can like a weight on the end of her arm. Before the boy could dodge it caught him full in the side of the head, knocking him howling to the ground, the knife flying from his fingers. "You want some too?" she shouted, advancing on the second boy. He was unarmed.

"No, I don't want no trouble," he begged, pulling at the first one's arm, then retreating when she approached. When she bent to pick up the fallen knife, he managed to drag the other boy to his feet and half carry him around the corner. It had only taken a few seconds and all the time Shirl had stood with her back to the wall, trembling with fear.

"They got some surprise," the woman crowed, holding the worn carving knife up to admire it. "I can use this better than they can. Just punks, kids." She was excited and happy. During the entire time she had never released her grip on the child's hand; it was sobbing louder.

There was no more trouble and the woman went with Shirl as far as her door. "Thank you very much," Shirl said. "I don't know what I would have done . . ."

"That's no trouble," the woman beamed. "You saw what I did to him—and who got the knife now!" She stamped away, hauling the heavy can in one hand, the child in the other. Shirl went in.

"Where have you been?" Andy asked when she pushed open the door. "I was beginning to wonder what had happened to you." It was warm in the room, with a faint odor of fishy smoke, and he and Sol were sitting at the table with drinks in their hands.

"It was the water, the line must have been a block long. They only gave me six quarts, the ration has been cut again." She saw his black look and decided not to tell him about the trouble on the way back. He would be twice as angry then and she didn't want this meal to be spoiled.

"That's really wonderful," Andy said sarcastically. "The ration was already too small—so now they lower it even more. Better get out of those wet things, Shirl, and Sol will pour you a Gibson. His homemade vermouth has ripened and I bought some vodka."

"Drink up," Sol said, handing her the chilled glass. "I made some soup with that ener-G junk, it's the only way it's edible, and it should be just about ready. We'll have that for the first course, before—" He finished the sentence by jerking his head in the direction of the refrigerator.

"What's up?" Andy asked. "A secret?"

"No secret," Shirl said, opening the refrigerator, "just a surprise. I got these today in the market, one for each of us." She took out a plate with three small soylent burgers on it. "They're the new ones, they had them on TV, with the smoky-barbecue flavor."

"They must have cost a fortune," Andy said. "We won't eat for the rest of the month."

"They're not as expensive as all that. Anyway, it was my own money, not the budget money, I used."

"It doesn't make any difference, money is money. We could probably live for a week on what these things cost."

"Soup's on," Sol said, sliding the plates onto the table. Shirl had a lump in her throat so she couldn't say anything; she sat and looked at her plate and tried not to cry.

"I'm sorry," Andy said. "But you know how prices are going up—we have to look ahead. City income tax is higher, eighty per cent now, because of the raised Welfare payment, so it's going to be rough going this winter. Don't think I don't appreciate it. . . ."

"If you do, so why don't you shut up right there and eat your soup?" Sol said.

"Keep out of this, Sol," Andy said.

"I'll keep out of it when you keep the fight out of my room. Now come on, a nice meal like this, it shouldn't be spoiled."

Andy started to answer him, then changed his mind. He reached over and took Shirl's hand. "It is going to be a good dinner," he said. "Let's all enjoy it."

"Not that good," Sol said, puckering his mouth over a spoonful of soup. "Wait until you try this stuff. But the burgers will take the taste out of our mouths."

There was silence after that while they spooned up the soup, until Sol started on one of his Army stories about New Orleans and it was so impossible they had to laugh, and after that things were better. Sol shared out the rest of the Gibsons while Shirl served the burgers.

"If I was drunk enough this would almost taste like meat," Sol announced, chewing happily.

"They are good," Shirl said. Andy nodded agreement. She finished the burger quickly and soaked up the juice with a scrap of weedcracker, then sipped at her drink. The trouble on the way home with the water already seemed far distant. What was it the woman had said was wrong with the child?

"Do you know what 'kwash' is?" she asked.

Andy shrugged. "Some kind of disease, that's all I know. Why do you ask?"

"There was a woman next to me in line for the water, I was talking to her. She had a little boy with her who was sick with this kwash. I don't think she should have had him out in the rain, sick like that. And I was wondering if it was catching."

"That you can forget about," Sol said. " 'Kwash' is short for 'kwashiorkor.' If, in the interest of good health, you watched the medical programs like I do, or opened a book, you would know all about it. You can't catch it because it's a deficiency disease like beriberi."

"I never heard of that either," Shirl said.

"There's not so much of that, but there's plenty of kwash. It comes from not eating enough protein. They used to have it only in Africa but now they got it right across the whole U.S. Isn't that great? There's no meat around, lentils and soybeans cost too much, so the mamas stuff the kids with weedcrackers and candy, whatever is cheap. . . ."

The light bulb flickered, then went out. Sol felt his way across the room and found a switch in the maze of wiring on top of the refrigerator. A dim bulb lit up, connected to his batteries. "Needs a charge," he said, "but it can wait until morning. You shouldn't exercise after eating, bad for the circulation and digestion."

"I'm sure glad you're here, doctor," Andy said. "I need some medical advice. I've got this trouble. You see—everything I eat goes to my stomach. . . ."

"Very funny, Mr. Wiseguy. Shirl, I don't see how you put up with this joker."

They all felt better after the meal and they talked for a while, until Sol announced he was turning off the light to save the juice in the batteries. The small bricks of seacoal

had burned to ash and the room was growing cold. They
said good night and Andy went in first to get his flashlight;
their room was even colder than the other.

"I'm going to bed," Shirl said. "I'm not really tired, but
it's the only way to keep warm."

Andy flicked the overhead light switch uselessly. "The
current is still off and there are some things I have to do.
What is it—a week now since we had any electricity in the
evening?"

"Let me get into bed and I'll work the flash for you—will
that be all right?"

"It'll have to do."

He opened his notepad on top of the dresser, lay one of
the reusable forms next to it, then began copying information into the report. With his left hand he kept a slow
and regular squeezing on the flashlight that produced
steady illumination. The city was quiet tonight with the
people driven from the streets by the cold and the rain;
the whir of the tiny generator and the occasional squeak of
the stylo on plastic sounded unnaturally loud. There was
enough light from the flash for Shirl to get undressed by. She
shivered when she took off her outer clothes and quickly
pulled on heavy winter pajamas, a much-darned pair of
socks she used for sleeping in, then put her heavy sweater on
top. The sheets were cold and damp, they hadn't been
changed since the water shortage, though she did try to air
them out as often as she could.

"What are you writing up?" she asked.

"Everything I have on Billy Chung, they're still after me
to find him—it's the most stupid thing I ever heard of." He
slammed the stylo down and paced angrily back and forth,
the flashlight in his hand throwing twisting shadows across
the ceiling. "We've had two dozen killings in the precinct
since O'Brien was murdered. We caught one killer while his
wife was still bleeding to death—but all of the other
murders have been forgotten, almost the same day they
happened. What can be so important about Big Mike? No
one seems to know—yet they still want reports. So after I
put in a double shift I'm expected to keep on looking for the
kid. I should be out tonight, running down another phony
spotting report, but I'm not going to—even though Grassy
will ream me out tomorrow. Do you know how much sleep
I've been getting lately?"

"I know," she said softly.

"A couple of hours a night—if that. Well, tonight I'm going to catch up. I have to sign in again by seven in the morning, there's another protest rally in Union Square, so I won't get much sleep anyway." He stopped pacing and handed her the flashlight, which dimmed, then brightened again as she worked the lever. "I'm making all the noise— but you're really the one who should be complaining, Shirl. You had it a lot better before you ever met me."

"It's bad for everyone this fall, I've never seen anything like it. First the water, now this thing about a fuel shortage, I don't understand it. . . ."

"That's not what I mean, Shirl—will you shine the light on this drawer?" He took out a can of oil and his cleaning kit, spreading the contents out on a rag on the floor next to the bed. "It's about you and me personally. Things here aren't up to the standards you've been used to."

She skirted around mentioning her stay with Mike just as carefully as he did. It was something they never talked about. "My father's place is in a neighborhood just like this one," she said. "Things aren't that different."

"I'm not talking about that." He squatted and broke open his revolver, then ran the cleaning brush back and forth through its barrel. "After you left home things went a lot better for you, I know that. You're a pretty girl, more than just pretty, there must have been a lot of guys who were running after you." He spoke haltingly, looking at his work.

"I'm here because I want to be here," she said, putting into words what he had not been able to say. "Being attractive makes things easier for a girl, I know that, but it doesn't make everything all right. I want . . . I don't know exactly . . . happiness, I suppose. You helped me when I really needed help and we had more fun than I ever had before in my life. I never told you before, but I was hoping you would ask me to come here, we got along so well."

"Is that the only reason?"

They had never talked about this since the night he had asked her here, and now he wanted to know all about her feelings without revealing any of his own.

"Why did you ask me here, Andy? What were your reasons?" She avoided his question.

He clicked the cylinder back into the gun without looking up at her, and spun it with his thumb. "I liked you—liked you a lot. In fact, if you want to know," he lowered his voice as though the words were shameful, "I love you."

Shirl didn't know what to say and the silence lengthened. The dynamo in the flashlight whirred and on the other side of the partition there was a creaking of springs and a subdued grunt as Sol climbed into bed.

"What about you, Shirl?" Andy said, in a low voice so Sol wouldn't hear them. He raised his face for the first time and looked at her.

"I . . . I'm happy here, Andy, and I want to be here. I haven't thought much more about it."

"Love, marriage, kids? Have you thought about those things?" There was a sharp edge to his voice now.

"Every girl thinks about things like that, but . . ."

"But not with a slob like me in a broken-down rat trap like this, is that what you mean?"

"Don't put words into my mouth, I didn't say that or even think it. I'm not complaining—except maybe about the awful hours you're away."

"I have my job to do."

"I know that—it's just that I never see you any more. I think we were together more in those first weeks after I met you. It was fun."

"Spending loot is always fun, but the world can't be like that all the time."

"Why not? I don't mean all the time, but just once in a while or in the evenings, or even a Sunday off. It seems like weeks since we have even talked together. I'm not saying it has to be romance all the time. . . ."

"I have my job. Just how much romance do you think there would be in living if I gave it up?"

Shirl found herself close to tears. "Please, Andy—I'm not trying to fight with you. That's the last thing I want. Don't you understand . . . ?"

"I understand damn well. If I was a big man in the syndicate and running girls and hemp and LSD, things might be different. But I'm just a crummy cop trying to hold things together while the rest of the bastards are taking them apart."

He stabbed the bullets into the cylinder while he talked, not looking at her and not seeing the silent tears that ran down her face. She hadn't cried at the dinner table, but she could not stop it now. It was the cold weather, the boy with the knife, the water shortage, everything—and now this. When she laid the flashlight on the floor the light faded and almost went out as the flywheel slowed. Before it brightened again in his hand she had turned her face to the wall and had pulled the covers up over her head.

She did like Andy, she knew that—but did she love him? It was so hard to decide anything when she hardly ever saw him. Why didn't he understand that? She wasn't trying to hide anything or avoid anything. Yet her life wasn't with him, it was in this terrible room where he hardly ever came, living on this street, the people, that boy with the knife. . . . She bit into her lip but could not stop crying.

When he came to bed he did not say anything, and she did not know what she could say. It was warmer with him there, though she could still smell the gun oil, it must have got on his hands and he could not wipe it all off, and when he was close she felt much better.

She touched his arm and whispered "Andy," but by then it was too late. He was sound asleep.

2

"I smell trouble brewing," Detective Steve Kulozik said as he finished adjusting the headband in the fiberglass helmet. He put it on and scowled out unhappily from under the projecting edge.

"You smell trouble!" Andy shook his head. "What a wonderful nose you got. They have the whole precinct, patrolmen and detectives, mixed together, like shock troops. We're issued helmets and riot bombs at seven in the morning, locked in here without any orders—and you smell trouble. What's your secret, Steve?"

"A natural talent," the fat detective said placidly.

"Let's have your attention here," the captain shouted. The voices and foot shuffling died away and the ranks of men were silent, looking expectantly toward the far end of the big room where the captain stood.

"We're going to have some special work today," the

captain said, "and Detective Dwyer here, of the Head-quarters Squad, will explain it to you."

There was an interested stir as the men in the back rows tried to see past the ranks ahead of them. The Headquarters Squad were trouble shooters, they worked out of Centre Street and took their orders directly from Detective Inspector Ross.

"Can you men in the rear there hear me?" Dwyer called out, then climbed onto a chair. He was a broad, bulky man with the chin and wrinkled neck of a bulldog, his voice a hoarse, bass rumble. "Are the doors locked, captain?" he asked. "What I have to say is for these men alone." There was a mumbled reassurance and he turned back to face them, looking over the rows of uniformed patrolmen and the drab-coated detectives in the rear.

"There's going to be a couple of hundred—or maybe a couple of thousand—people killed in this city by tonight," he said. "Your job is to keep that figure as low as possible. When you go out of here you better realize that there are going to be riots and trouble today and the faster you act to break them up the easier it's going to be for all of us. The Welfare stations won't open today and there won't be any food issued for at least three days."

His voice rose sharply over the sudden hum of voices. "Knock that noise off! What are you—police officers or a bunch of old women? I'm giving this to you straight so you can get ready for the worst, not just yak-yak about it." The silence was absolute.

"All right. The trouble has been coming for days now, but we couldn't act until we knew where we stood. We know now. The city has gone right along issuing full food rations until the warehouses are almost empty. We're going to close them now, build up a backlog and open again in three days. With a smaller ration—and *that* is classified and not to be repeated to anyone. Rations are going to stay small the rest of the winter, don't forget that, whatever you may hear to the contrary. The immediate cause of the shortage right now is that accident on the main line north of Albany, but that's just one of the troubles. The grain is going to start coming in again—but it still won't be enough. We had a professor from Columbia down at Centre Street to tell us about it so we could pass it on, but it gets technical and we haven't got that much time. But here's what it boils down to.

"There was a fertilizer shortage last spring, which means the crop wasn't as good as expected. There have been storms and flooding. The Dust Bowl is still growing. And there was that trouble with the poisoned soybeans from the insecticide. You all know just as much about it as I do, it was on TV. What it adds up to is that a lot of small things have piled up to make one big trouble. There have even been some mistakes made by the President's Emergency Food Planning Board and you're going to see some new faces there. So everyone in this town is going to have to tighten his belt a bit. There is going to be enough for all of us as long as we can keep law and order. I don't have to tell you what would happen if we had some real good riots, some fires, big trouble. We can't count on any outside help because the Army has got plenty of other things to worry about. It's going to be you men on foot out there that do the job. There isn't one operational hovercraft left, they've all either got parts missing or broken impeller blades, and there aren't any replacements. It's up to you. There are thirty-five million people here counting on us. If you don't want them to starve to death—do your jobs. Now . . . any questions?"

A buzz of whispered talk swept across the crowded room, then a patrolman hesitantly raised his hand and Dwyer nodded to him.

"What about the water, sir?"

"That trouble should be licked soon. Repairs on the aqueduct are almost finished and the water should be coming through within a week. But there is still going to be rationing because of the loss of ground water from the Island, and the low level of the reservoirs. And that brings up another thing. We been putting the announcement on TV every hour and we got as many guards as we can spare along the waterfront, but people are still drinking river water. I don't know how they can—the damned river is just an open sewer by the time it reaches us, and salty from the ocean —but people do it. And they're not boiling it, which is the same as taking poison. The hospitals are filling up with typhoid and dysentery cases and God knows what else, and *that* is going to get worse before the winter is over. There are lists of symptoms posted on the bulletin boards and I want you to memorize them and keep your eyes open, get word to the Health Department about anything you see and bring in any cases you think will get away. Keep your shots up to

date and you got nothing to worry about, the department
has all the vaccine you're going to need." He cupped his ear
toward the nearby ranks and frowned.

"I think I heard someone say 'political officer,' but maybe
they didn't. Let's say they didn't, but I've heard it before
and you may be hearing it again yourselves. So let's get one
thing straight. The Commies invented that name, and the
way they use it it means a guy who pushes the Party line to
the troops, sells them a snow job, a lot of crap. But that's
not the way we work it in this country. Maybe I'm a political
officer, but I'm leveling with you, telling you all the truth so
you can get out there and do your job knowing just what has
to be done. Any more questions?"

His big head looked around the room and the silence
lengthened; no one else was asking the question, so Andy
reluctantly raised his hand.

"Yes?" Dwyer said.

"What about the markets, sir?" Andy said, and the
nearby faces turned toward him. "There's the flea market in
Madison Square, they have some food there, and the
Gramercy Park market."

"That's a good question, because they are going to be our
sore spots today. A lot of you will be on duty in or near
those markets. We are going to have trouble at the
warehouses when they don't open, and there will be trouble
in Union Square with the Eldsters there—they are *always*
trouble." A duly appreciative laugh followed his words.
"The stores are going to sell out and board up, we're taking
care of that, but we can't control the markets the same way.
The only food on sale in this city will be there, and people
are going to realize it soon enough. Keep your eyes open and
if anything starts—stop it before it can spread. You've got
night sticks and you have gas, use them when you have to.
You've got guns and they're best left in their holsters. We
don't want indiscriminate killing, that only makes things
worse."

There were no more questions. Detective Dwyer left
before they had been given their assignments and they did
not see him again. The rain had almost stopped when they
went out, but had been replaced by a heavy cold mist that
swept in from the lower bay. There were two canvas-
covered trucks waiting at the curb, and an old city bus that

had been painted a dull olive drab. Half of its windows were boarded up.

"Put'cher fares in the box," Steve said as he followed Andy into the bus. "I wonder where they resurrected this antique from?"

"City Museum," Andy said. "The same place they got these riot bombs. Did you look at them?"

"I counted them, if that's what you mean," Steve said, swinging heavily into one of the cracked plastic seats next to Andy. They both had their satchels of bombs on their laps so there would be room to sit. Andy opened his and took out one of the green canisters.

"Read that," he said, "if you can read."

"I been to Delehanty's," Steve grunted. "I can read Irish as well as American. 'Grenade, pressurized—riot gas— MOA-397 . . .'"

"The fine print, down at the bottom."

"'. . . sealed St. Louis arsenal, April 1974.' So what, this stuff never gets old."

"I hope not. From what our political officer said it sounds like we might need them today."

"Nothing'll happen. Too wet for riots."

The bus shuddered to a halt on the corner where Broadway passed Worth Square and Lieutenant Grassioli pointed at Andy and jerked his thumb toward the door. "You're interested in markets, Rusch, take the beat from here down to Twenty-third. You too, Kulozik."

Behind them the door creaked shut and the bus pushed slowly away through the crowds. They streamed by on all sides, jostling and bumping into each other without being aware of it, a constantly changing but ever identical sea of people. An eddy formed naturally around the two detectives, leaving a small cleared area of wet pavement in the midst of the crowd. Police were never popular, and policemen in helmets, carrying yard-long, lead-filled riotclubs, were to be avoided even more. The cleared space moved with them as they crossed Fifth Avenue to the Eternal Light, now extinguished because of the fuel shortage.

"Almost eight," Andy said, his eyes moving constantly over the people around them. "That's when the Welfare

stations usually open. I suppose the announcement will go
on TV at the same time."

They went slowly toward Twenty-third Street, walking in
the street because the clustering stalls of the flea market had
pushed outward until they covered most of the sidewalk.
"Hubcaps, hubcaps, I got all the best," a merchant
droned as they passed, a small man who was almost lost in
the raveling folds of an immense overcoat, his shaved head
projecting above the collar like a vulture's from a ruff of
matted feathers. He rubbed his dripping nose with cracked
knuckles and appeared to be a little feebleminded.
"Get'cher hubcaps here, officer, all the best, make good
bowls, pots, soup pots, night pots, make good anything. . . ."
They passed out of earshot.

By nine o'clock there was a different feeling in the air, a
tension that had not been there before. The crowd seemed
to have a louder voice and to be stirring about faster, like
water about to boil. When the detectives passed the hubcap
stall again they saw that most of the stock had been locked
away and the few hubcaps left on the counter were rusty and
scarcely worth stealing. Their owner crouched among them
no longer shouting his wares, unmoving except for his
darting eyes.

"Did you hear that?" Andy asked, and they both turned
toward the market. Above the rising hum of voices there
was an angry shout, followed by others. "Let's take a look,"
Andy said, pushing into one of the narrow paths that
threaded through the market.

A shouting crowd was jammed solid between the stalls
and pushcarts, blocking their way, and only stirred without
moving aside when they blew their whistles. The clubs
worked better, they rapped at the barricades of ankles and
legs and a reluctant opening was made for them. At the
center of the mob were three crumb stands, one of them
knocked off its legs and half overturned, with bags of
weedcrumbs dribbling to the ground.

"They been jacking the price!" a thin-faced harridan
screamed. "Against the law jacking the price. They asking
double for crumbs."

"No law says, we can ask what we want," a stall owner
shouted back, clearing the area in front of him with wild
swings of an old connecting rod. He was ready to defend
with his life his stock of broken bits of weedcracker.

Weedcrumbs, the cheapest and most tasteless nourishment ever consumed by man.

"You got no rights, crumby, those prices don't go!" a man called out, and the crowd heaved and surged.

Andy blasted on his whistle. "Hold on!" he shouted above the voice of the mob. "I'll settle this—just hold on." Steve stood and faced the angry crowd, swinging his club before him, as Andy turned to the stall owner and talked in a low voice. "Don't be stupid. Ask a fair price and sell your stock out. . . ."

"I can ask any price I want. There ain't no law—" he protested and broke off when Andy slammed his club against the side of the stall.

"That's right—there's no law unless the law is standing right here. Do you want to lose everything, including your own stupid head? Fix a price and sell out, because if you don't I'm just going to walk away from here and let these people do whatever they want."

"He's right, Al," the crumby from the next stall said, he had sidled over to listen to Andy. "Sell out and get out, they gonna walk all over us if we don't. I'm knocking the price back."

"You're a jerk—look at the loot!" Al protested.

"Balls! Look at the hole in my head if we don't. I'm selling."

There was still a lot of noise, but as soon as the crumbies started selling at a lower price there were enough people who wanted to buy so that the unity of the crowd broke up. Other shouts could be heard, on the Fifth Avenue side of the Square.

"This'll keep here," Steve said. "Let's get circulating."

Most of the stalls were locked now and there were gaps between them where the pushcart owners had closed up and moved shop. A tattered woman was sprawled, sobbing, in the wreckage of her beanwich stall, her stock, cooked beans pressed between weedcrackers, looted and gone.

"Lousy cops," she choked out when they passed. "Why didn' you stop them, do something? Lousy cops." They went by without looking at her, out into Fifth Avenue. The crowd was in a turmoil and they had to force their way through.

"Do you hear that, coming north?" Steve asked. "Sounds like singing or shouting."

The surging of the crowd became more directed, taking on a unity of movement heading uptown. Each moment the massed chanting grew louder, punctuated by the stentorian rasp of an amplified voice.

"Two, four, six, eight—Welfare rations come too late.
Three, five, seven, nine—Medicare is still behind."

"It's the Eldsters," Andy said. "They're marching on Times Square again."

"They picked the right day for it—everything is happening today."

As the crowd pressed back to the curb the first marchers appeared, preceded by a half-dozen uniformed patrolmen, their clubs swinging in easy arcs before them. Behind them was the first wave of the elderly legion, a gray-haired, balding group of men led by Kid Reeves. He limped a bit as he walked, but he stayed out in front, carrying a compact, battery-operated bull horn: a gray metal trumpet with a microphone set into the end. He raised it to his mouth and his amplified voice boomed over the noise of the crowd.

"All you people there on the curbs, join in. March with us. Join this protest, raise your voices. We're not marching for ourselves alone, but for all of you as well. If you are a senior citizen you are with us in your heart because we're marching to help you. If you are younger you must know that we are marching to help your mother and father, to get the help that you yourself will need one day. . . ."

People were being pushed in from the mouth of Twenty-fourth Street, being driven across the path of the marchers, looking back over their shoulders as the force of the crowd behind them drove them forward. The Eldsters' march slowed to a crawl, then stopped completely in a jumble of bodies. Police whistles shrilled in the distance and the policemen who had been marching in front of the Eldsters fought vainly to stop the advance, but were swallowed up and lost in a moment as the narrow exit from Twenty-fourth Street disgorged a stampede of running figures. They crashed into the crowd and merged with the advance guard of the Eldsters.

"Stop there, stop!" Reeves's amplified shout boomed out. "You're interfering with this march, a legal march. . . ." The newcomers pushed against him and a heavy-set man, streaked with blood on the side of his head, grabbed for the bull horn. "Give me that!" he ordered and his words were amplified and mixed with Reeves's in a thunderous jumble.

Andy could clearly see what was happening, but could do nothing to stop it since the crowd had separated him from Steve and carried him back against the quacking row of stalls.

"Give it to me!" the voice bellowed again, overridden by a scream from Reeves as the bull horn was twisted violently from his hands.

"They're trying to starve us!" the amplified sound hammered across the crowd; white faces turned toward it. "The Welfare station is full of food but they locked it up, won't give us any. Open it up and get the food out! Let's open it up!"

The crowd roared agreement and surged back into Twenty-fourth Street, trampling over many of the Eldsters, pushing them to the ground, driven on by the rancorous voice. The crowd was turning into a mob and the mob would turn into a riot if they were not stopped. Andy lashed out with his club at the people nearby, forcing his way through them, trying to get close enough to the man with the bull horn so that he could stop him. A group of Eldsters had locked arms about their injured leader, Reeves, who was shouting something unheard in the uproar, holding his right forearm in his left hand to protect it; it dangled at an odd angle, broken. Andy flailed out but saw that he would never get through, the mob was surging away, faster than he could move.

". . . keeping the food for themselves—anyone ever see a skinny cop! And the politicians, they're eating our food and they don't care if we starve!" The nagging boom of the voice drove the crowd closer and closer to riot. People, mostly Eldsters, had already fallen and been trampled. Andy tore open his satchel and grabbed out one of the riot bombs. They were timed to explode and release their clouds of gas three seconds after the fuse was pulled. Andy held the bomb low, tore out the ring, then hurled it straight-armed toward the man with the bull horn. The green canister arched high and fell into the crowd next to him. It didn't go off.

"Bombs!" the man bellowed. "The cops are trying to kill us so we don't get that food. They can't stop us—let's go —let's get it! Bombs!"

Andy cursed and tore out another gas grenade. This one had better work, the first one had only made things worse. He pushed the nearest people away with his club to make room to swing, pulled the pin and counted to two before he threw.

The canister exploded with a dull thud almost on top of the man with the stolen bull horn, the tearing sound of his retching cut across the roar of voices. The crowd surged, its unity of purpose lost as people tried to flee the cloud of vapor, blinded by the tear gas, with their guts twisted by the regurgitants. Andy tore the gas mask from the bottom of his satchel and swiftly and automatically put it on by gas-drill procedure. His helmet slid down his left arm, hanging from its strap, while he used both hands, thumbs inside, to shake out the mask and free the head straps. Holding his breath, he bent his head and tucked his chin into the mask and, with a single swift motion, pulled the straps over his head that held the mask in place. His right palm sealed the exhaust valve over his mouth as he expelled the air violently from his lungs, it rushed out of the vibrating sides of the mask clearing away any traces of gas. Even as he did this he was straightening up and putting his helmet back on with his other hand.

Though the whole operation of donning the mask had taken no more than three seconds, the scene before him had changed dramatically. People were pushing out in all directions, trying to escape from the spreading cloud of gas that drifted in a thin haze over a widening area of road. The only ones remaining were sprawled on the pavement or bent over, racked by uncontrolled vomiting. It was a potent gas. Andy ran to the man who had grabbed the bull horn. He was down on all fours, blinded and splattered by his own disgorgement, but still holding on to the loudspeaker and cursing between racking spasms. Andy tried to take it away from him, but he fought back viciously and blindly, clutching it with a grip of death, until Andy was forced to rap him on the base of the skull with his club. He collapsed onto the fouled street and Andy pulled the bull horn away.

This was the hardest part. He scratched the microphone with his finger and an amplified clattering rolled out; the thing was still working. Andy took a deep breath, filling his lungs against the resistance of the filters in the canister, then tore the mask from his face.

"This is the police," he said, and faces turned toward his amplified voice. "The trouble is over. Go quietly to your homes, disperse, the trouble is over. There will be no more gas if you disperse quietly." There was a change in the sound of the crowd when they heard the word "gas," and the force of their movement began to change. Andy fought against the nausea that gripped his throat. "The police are in charge here and the trouble is over. . . ."

He clutched his hand over the microphone to deaden it as he doubled over with agony and vomited.

3

New York City trembled on the brink of disaster. Every locked warehouse was a nucleus of dissent, surrounded by crowds who were hungry and afraid and searching for someone to blame. Their anger incited them to riot, and the food riots turned to water riots and then to looting, wherever this was possible. The police fought back, only the thinnest of barriers between angry protest and bloody chaos.

At first night sticks and weighted clubs stopped the trouble, and when this failed gas dispersed the crowds. The tension grew, since the people who fled only reassembled again in a different place. The solid jets of water from the riot trucks stopped them easily when they tried to break into the Welfare stations, but there were not enough trucks, nor was there more water to be had once they had pumped dry their tanks. The Health Department had forbid the use of river water: it would have been like spraying poison. The little water that was available was badly needed for the fires that were springing up throughout the city. With the streets blocked in many places the fire-fighting equipment could not get through and the trucks were forced to make long detours. Some of the fires were spreading and by noon all of the equipment had been committed and was in use.

The first gun was fired a few minutes past twelve, by a Welfare Department guard who killed a man who had broken open a window of the Tompkins Square food depot and had tried to climb in. This was the first but not the last shot fired—nor was it the last person to be killed.

Flying wire sealed off some of the trouble areas, but there was only a limited supply of it. When it ran out the copters fluttered helplessly over the surging streets and acted as aerial observation posts for the police, finding the places where reserves were sorely needed. It was a fruitless labor because there were no reserves, everyone was in the front line.

After the first conflict in Madison Square nothing else made a strong impression on Andy. For the rest of the day and most of the night, he along with every other policeman in the city was braving violence and giving violence to restore law and order to a city torn by battle. The only rest he had was after he had fallen victim to his own gas and had managed to make his way to the Department of Hospitals ambulance for treatment. An orderly washed out his eyes and gave him a tablet to counteract the gut-tearing nausea. He lay on one of the stretchers inside, clutching his helmet, bombs and club to his chest, while he recovered. The ambulance driver sat on another stretcher by the door, armed with a .30-caliber carbine, to discourage anyone from too great an interest in the ambulance or its valuable surgical contents. Andy would like to have lain there longer, but the cold mist was rolling in through the open doorway, and he began to shiver so hard that his teeth shook together. It was difficult to drag to his feet and climb to the ground, yet once he was moving he felt a little better—and warmer. The attack on the Welfare center had been broken up, maybe his grabbing the bull horn had helped, and he moved slowly to join the nearest cluster of blue-coated figures, wrinkling his nose at the foul odor of his clothes.

From this point on, the fatigue never left him and he had memories only of shouting faces, running feet, the sound of shots, screams, the thud of gas grenades, of something unseen that had been thrown at him and hit the back of his hand and raised an immense bruise.

By nightfall it was raining, a cold downpour mixed with sleet, and it was this and exhaustion that drove the people from the streets, not the police. Yet when the crowds were gone the police found that their work was just beginning.

Gaping windows and broken doorways had to be guarded until they could be repaired, the injured had to be found and brought in for treatment, while the Fire Department needed aid in halting the countless fires. This went on through the night and at dawn Andy found himself slumped on a bench in the precinct, hearing his name being called off from a list by Lieutenant Grassioli.

"And that's all that can be spared," the lieutenant added. "You men draw rations before you leave and turn in your riot equipment. I want you all back here at eighteen-hundred and I don't want excuses. Our troubles aren't over yet."

Sometime during the night the rain had stopped. The rising sun cast long shadows down the crosstown streets, putting a golden sheen on the wet, black pavement. A burned-out brownstone was still smoking and Andy picked his way through the charred wreckage that littered the street in front of it. On the corner of Seventh Avenue were the crushed wrecks of two pedicabs, already stripped of any usable parts, and a few feet farther on, the huddled body of a man. He might be asleep, but when Andy passed, the upturned face gave violent evidence that the man was dead. He walked on, ignoring it. The Department of Sanitation would be collecting only corpses today.

The first cavemen were coming out of the subway entrance, blinking at the light. During the summer everyone laughed at the cavemen—the people whom Welfare had assigned to living quarters in the stations of the now-silent subways—but as the cold weather approached, the laughter was replaced by envy. Perhaps it was filthy down there, dusty, dark, but there were always a few electric heaters turned on. They weren't living in luxury, but at least Welfare didn't let them freeze. Andy turned into his own block.

Going up the stairs in his building, he trod heavily on some of the sleepers but was too fatigued to care—or even notice. He had trouble fumbling his key into the lock and Sol heard him and came to open it.

"I just made some soup," Sol said. "You timed it perfectly."

Andy pulled the broken remains of some weedcrackers from his coat pocket and spilled them onto the table.

"Been stealing food?" Sol asked, picking up a piece and nibbling on it. "I thought no grub was being given out for two more days?"

"Police ration."

"Only fair. You can't beat up the citizenry on an empty stomach. I'll throw some of these into the soup, give it some body. I guess you didn't see TV yesterday so you wouldn't know about all the fun and games in Congress. Things are really jumping. . . ."

"Is Shirl awake yet?" Andy asked, shucking out of his coat and dropping heavily into a chair.

Sol was silent a moment, then he said slowly, "She's not here."

Andy yawned. "It's pretty early to go out. Why?"

"Not today, Andy." Sol stirred the soup with his back turned. "She went out yesterday, a couple of hours after you did. She's not back yet—"

"You mean she was out all the time during the riots—and last night too? What did you do?" He sat upright, his bone-weariness forgotten.

"What could I do? Go out and get myself trampled to death like the rest of the old fogies? I bet she's all right, she probably saw all the trouble and decided to stay with friends instead of coming back here."

"What friends? What are you talking about? I have to go find her."

"Sit!" Sol ordered. "What can you do out there? Have some soup and get some sleep, that's the best thing you can do. She'll be okay. I know it," he added reluctantly.

"What do you know, Sol?" Andy took him by the shoulders, half turning him from the stove.

"Don't handle the merchandise!" Sol shouted, pushing the hand away. Then, in a quieter voice: "All I know is she just didn't go out of here for nothing, she had a reason. She had her old coat on, but I could see what looked like a real nifty dress underneath. And nylon stockings. A fortune on her legs. And when she said so long I saw she had lots of makeup on."

"Sol—what are you trying to say?"

"I'm not trying—I'm saying. She was dressed for visiting, not for shopping, like she was on the way out to see someone. Her old man, maybe, she could be visiting him."

"Why should she want to see him?"

"You tell me? You two had a fight, didn't you? Maybe she went away for a while to cool off."

"A fight . . . I guess so." Andy dropped back into the chair, squeezing his forehead between his palms. Had it only been last night? No, the night before last. It seemed a hundred years since they had had that stupid argument. He looked up with sudden fear. "She didn't take her things—anything with her?" he asked.

"Just a little bag," Sol said, and put a steaming bowl on the table in front of Andy. "Eat up. I'll pour one for myself." Then, "She'll be back."

Andy was almost too tired to argue—and what could be said? He spooned the soup automatically, then realized as he tasted it that he was very hungry. He ate with his elbow on the table, his free hand supporting his head.

"You should have heard the speeches in the Senate yesterday," Sol said. "Funniest show on earth. They're trying to push this Emergency Bill through—some emergency, it's only been a hundred years in the making—and you should hear them talking all around the little points and not mentioning the big ones." His voice settled into a rich Southern accent. "Faced by dire straits, we propose a survey of all the ee-mense riches of this the greatest ee-luvial basin, the delta, suh, of the mightiest of rivers, the Mississippi. Dikes and drains, suh, science, suh, and you will have here the richest farmlands in the Western World!" Sol blew on his soup angrily. " 'Dikes' is right—another finger in the dike. They've been over this ground a thousand times before. But does anyone mention out loud the sole and only reason for the Emergency Bill? They do not. After all these years they're too chicken to come right out and tell the truth, so they got it hidden away in one of the little riders tacked onto the bottom."

"What are you talking about?" Andy asked, only half listening.

"Birth control, that's what. They are finally getting around to legalizing clinics that will be open to anyone—married or not—and making it a law that all mothers *must* be supplied with birth-control information. Boy, are we going to hear some howling when the bluenoses find out about that!"

"Not now, Sol, I'm tired. Did Shirl say anything about when she would be back?"

"Just what I told you . . ." He stopped and listened to the sound of footsteps coming down the hall. They stopped—and there was a light knocking on the door.

Andy was there first, twisting at the knob, tearing the door open.

"Shirl!" he said. "Are you all right?"

"Yes, sure—I'm fine."

He held her to him, tightly, almost cutting off her breath. "With the riots—I didn't know what to think," he said. "I just came in a little while ago myself. Where have you been? What happened?"

"I just wanted to get out for a while, that's all." She wrinkled her nose. "What's that funny smell?"

He stepped away from her, anger welling up through the fatigue. "I caught some of my own puke gas and heaved up. It's hard to get off. What do you mean that you wanted to get out for a while?"

"Let me get my coat off."

Andy followed her into the other room and closed the door behind them. She was taking a pair of high-heeled shoes out of the bag she carried and putting them into the closet. "Well?" he said.

"Just that, it's not complicated. I was feeling trapped in here, with the shortages and the cold and everything, and never seeing you, and I felt bad about the fight we had. Nothing seemed to be going right. So I thought if I dressed up and went to one of the restaurants where I used to go, just have a cup of kofee or something, I might feel better. A morale booster, you know." She looked up at his cold face, then glanced quickly away.

"Then what happened?" he asked.

"I'm not in the witness box, Andy. Why the accusing tone?"

He turned his back and looked out the window. "I'm not accusing you of anything, but—you were out all night. How do you expect me to feel?"

"Well, you know how bad it was yesterday, I was afraid to come back. I was up at Curley's—"

"The meateasy?"

"Yes, but if you don't eat anything it's not expensive. It's just the food that costs. I met some people I knew and we talked, they were going to a party and invited me and I went along. We were watching the news about the riots on TV and no one wanted to get out, so the party just went on and on. That's about all, a lot of people stayed overnight and so did I." She slipped off her dress and hung it up, then put on wool slacks and a heavy sweater.

"Is that all you did, just spend the night?"

"Andy, you're tired. Why don't you get some sleep? We can talk about this some other time."

"I want to talk about it now."

"Please, there's nothing more to be said. . . ."

"Yes there is. Whose apartment was it?"

"No one you know. He's not a friend of Mike's, just someone I used to see at parties."

"He?" The silence stretched tight, until Andy's question snapped it. "Did you spend the night with him?"

"Do you really want to know?"

"Of course I want to know. What do you think I'm asking you for? You slept with him, didn't you?"

"Yes."

The calmness of her voice, the suddenness of her answer stopped him, as though he had asked the question hoping to get another answer. He groped for the words to express what he felt and, finally, all he could ask was "Why?"

"Why?" This single word opened her lips and spilled out the cold anger. "Why? What other choice did I have? I had dinner and drinks and I had to pay for it. What else do I have to pay with?"

"Stop it, Shirl, you're being . . ."

"I'm being what? Truthful? Would you let me stay here if I didn't sleep with you?"

"That's different!"

"Is it?" She began to tremble. "Andy, I hope it is, it should be—but I just don't know any more. I want us to be happy, I don't know why we fight. That's not what I want. But things seem to be going so wrong. If you were here, if I was with you more . . ."

"We settled that the other night. I have my work—what else can I do?"

"Nothing else, I suppose, nothing . . ." She clasped her fingers together to stop their shaking. "Go to sleep now, you need the rest."

She went into the other room and he did not stir until the

door clicked shut. He started to follow her, then stopped
and sat on the edge of the bed. What could he say to her?
Slowly he pulled off his shoes and, fully dressed, stretched
out and pulled the blanket over him.

Tired and exhausted as he was, he did not fall asleep for a
very long time.

4

Since most people don't like to get up while it is still dark,
the morning line for the water ration was always the shortest
of the day. Yet there were still enough people about when
Shirl hurried to get a place in line so that no one ever
bothered her. By the time she had her water the sun would
be up and the streets were a good deal safer. Besides that,
she and Mrs. Miles had fallen into the habit of meeting
every day, whoever came first saved a place in line, and
walking back together. Mrs. Miles always had the little boy
with her who still seemed to be ill with the kwash.
Apparently her husband needed the protein-rich peanut
butter more than the child did. The water ration had been
increased. This was so welcome that Shirl tried not to notice
how much harder it was to carry, and how her back hurt
when she climbed the stairs. There was even enough water
now to wash with. The water points were supposed to open
again by mid-November at the very latest, and that wasn't
too far away. This morning, like most of the other
mornings, Shirl was back before eight and when she came
into the apartment she saw that Andy was dressed and just
ready to leave.

"Talk to him, Shirl," Andy said. "Convince him that he is
being a chunkhead. It must be senility." He kissed her good-
by before he went out. It had been three weeks since the
fight and on the surface things were the same as before, but
underneath something had changed, some of the feeling of
security—or perhaps love—had been eroded away. They
did not talk about it.

"What's wrong?" she asked, peeling off the outer layers

of clothing that swaddled her. Andy stopped in the doorway.

"Ask Sol, I'm sure he'll be happy to tell you in great detail. But when he's all through remember one thing. He's wrong."

"Every man to his own opinion," Sol said placidly, rubbing the grease from an ancient can of dubbing onto an even more ancient pair of Army boots.

"Opinion nothing," Andy said. "You're just asking for trouble. I'll see you tonight, Shirl. If it's as quiet as yesterday I shouldn't be too late." He closed the door and she locked it behind him.

"What on earth is he talkng about?" Shirl asked, warming her hands over the brick of seacoal smoldering in the stove. It was raw and cold out, and the wind rattled the window in its frame.

"He's talking about protest," Sol said, admiring the buffed, blackened toe of the boot. "Or maybe better he's talking against protest. You heard about the Emergency Bill? It's been schmeared all over TV for the last week."

"Is that the one they call the Baby-killer Bill?"

"They?" Sol shouted, scrubbing angrily at the boot. "Who are they? A bunch of bums, that's who. People with their minds in the Middle Ages and their feet in a rut. In other words—bums."

"But, Sol—you can't force people to practice something they don't believe in. A lot of them still think that it has something to do with killing babies."

"So they think wrong. Am I to blame because the world is full of fatheads? You know well enough that birth control has nothing to do with killing babies. In fact it saves them. Which is the bigger crime—letting kids die of disease and starvation or seeing that the unwanted ones don't get born in the first place?"

"Putting it that way sounds different. But aren't you forgetting about natural law? Isn't birth control a violation of that?"

"Darling, the history of medicine is the history of the violation of natural law. The Church—and that includes the Protestant as well as the Catholic—tried to stop the use of anesthetics because it was natural law for a woman to have pain while giving birth. And it was natural law for people to die of sickness. And natural law that the body not be cut open and repaired. There was even a guy named Bruno that got burned at the stake because he didn't believe in absolute truth and natural laws like these. *Everything* was against natural law once, and now birth control has got to join the rest. Because all of our troubles today come from the fact that there are too many people in the world."

"That's too simple, Sol. Things aren't really that black and white. . . ."

"Oh yes they are, no one wants to admit it, that's **all.** Look, we live in a lousy world today and our troubles come from only one reason. Too goddamn many people. Now, how come that for ninety-nine per cent of the time that people have been on this earth we never had any over-population problems?"

"I don' know—I never thought about it."

"You're not the only one. The reason—aside from wars and floods and earthquakes, unimportant things like that— was that everybody was sick like dogs. A lot of babies died, a lot of kids died, and everybody else died young. A coolie in China living on nothing but polished rice used to die of old age before he was thirty. I heard that on TV last night, and I believe it. And one of the Senators read from a hornbook, that's a schoolbook they used to have for kids back in colonial America, that said something like 'be kind to your little sister or brother, he won't be with you very long'. They bred like flies and died like flies. Infant mortality—boy! And not so long ago, I tell you. In 1949 after I got out of the Army, I was in Mexico. Babies there die from more diseases than you or I ever heard of. They never baptize the kids until after they are a year old because most of them are dead by that time and baptisms cost a lot of money. That's why there never used to be a population problem. The whole world used to be one big Mexico, breeding and dying and just about staying even."

"Then—what changed?"

"I'll tell you what changed." He shook the boot at her. "Modern medicine arrived. Everything had a cure. Malaria was wiped out along with all the other diseases that had been killing people young and keeping the population down. Death control arrived. Old people lived longer. More babies lived who would have died, and now they grow up into old people who live longer still. People are still being fed into the world just as fast—they're just not being taken out of it at the same rate. Three are born for every two that die. So the population doubles and doubles—and keeps on doubling at a quicker rate all the time. We got a plague of people, a disease of people infesting the world. We got more people who are living longer. Less people have to be born, that's the answer. We got death control—we got to match it with birth control."

"I still don't see how you can when people still think it has something to do with killing babies."

"Stop with the dead babies!" Sol shouted, and heaved the boot the length of the room. "There are no babies involved in this—alive or dead—except in the pointed heads of the idiots who repeat what they have heard without understanding a word of it. Present company excepted," he added in a not too sincere voice. "How can you kill something that never existed? We're all winners in the ovarian derby, yet I never heard anyone crying about the—if you will excuse the biological term—the sperm who were the losers in the race."

"Sol—what on earth are you talking about?"

"The ovarian derby. Every time an egg is fertilized there are a couple of million sperm swimming along, racing along trying to do the job. Only one of them can win the derby, since the very instant fertilization takes place all the rest of them are out in the cold. Does anyone give a damn about the millions of sperm that don't make it? The answer is no. So what are all the complicated rhythm charts, devices, pills, caps and drugs that are used for birth control? Nothing but ways of seeing that *one* other sperm doesn't make it either. So where do the babies come in? I don't see any babies."

"When you put it that way, I guess they don't. But if it is that simple how come nothing was ever done before this?"

Sol breathed a long and tremulous sigh and gloomily retrieved the boot and went back to polishing it.

"Shirl," he said, "if I could answer that they would probably make me President tomorrow. Nothing is ever that simple when it comes down to finding an answer. Everyone has got their own ideas and they push them and say to hell with everyone else. That's the history of the human race. It got us on top, only now it is pushing us off. The thing is that people will put up with any kind of discomfort, and dying babies, and old age at thirty as long as it has always been that way. Try to get them to change and they fight you, even while they're dying, saying it was good enough for grandpa so it's good enough for me. Bango, dead. When the UN sprayed the houses with DDT in Mexico—to kill the mosquitoes who carried malaria that killed the people— they had to have soldiers hold the people back so they could spray. The locals didn't like that white stuff on the furniture, didn't look good. I saw it myself. But that was the rarity. Death control slid into the world mostly without people even knowing it. Doctors used better and better drugs, water supplies improved, public health people saw to it that diseases didn't spread the way they used to. It came about almost naturally without hardly being noticed, and now we got too many people in the world. And something has to be done about it. But doing *something* means that people must change, make an effort, use their minds, which is what most people do not like to do."

"Yet it does seem an intrusion of privacy, Sol. Telling people they can't have any children."

"Stop it! We're almost back to the dead babies again! Birth control doesn't mean no children. It just means that people have a choice how they want to live. Like rutting, unthinking, breeding animals—or like reasoning creatures. Will a married couple have one, two or three children— whatever number will keep the world population steady and provide a full life of opportunity for everyone? Or will they have four, five or six, unthinking and uncaring, and raise them in hunger and cold and misery? Like that world out there," he added, pointing out of the window.

"If the world is like that—then everyone must be unthinking and selfish, like you say."

"No—I think better of the human race. They've just never been told, they've been born animals and died animals, too many of them. I blame the stinking politicians and so-called public leaders who have avoided the issue and covered it up because it was controversial and what the hell, it will be years before it matters and I'm going to get mine now. So mankind gobbled in a century all the world's resources that had taken millions of years to store up, and no one on the top gave a damn or listened to all the voices that were trying to warn them, they just let us overproduce and overconsume, until now the oil is gone, the topsoil depleted and washed away, the trees chopped down, the animals extinct, the earth poisoned, and all we have to show for this is seven billion people fighting over the scraps that are left, living a miserable existence—and still breeding without control. So I say the time has come to stand up and be counted."

Sol pushed his feet into the boots, laced them up and tied them. He put on a heavy sweater, then took an ancient, moth-eaten battle jacket from the wardrobe. A row of ribbons drew a line of color across the olive drab, and under them were a sharpshooter's medal and a technical-school badge. "It must have shrunk," Sol said, grunting as he struggled to close it over his stomach. Then he wrapped a scarf around his neck and shrugged into his ancient, battered overcoat.

"Where are you going?" Shirl asked, baffled.

"To make a statement. To ask for trouble as our friend Andy told me. I'm seventy-five years old and I reached this venerable state by staying out of trouble, keeping my mouth shut and not volunteering, just like I learned in the Army. Maybe there were too many guys in the world like me, I don't know. Maybe I should have made my protest a lot earlier, but I never saw anything I felt like protesting about—which I do now. The forces of darkness and the forces of light, they're meeting today. I'm going to join with the forces of light." He jammed a woolen watch cap down over his ears and stalked to the door.

"Sol, what on earth are you talking about? Tell me, please," Shirl begged, not knowing whether to laugh or to cry.

"There's a rally. The Save Our Babies nuts are marching on City Hall, trying to lick the Emergency Bill. There's another meeting, of people in favor of the bill, and the bigger the turnout there, the better. If enough people stand up and shout they might be heard, maybe the bill will get through Congress this time. Maybe."

"Sol . . ." she called out, but the door was closed.

Andy brought him home, late that night, helping the two ambulance men carry the stretcher up the stairs. Sol was strapped to the stretcher, white faced and unconscious, breathing heavily.

"There was a street fight," Andy said, "almost a riot when the march started. Sol was in it. He got knocked down. His hip is broken." He looked at her, unsmiling and tired, as the stretcher was carried in.

"That can be very serious with old people," he said.

5

There was a thin crust of ice on the water, and it crackled and broke when Billy pushed the can down through it. As he climbed back up the stairs he saw that another rusted metal step had been exposed. They had dipped a lot of water out of the compartment, but it still appeared to be at least half full.

"There's a little ice on top, but I don't think it can freeze all the way down solid," he told Peter as he closed and dogged shut the door. "There's still plenty of water there, plenty."

He measured the water carefully every day and locked the door on it as though it were a bank vault full of money. Why not? It was as good as money. As long as the water shortage continued they could get a good price for it, all the D's they needed to keep warm and eat well.

"How about that, Pete?" he said, hanging the can from the bracket over the seacoal fire. "Did you ever stop to think that we can eat this water? Because we can sell it and buy food, that's why."

Peter squatted on his hams, staring fixedly out the door, and paid no attention until Billy shouted to him and repeated what he had said. Peter shook his head, unhappily.

"Whose God is their belly, and whose glory is in their shame," he intoned. "I have explained to you, Billy, we are approaching the end of all material things. If you covet them you are lost. . . ."

"So—are you lost? You're wearing clothes bought with that water and eating the grub—so what do you mean?"

"I eat simply to exist for the Day," he answered solemnly, squinting through the open door at the watery November sun. "We are so close, just a few weeks now, it is hard to believe. Soon it will be days. What a blessing that it should come during our lifetimes." He pulled himself to his feet and went out; Billy could hear him climbing down to the ground.

"World coming to an end," Billy muttered to himself as he stirred ener-G granules into the water. "Nuts, plain nuts."

This wasn't the first time he had thought that—but only to himself, never aloud in Peter's hearing. Everything the man said did sound crazy but it could be true too. Peter could prove it with the Bible and other books, he didn't have the books now, but he had read them so much he could recite whole long pieces out of them. Why couldn't it be true? What other reason could there be for the world being like this? It hadn't always been this way, the old films on TV proved that, yet it had changed so much so quickly. There had to be a reason, so maybe it was like Peter said, the world would end and New Year's Day would be Doomsday.

. . .

"It's a nutty idea," he said out loud, but he shivered at the same time and held his hands over the smoking fire.

Things weren't that bad. He was wearing two sweaters and an old suit jacket with pieces of inner tube sewed on to patch the elbows, warmer than anything he had ever worn before. And they ate well; he noisily sucked the ener-G broth from the spoon. Buying the Welfare cards had cost a lot of D's but it was worth it, well worth it. They got Welfare food rations now, and even water rations so they could save their own water to sell. And he had been sniffing LSD dirt at least once a week. The world wasn't going to come to an end for a long while yet. The hell with that, the world was all right as long as you kept your eyes open and looked out for yourself.

A jingling clank sounded outside, from one of the pieces of rusty metal hanging from the bare ribs of the ship. Anyone who tried to climb up to the cabin now had to push past these dangling obstacles and give clear warning of their approach. Since the discovery of the water they had to be wary of any others who might want to move in as occupants. Billy picked up the crowbar and walked to the door.

"I made us some food, Peter," he said, leaning over the edge. A strange, bristle-bearded face looked up at him.

"Get down from there!" Billy shouted. The man mumbled something around the length of sharpened automobile leaf spring that he had clamped in his mouth, then hung by one hand and took out the weapon with his free hand.

"Bettyjo!" he shouted in a hoarse voice, and Billy jumped as something whizzed by his ear and crashed into the metal bulkhead behind him.

A squat woman with an immense tangle of blond hair stood among the ribs of the ship below, and Billy dodged as she hurled another lump of broken concrete at him. "Go on, Donald!" she screeched. "Get up there!"

A second man, hairy and filthy enough to be a twin to the first one, scrambled over the rusty metal and began to climb up on the other side of the ship. Billy saw the trap at once. He could brain anyone who tried to get to the strip of deck in front of the door—but only one at a time. He couldn't guard both sides at once. While he was beating off one attacker the other would climb up behind him.

"Peter!" he shouted as loud as he could. "Peter!"

Another piece of concrete burst into dust behind him. He ran to the edge and swung his crowbar at the first man, who bent lower and let it clang against the beam above his head. The noise gave Billy an idea and he jumped back and pounded his crowbar against the metal wall of the deckhouse until the hammering boom rolled out across the shipyard. "Peter!" he shouted once more, desperately, then leaped for the other end where the second man had thrown an arm over the edge. The man withdrew it hurriedly and swung down out of range of his weapon, jeering up at him.

When Billy turned back he saw that the first man had both arms over the edge and was pulling himself up. Screaming, more afraid than angry, Billy ran at him swinging down his crowbar; it grazed the man's head and thudded into his shoulder, knocking the auto spring out of his mouth at the same time. The man roared with rage but did not fall. Billy swung his weapon up for another blow but found himself caught roughly from behind by the second man. He couldn't move—could scarcely breathe—as the man before him spat out fragments of teeth. Blood ran down into his beard and he gurgled as he pulled himself all the way up and began beating Billy with granite fists. Billy howled with pain, lashed out with his feet, tried to break free, but there was no escape. The two men, laughing now, pushed him over the edge of the deck, prying at his clutching hands, sending him toward destruction on the jagged metal twenty feet below.

He was hanging by his hands as they stamped at his fingers when they suddenly jumped back. This was the first that Billy realized Peter had returned and climbed up behind him, swinging his length of pipe at the two men above. In the moment's respite Billy transferred his grip to the skeletal side of the ship and eased his aching body toward the ground that looked impossibly far below. The invaders had occupied the ship and had the advantage now. Peter dodged a swing of the leaf spring and joined Billy in a retreat to the ground. Words penetrated and Billy realized that the woman was screaming curses, and had been for some time.

"Kill 'em both!" she shouted. "He hit me, knocked me down. Kill 'em!" She was hurling lumps of concrete again, but was so carried away by rage that none of them came close. When Peter and Billy reached the ground she waddled quickly away, calling curses over her shoulder, her mass of yellow hair flying around her head. The two men above blinked down at them, but said nothing. They had done their job. They were in possession of the ship.

"We shall leave," Peter said, putting his arm around Billy to help him walk, using his pipe as a staff to lean upon. "They are strong and have the ship now—and the water. And they are wise enough to guard it well, at least the harlot Bettyjo is. I know her, a woman of evil who gives her body to those two so they will do what she asks. Yes, it is a sign. She is a harlot of Babylon, displacing us . . ."

"We have to get back in," Billy gasped.

". . . showing us that we must go to the greater harlot of Babylon, there across the river. There is no turning back."

Billy sank to the ground, gasping for breath and trying to knead some of the pain from his fingers, while Peter calmly looked back at the ship that had been their home and fortune. Three small figures capered on the high deck and their jeers came faintly through the cold wind from the bay. Billy began to shiver.

"Come," Peter said gently, and helped him to his feet. "There is no place to stay here, no dwelling any more. I know where we can get shelter in Manhattan, I have been there many times before."

"I don't want to go there," Billy said, drawing back, remembering the police.

"We must. We will be safe there."

Billy walked slowly after him. Why not? he thought; the cops would have forgotten about him a long time ago. It might be all right, specially if Peter knew some place to go. If he stayed here he would have to stay alone; the fear of that was greater than any remembered fear of the police. They would make out as long as they stuck together.

They were halfway across Manhattan Bridge before Billy realized that one of his pockets had been torn away in the fight. "Wait," he called to Peter, then, more frightened, "wait!" as he searched through his clothing in growing panic. "They're gone," he finally said, leaning against the railing. "The Welfare cards. They must have got lost during the fight. Maybe you have them?"

"No, as you recall, you took them to get the water yesterday. They are not important."

"Not important!" Billy sobbed.

They had the bridge to themselves, an aching winter aloneness. The color of the slate-gray water below was reflected in the lowering clouds above, which were driven along by the icy wind that cut sharply through their clothes. It was too cold to stay and Billy started forward, Peter followed.

"Where are we going?" Billy asked when they came off the bridge and turned down Division Street. It seemed a little warmer here, surrounded by the shuffling crowds. He always felt better with people around.

"To the lots. There are a large number of them near the housing developments," Peter said.

"You're nuts, the lots are full, they always have been."

"Not this time of year," Peter answered, pointing to the filthy ice that filled the gutter. "Living in the lots is never easy, and this time of year it is particularly hard for the older people and invalids."

It was only on the television screen that Billy had seen the streets of the city filled with cars. For him it was a historical—and therefore uninteresting—fact, because the lots had been there for as long as he could remember, a permanent and decaying part of the landscape. As traffic had declined and operating automobiles became rarer, there was no longer a need for the hundreds of parking lots scattered about the city. They began to gradually fill up with abandoned cars, some hauled there by the police and others pushed in by hand. Each lot was now a small village with people living in every car because, uncomfortable as the cars were, they were still better than the street. Though each car had long since had its full quota of inhabitants, vacancies occurred in the winter when the weaker ones died.

They started to work their way through the big lot behind the Seward Park Houses, but were driven off by a gang of teen-agers armed with broken bricks and homemade knives. Walking down Madison Street, they saw that the fence around the small park next to the La Guardia Houses had been pushed down years earlier, and that the park was now filled with the rusting, wheelless remains of cars. There were no aggressive teen-agers here and the few people walking about had a shuffling, hopeless look. Smoke rose from only one of the chimneys that projected from most of the automobiles. Peter and Billy pushed their way between the cars, peering in through windshields and cracked windows, scraping clear patches in the frost when they couldn't see in. Pale, ghostlike faces turned to look up at them or forms stirred inside as they worked their way through the lot.

"This looks like a good one," Billy said, pointing to a hulking ancient Buick turbine sedan with its brake drums half sunk into the dirt. The windows were heavily frosted on both sides, and there was only silence from inside when they tried all the locked doors. "I wonder how they get in?" Billy said, then climbed up on the hood. There was a sliding sunroof over the front seat and it moved a little when he pushed at it. "Bring the pipe up here, this might be it," he called down to Peter.

The cover shifted when they levered at it with the pipe, then slid back. The gray light poured down on the face and staring eyes of an old man. He had an evil-looking club clutched in one hand, a bar of some kind bound about with lengths of knotted cord that held shards of broken, pointed glass into place. He was dead.

"He must have been tough to hold on to a big car like this all by himself," Billy said.

He was a big man and stiff with the cold and they had to work hard to get him up through the opening. They had no need for the filthy rags bound around him, though they did take his Welfare card. Peter dragged him out to the street for the Department of Sanitation to find, while Billy waited inside the car, standing with his head out of the opening, glowering in all directions, the glass-studded club ready if anyone wanted to dispute the occupation of their new home.

6

"My, that does look good," Mrs. Miles said, waiting at the end of the long counter, watching as the Welfare clerk slid the small package across the counter to Shirl. "Someone sick in your fambly?"

"Where's the old package, lady?" the clerk complained. "You know you don't get the new one without turning in the old. And three D's."

"I'm sorry," Shirl said, taking the crumpled plastic envelope from her shopping bag and handing it to him along with the money. He grumbled something and made a check on one of his record boards. "Next," he called out.

"Yes," Shirl told Mrs. Miles, who was squinting at the package and shaping the words slowly with her mouth as she spelled out the printing on it. "It's Sol, he had an accident. He shares the apartment with us and he must be over seventy. He broke his hip and can't get out of bed! This is for him."

"Meat flakes, that sure sounds nice," Mrs. Miles said, handing back the package and following it with her eyes as it vanished into Shirl's bag. "How do you cook them?"

"You can do whatever you like with them, but I make a thick soup with weedcrumbs, it's easier to eat that way. Sol can't sit up at all."

"A man like that should be in the hospital, specially when he's so old."

"He was in the hospital, but there's no room at all now. As soon as they found out he lived in an apartment they got in touch with Andy and made him take Sol home. Anyone who has a place they can go to has to leave. Bellevue is full up and they have been taking over whole units in Peter Cooper Village and putting in extra beds, but there still isn't room enough." Shirl realized that there was something different about Mrs. Miles today: this was the first time she had seen her without the little boy in tow. "How is Tommy—is he worse?"

"No better, no worse. Kwash stays the same all the time, which is okay because I keep drawing the ration." She pointed to the plastic cup in her bag, into which had been dropped a small dollop of peanut butter. "Tommy gotta stay home while the weather is so cold, there ain't enough clothes for all the kids to go around, not with Winny going out to school every day. She's smart. She's going to finish the whole three years. I haven't seen you at the water ration a long time now."

"Andy goes to get it, I have to stay with Sol."

"You're lucky having someone sick in the house, you can get in here for a ration. It's going to be weedcrackers and water for the rest of the city this winter, that's for sure."

Lucky? Shirl thought, knotting her kerchief under her chin, looking around the dark bare room of the Welfare Special Ration section. The counter divided the room in half, with the clerks and the tiers of half-empty shelves on one side, the shuffling lines of people on the other. Here were the tight-drawn faces and trembling limbs of the sick, the ones in need of special diets. Diabetics, chronic invalids, people with deficiency diseases and the numerous pregnant women. Were these the lucky ones?

"What you going to have for dinner tomorrow?" Mrs. Miles asked, peering through the dirt-filmed window, trying to see the sky outside.

"I don't know, the same as always I guess. Why?"

"It might snow. Maybe we might have a white Thanksgiving like we used to have when I was a little girl. We're going to have a fish, I been saving for it. Tomorrow's Thursday, the twenty-fifth of November. Didn't you remember?"

Shirl shook her head. "I guess not. Things have been turned upside down since Sol has been sick."

They walked, heads lowered to escape the blast of the wind, and when they turned the corner from Ninth Avenue into Nineteenth Street, Shirl walked into someone coming in the opposite direction, jarring the woman back against the wall.

"I'm sorry," Shirl said. "I didn't see you. . . ."

"You're not blind," the other woman snapped. "Walking around running into people." Her eyes widened as she looked at Shirl. "You!"

"I said I was sorry, Mrs. Haggerty. It was an accident." She started to walk on but the other woman stepped in front of her, blocking her way.

"I knew I'd find you," Mrs. Haggerty said triumphantly. "I'm going to have the court of law on you, you stole all my brother's money and he didn't leave me none, none at all. Not only that but all the bills I had to pay, the water bill, everything. They were so high I had to sell all the furniture to pay them, and it still wasn't enough and they're after me for the rest. You're going to pay!"

Shirl remembered Andy taking the showers and something of her thoughts must have shown on her face because Mary Haggerty's shout rose to a shrill screech.

"Don't laugh at me, I'm an honest woman! A thing like you can't stand in a public street smiling at me. The whole world knows what you are, you. . . ."

Her voice was cut off by a sharp crack as Mrs. Miles slapped her hard across the face. "Just hold on to that dirty tongue, girlie," Mrs. Miles said. "No one talks to a friend of mine like that."

"You can't do that to me!" Mike's sister shrieked.

"I already done it—and you'll get more if you keep hanging around here."

The two women faced each other and Shirl was forgotten for the moment. They were alike in years and background, though Mary Haggerty had come up a bit in the world since she had been married. But she had grown up in these streets and she knew the rules. She had to either fight or back down.

"This is none of your business," she said.

"I'm making it my business," Mrs. Miles said, balling her fist and cocking back her arm.

"It's none of your business," Mike's sister said, but she scuttled backward a few steps at the same time.

"Blow!" Mrs. Miles said triumphantly.

"You're going to hear from me again!" Mary Haggerty called over her shoulder as she drew together the shreds of her dignity and stalked away. Mrs. Miles laughed coldly and spat after the receding back.

"I'm sorry to get you involved," Shirl said.

"My pleasure," Mrs. Miles said. "I wish she really had started some trouble. I would have slugged her. I know her kind."

"I really don't owe her any money. . . ."

"Who cares? It would be better if you did. It would be a pleasure to stiff someone like that."

Mrs. Miles left her in front of her building and stamped solidly away into the dusk. Suddenly weary, Shirl climbed the long flights to the apartment and pushed through the unlocked door.

"You look bushed," Sol told her. He was heaped high with blankets and only his face showed; his woolen watch cap was pulled down over his ears. "And turn that thing off, will you. It's an even chance whether I go blind or deaf first."

Shirl put down her bag and switched off the blaring TV. "It's getting cold out," she said. "It's even cold in here. I'll make a fire and heat some soup at the same time."

"Not more of that *drecky* meat flake stuff," Sol complained, and made a face.

"You shouldn't talk like that," Shirl said patiently. "It's real meat, just what you need."

"What I need, you can't get any more. Do you know what meat flakes are? I heard all about it on TV today, not that I wanted to but how could I turn the damn thing off? A big sales pitch program on taming the wilds in Florida. Some wilds, they should hear about that in Miami Beach. They stopped trying to drain all the swamps and are doing all kinds of fancy things with them instead. Snail ranches—how do you like that? Raising the giant West African snail, three-quarters of a pound of meat in every shell. Plucked, cut, dehydrated, radiated, packed and sealed and sent to the starving peasants here in the frigid North. Meat flakes. What do you think of that?"

"It sounds very nice," Shirl said, stirring the brown, woodlike chips of meat into the pot. "I saw a movie once on TV where they were eating snails, in France I think it was. They were supposed to be something very special."

"For Frenchmen maybe, not for me . . ." Sol broke into a

fit of coughing that left him weak and white faced on the pillow, breathing rapidly.

"Do you want a drink of water?" Shirl asked.

"No—that's all right." His anger seemed to have drained away with the coughing. "I'm sorry to take it out on you, kid, you taking care of me and everything. It's just that I'm not used to lying around. I stayed in shape all my life, regular exercise that's the answer, looked after myself, never asked anybody for anything. But there's one thing you can't stop." He looked down gloomily at the bed. "Time marches on. The bones get brittle. Fall down and bango, they got you in a cast to your chin."

"The soup's ready—"

"Not right now, I'm not hungry. Maybe you could turn on the TV—no, leave it off. I had enough. On the news they said that it looks like the Emergency Bill is going to pass after only a couple of months of yakking in Congress. I don't believe it. Too many people don't know about it or don't care about it, so there is no real pressure on Congress to do anything about it. We still have women with ten kids who are starving to death, who believe there is something evil about having smaller families. I suppose we can mostly blame the Catholics for that, they're still not completely convinced that controlling births is a good thing."

"Sol, please, don't be anti-Catholic. My mother's family . . ."

"I'm not being anti-nothing, and I love your mother's family. Am I anti-Puritan because I say Cotton Mather was a witch-burning bum who helped to cook old ladies? That's history. Your Church has gone on record and fought publicly against any public birth control measures. That's history too. The results—which prove them wrong—are just outside that window. They have forced their beliefs on the rest of us so we're all going down the drain together."

"It's not really that bad. The Church is not really against the idea of birth control, just the way it is done. They have always approved of the rhythm technique. . . ."

"Not good enough. Neither is the Pill, not for everybody. When are they going to say okay to the Loop? This is the one that really works. And do you know how long it has been around and absolutely foolproof and safe and harmless and all the rest? Since 1964, when the bright boys at Johns Hopkins licked all the problems and side effects, that's how long. For thirty-five years they've had this little piece of plastic that costs maybe a couple of cents. Once inserted it stays in for years, it doesn't interfere with any of the body processes, it doesn't fall out, in fact the woman doesn't even know it is there—but as long as it is she is not going to get pregnant. Remove it and she can have kids again, nothing is changed. And the funny part is that no one is even sure how it works. It's a mystery. Maybe it should be spelled with a capital *M*, Mystery, so your Church could accept it and say it's God's will whether the thing is going to work or not."

"Sol—you're being blasphemous."

"Me? Never! But I got just as much right as the next guy to take a guess as to what God is thinking. Anyway, it really has nothing to do with Him. I'm just trying to find an excuse for the Catholic Church to accept the thing and give the suffering human race a break."

"They're considering it now."

"That's great. They're only about thirty-five years too late. Still, it might work out, though I doubt it. It's the old business of too little and too late. The world's gone—not going—to hell in a hand basket, and it's all of us who pushed it there."

Shirl stirred the soup and smiled at him. "Aren't you exaggerating maybe a *little* bit? You can't really blame all our troubles on overpopulation."

"I damned well can, if you'll pardon the expression. The coal that was supposed to last for centuries has all been dug up because so many people wanted to keep warm. And the oil too, there's so little left that they can't afford to burn it, it's got to be turned into chemicals and plastics and stuff. And the rivers—who polluted them? The water—who drank it? The topsoil—who wore it out? Everything has been gobbled up, used up, worn out. What we got left—our one natural resource? Old-car lots, that's what. Everything else has been used up and all we got to show for it is a couple of billion old cars that are rusting away. One time we had the whole world in our hands, but we ate it and burned it and it's gone now. One time the prairie was black with buffalo, that's what my schoolbooks said when I was a kid, but I never saw them because they had all been turned into steaks and moth-eaten rugs by that time. Do you think that made any impression on the human race? Or the whales and

passenger pigeons and whooping cranes, or any of the
hundred other species that we wiped out? In a pig's eye it
did. In the fifties and the sixties there was a lot of talk about
building atomic power plants to purify sea water so the
desert would bloom and all that jazz. But it was just talk.
Just because some people saw the handwriting on the wall
didn't mean they could get anyone else to read it too. It
takes at least five years to build just one atomic plant, so the
ones that should have supplied the water and electricity we
need *now* should have been built *then*. They weren't. Simple
enough."

"You make it sound simple, Sol, but isn't it too late to
worry about what people should have done a hundred years
ago?"

"Forty, but who's counting."

"What can we do today? Isn't that what we should be
thinking about?"

"You think about it, honeybunch, I get gloomy when I
do. Run full speed ahead just to stay even, and keep our
fingers crossed, that's what we can do today. Maybe I live in
the past, and if I do I got good reasons. Things were a lot
better then, and the trouble would always be coming tomorrow, so the hell with it. There was France, a great big
modern country, home of culture, ready to lead the world in
progress. Only they had a law that made birth control
illegal, and it was a crime for even doctors to talk about
contraception. Progress! The facts were clear enough if
anybody had bothered to look. The conservationists kept
telling us to change our ways or our resources would soon
be gone. They're gone. It was almost too late then, but
something could have been done. Women in every country
in the world were begging for birth control information so
they could limit the size of their families to something
reasonable. All they got was a lot of talk and damn little
action. If there had been five thousand family-planning
clinics for every one there was it still wouldn't have been
enough. Babies and love and sex are probably the most
emotionally important and the most secret things known to
mankind, so open discussion was almost impossible. There
should have been free discussion, tons of money for fertility
research, world-wide family planning, educational programs on the importance of population control—and most

important of all, free speech for free opinion. But there never was, and now it is 1999 and the end of the century. Some century! Well, there's a new century coming up in a couple of weeks, and maybe it really will be a new century for the knocked-out human race. I doubt it—and I don't worry about it. I won't be here to see it."

"Sol—you shouldn't talk like that."

"Why not? I got an incurable disease. Old age."

He started coughing again, longer this time, and when he was through he just lay on the bed, exhausted. Shirl came over to straighten his blankets and tuck them back in, and her hand touched his. Her eyes opened wide and she gasped.

"You're warm—hot. Do you have a fever?"

"Fever?" He started to chuckle but it turned to a fit of coughing that left him weaker than before. When he spoke again it was in a low voice. "Look, darling, I'm an old cocker. I'm flat on my back in bed all busted up and I can't move and it's cold enough to freeze a brass monkey in here. The least I should get is bedsores, but the chances are a lot better that I get pneumonia."

"No!"

"Yes. You don't get anywheres running away from the truth. If I got it, I got it. Now, be a good girl and eat the soup, I'm not hungry, and I'll take a little nap." He closed his eyes and settled his head into the pillow.

It was after seven that evening when Andy came home. Shirl recognized his footsteps in the hall and met him with her finger to her lips, then led him quietly toward the other room, pointing to Sol, who was still asleep and breathing rapidly.

"How is he feeling?" Andy asked, unbuttoning his sodden topcoat. "What a night out, rain mixed with sleet and snow."

"He has a fever," Shirl said, her fingers twisting together. "He says that it's pneumonia. Can it be? What can we do?"

Andy stopped, halfway out of his coat. "Does he feel very warm? Has he been coughing?" he asked. Shirl nodded. Andy opened the door and listened to Sol's breathing, then closed it again silently and put his coat back on.

"They warned me about this at the hospital," he said. "There's always a chance with old people who have to stay in bed. I have some antibiotic pills they gave me. We'll give those to him, then I'll go to Bellevue to see if I can get some more—and see if they won't readmit him. He should be in an oxygen tent."

Sol barely woke up when he swallowed the pills, and his skin felt burning hot to Shirl when she held up his head. He was still asleep when Andy returned, less than an hour later. Andy's face was empty of expression, unreadable, what she always thought of as his professional face. It could mean only one thing.

"No more antibiotics," he whispered. "Because of the flu epidemic. The same with the oxygen tents and the beds. None available, filled up. I never even saw any of the doctors, just the girl at the desk."

"They can't do that. He's terribly sick. It's like murder."

"If you go into Bellevue it looks as though half the city is sick, people everywhere, even in the street outside. There just isn't enough medicine to go around, Shirl. I think just the children are getting it, everyone else has to take their chances."

"Take their chances!" She leaned her face against his wet coat and began to sob helplessly. "But there is no chance at all here. It's murder. An old man like that, he needs some help, he just can't be left to die."

He held her to him. "We're here and we can look after him. There are still four of the tablets left. We'll do everything that we can. Now come inside and lie down. You're going to get sick too if you don't take better care of yourself."

7

"No, Rusch, impossible. Can't be done—and you should know better than to ask me." Lieutenant Grassioli held his knuckle against the corner of his eye, but it did not stop the twitching.

"I'm sorry, lieutenant," Andy said. "I'm not asking for myself. It's a family problem. I've been on duty nine hours now and I'll take double tours the rest of the week—"

"A police officer is on duty twenty-four hours a day."

Andy held tight to his temper. "I know that, sir. I'm not trying to avoid anything."

"No. Now that's the end of it."

"Then let me off for a half an hour. I just want to go to my place, then I'll report right back to you. After that I can work through until the day-duty men come on. You're going to be shorthanded here after midnight anyway, and if I stay around I can finish off those reports that Centre Street has been after all week."

It would mean working twice around the clock without any rest, but this would be the only way to get any grudging aid out of Grassy. The lieutenant couldn't order him to work hours like this—if it wasn't an emergency—but he could use the help. Most of the detective staff had been turned out again on riot duty so that the routine work had fallen far behind. Headquarters on Centre Street did not think this a valid excuse.

"I never ask a man to do extra duty," Grassioli said, grabbing the bait. "But I believe in fair play, give and take. You can take a half an hour now—but no more, understand—and make it up when you come back. If you want to stay around later, that's your choice."

"Yes, sir," Andy said. Some choice. He was going to be here when the sun came up.

The rain that had been falling for the past three days had turned to snow, big, slow flakes that fell silently through the wide-spaced pools of light along Twenty-third Street. There were few other pedestrians, though there were still dark figures curled up in knots around the supporting pillars of the expressway. Most of the other street sleepers had sought the expressway. Most of the other street sleepers had sought were unseen, their crowded numbers, along with the other citizens of the city, pressed out from the buildings with an almost tangible presence. Behind every wall were hundreds of people, seen now only as dark shapes in doorways or the sudden silhouette against a window. Andy lowered his head to keep the snow out of his face and walked faster, worry pushing him on until he had to slow down, panting to catch his breath.

Shirl hadn't wanted him to leave that morning, but he had no other choice. Sol had been no better—or worse—than he had been for the past three days. Andy would have liked to have stayed with him, to help Shirl, but he had no choice. He had to leave, he was on duty. She had not understood this and they had almost fought over it, in whispers so that Sol wouldn't hear. He had hoped to be back early, but the riot duty had taken care of that. At least he could look in for a few minutes, talk to them both, see if he could help in any way. He knew it wasn't easy for Shirl to be alone with the sick old man—but what else was there to do?

Music and the canned laughter of television sounded from most of the doors along the hall, but his own apartment was silent; he felt a sudden cold premonition. He unlocked the door and opened it quietly. The room was dark.

"Shirl?" he whispered. "Sol?"

There was no answer, and something about the silence struck him at once. Where was the fast, rasping breathing that had filled the room? His flashlight whirred and the beam struck across the room and moved to the bed, to Sol's still, pale face. He looked as though he were sleeping quietly, perhaps he was, yet Andy knew—even before his fingertips touched—that the skin would be cold and that Sol was dead.

Oh, God, he thought, she was alone with him here, in the dark, while he died.

He suddenly became aware of the almost soundless, heartbreaking sobbing from the other side of the partition.

8

"I don't want to hear about it any more!" Billy shouted, but Peter kept talking just as if Billy hadn't been there, lying right next to him, and hadn't said a word.

"'. . . and I saw a new heaven and a new earth: for the first heaven and the first earth were passed away; and there was no more sea,' that is the way it is written in Revelation, the truth is there if we look for it. A revelation to us, a glimpse of tomorrow . . ."

"SHUT UP!"

It had no effect, and the monotonous voice went on steadily, against the background of the wind that swept around the old car and keened in through the cracks and holes. Billy pulled a corner of the dusty cover over his head to deaden the sound, but it didn't help much and he could hardly breathe. He slipped it below his chin and stared up at the gray darkness inside the car, trying to ignore the man beside him. With the seats removed the sedan made a single, not too spacious room. They slept side by side on the floor, seeking what warmth they could from the tattered mound of firewall insulation, cushion stuffing and rumpled plastic seat covering that made up their bedding. There was the sudden reek of iodine and smoke as the wind blew down the exhaust-pipe chimney and stirred the ashes in the trunk, which they used for a stove. The last chunk of seacoal had been burned a week before.

Billy had slept, he didn't know how long, until Peter's droning voice had wakened him. He was sure now that the man was out of his head, talking to himself most of the time. Billy felt stifled by the walls and the dust, the closeness and the meaningless words that battered at him and filled the car. Getting to his knees, he turned the crank, lowered the rear window an inch and put his mouth to the opening, breathing in the cold freshness of the air. Something brushed against his lips, wetting them. He bent his head to look out through the opening and could see the white shapes of snowflakes drifting down.

"I'm going out," he said as he closed the window, but Peter gave no sign that he had heard him. "I'm going out. It stinks in here." He picked up the poncho made from the plastic covering that had been stripped from the front seat of the Buick, put his head through the opening in the center and wrapped it around him. When he unlocked the rear door and pushed it open a swirl of snow came in. "It stinks in here, and you stink—and I think you're nuts." Billy climbed out and slammed the door behind him.

When the snow touched the ground it melted, but it was piling up on the rounded humps of the automobiles. Billy scraped a handful from the hood of their car and put it in his mouth. Nothing moved in the darkness and, except for the muffled whisper of the falling snow, the night was silent. Picking his way through the white-shrouded cars he went to Canal Street and turned west toward the Hudson River. The street was strangely empty, it must be very late, and the occasional pedicab that passed could be heard a long way off by the hissing of its tires. He stopped at the Bowery and watched in a doorway as a convoy of five tugtrucks went past, guards walked on both sides and the tugmen were bent double as they dragged at the loads. Must be something valuable, Billy thought, food probably. His empty stomach grumbled painfully at this reminder and he kneaded it with his fingers. It was going on two whole days since he had last eaten. There was more snow here, clumped on an iron fence, and as he passed he scraped it off and wadded it into a ball that he put into his mouth. When he came to Elizabeth Street he crossed over and peered up at the spring-powered clock mounted on the front of the Chinese Community Center building, and he could just make out the hands. It was a little after three o'clock. That meant there were at least three or four more hours before it got light, plenty of time to get uptown and back.

As long as he was walking he felt warm enough, though the snow melted and ran down inside his clothes. But it was a long way up to Twenty-third Street and he was very tired; he had not eaten much the last few weeks. Twice he halted to rest, but the cold bit through him as soon as he stopped moving, and after only a few minutes he struggled to his feet and went on. The farther north he walked, the larger the fear became.

Why shouldn't I come up here? he asked himself, looking around unhappily at the darkness. The cops have forgotten all about me by now. It was too long ago, it was—he counted off on his fingers—four months ago, going on five now in December. Cops never followed a case more than a couple of weeks, not unless somebody shot the mayor or stole a million D's or something. As long as no one saw him he was safe as houses. Twice before he had come north, but as soon as he had got near the old neighborhood he had stopped. It wasn't raining hard enough or there were too many people around or something. But tonight was different, the snow was like a wall around him—it seemed to be coming down heavier—and he wouldn't be seen. He would get to the *Columbia Victory* and go down to the apartment and wake them up. They were his family, they would be glad to see him, no matter what he had done, and he could explain that it was all a frameup, he wasn't guilty.

And food! He spat into the darkness. They had rations for four and his mother always hoarded some of it. He would eat his fill. Oatmeal, slabs of it, maybe even fresh cooked and hot. Clothes too, his mother must still have all of his clothes. He would put on some warm things and get the pair of heavy shoes that had been his father's. There was no risk, no one would know he had been there. Just stay a few minutes, a half an hour at the most, then get out. It would be worth it.

At Twentieth Street he crossed under the elevated highway and worked his way out on Pier 61. The barnlike building of the pier was jammed full of people and he did not dare pass through it. But a narrow ledge ran around the outside, on top of the row of piles, and he knew it well, though this was the first time he had ever gone there at night—with the ledge slippery with moist snow. He sidled along, feeling for each step with his back to the building, hearing the slapping of waves against the piles below. If he fell in there would be no way to get back up, it would be a cold, wet death. Shivering, he slid his foot forward and almost tripped over a thick mooring line. Above him, almost invisible in the darkness, was the rusty flank of the outermost hulk of Shiptown. This was probably the longest way to get to the *Columbia Victory*, which meant it would be the safest. There was no one in sight as he eased up the gangplank and onto the deck.

As he crossed the floating city of ships Billy had the sudden feeling that it was going to be all right. The weather was on his side, snowing just as hard as ever, wrapping around and protecting him. And he had the ships to himself, no one else was topside, no one saw him pass. He had it all figured out, he had been preparing for this night for a long time. If he went down the passageway he might be heard while he was trying to wake someone inside his apartment, but he wasn't that stupid. When he reached the deck he stopped and took out the braided wire he had made weeks earlier by splicing together the ignition wires from a half-dozen old cars. At the end of the wire was a heavy bolt. He carefully payed it out until the bolt reached the window of the compartment where his mother and sister slept. Then, swinging it out and back, he let it knock against the wooden cover that sealed the window. The tiny sound was muffled by the snow, lost among the creakings and rattlings of the anchored fleet. But inside the room it would sound loud enough, it would wake someone up.

Less than a minute after he started the thumping he heard a rattle below and the cover moved, then vanished inside. He pulled up the wire as a dark blur of a head protruded through the opening.

"What is it? Who is there?" his sister's voice whispered.

"The eldest brother," he hissed back in Cantonese. *"Open the door and let me in."*

9

"I feel so bad about Sol," Shirl said. "It seems so cruel."

"Don't," Andy said, holding her close in the warmth of the bed and kissing her. "I don't think he felt as unhappy about it as you do. He was an old man, and in his life he saw and did a lot. For him everything was in the past and I don't think he was very happy with the world the way it is today. Look—isn't that sunshine? I think the snow has stopped and the weather is clearing up."

"But dying like that was so useless, if he hadn't gone to that demonstration—"

"Come on, Shirl, don't beat it. What's done is done. Why don't you think about today? Can you imagine Grassy giving me a whole day off—just out of sympathy?"

"No. He's a terrible man. I'm sure he had some other reason and you'll find out about it when you go in tomorrow."

"Now you sound like me," he laughed. "Let's have some breakfast and think about all the good things we want to do today."

Andy went in and lit the fire while she dressed, then checked the room again to make sure that he had put all of Sol's things out of sight. The clothes were in the wardrobe and he had swept shelves clear and stuffed the books in on top of the clothes. There was nothing he could do about the bed, but he pulled the cover up and put the pillow in the wardrobe too so that it looked more like a couch. Good enough. In the next few weeks he would get rid of the things one by one in the flea market; the books should bring a good price. They would eat better for a while and Shirl wouldn't have to know where the extra money came from.

He was going to miss Sol, he knew that. Seven years ago, when he had first rented the room, it had been just a convenient arrangement for both of them. Sol had explained later that rising food prices had forced him to divide the room and let out half, but he didn't want to share it with just any bum. He had gone to the precinct and told them about the vacancy. Andy, who had been living in the police barracks, had moved in at once. So Sol had had his money—and an armed protection at the same time. There had been no friendship in the beginning, but this had come. They had become close in spite of their difference in ages: Think young, be young, Sol had always said, and he had lived up to his own rule. It was funny how many things Sol had said that Andy could remember. He was going to keep on remembering these things. He wasn't going to get sentimental over it—Sol would have been the first one to laugh at that, and give what he called his double razzberry—but he wasn't going to forget him.

The sun was coming in the window now and, between that and the stove, the chill was gone and the room was comfortable. Andy switched on the TV and found some music, not the kind of thing he liked, but Shirl did, so he kept it on. It was something called *The Fountains of Rome,* the title was on the screen, superimposed on a picture of the bubbling fountains. Shirl came in, brushing her hair and he pointed to it.

"Doesn't it give you a thirst, all that splashing water?" Andy asked.

"Makes me want to take a shower. I bet I smell something terrible."

"Sweet as perfume," he said, watching her with pleasure as she sat on the windowsill, still brushing her hair, the sun touching it with golden highlights. "How would you like to go on a train ride—and a picnic today?" he asked suddenly.

"Stop it! I can't take jokes before breakfast."

"No, I mean it. Move aside for a second." He leaned close to the window and squinted out at the ancient thermometer that Sol had nailed to the wooden frame outside. Most of the paint and numbers had flaked away, but

Sol had scratched new ones on in their place. "It's fifty already—in the shade—and I bet it goes up close to fifty-five today. When you get this kind of weather in December in New York—grab it. There might be five feet of snow tomorrow. We can use the last of the soypaste to make sandwiches. The water train leaves at eleven, and we can ride in the guard car."

"Then you meant it?"

"Of course, I don't joke about this kind of thing. A real excursion to the country. I told you about the trip I made, when I was with the guard last week. The train goes up along the Hudson River to Croton-on-Hudson, where the tank cars are filled. This takes about two, three hours. I've never seen it, but they say you can walk over to Croton Point Park—it's right out in the river—and they still have some real trees there. If it's warm enough we can have our picnic, then go back on the train. What do you say?"

"I say it sounds wonderfully impossible and unbelievable. I've never been that far from the city since I was a little girl, it must be miles and miles. When do we go?"

"Just as soon as we have some breakfast. I've already put the oatmeal up—and you might stir it a bit before it burns."

"Nothing can burn on a seacoal fire." But she went to the stove and took care of the pot as she said it. He didn't remember when he had seen her smiling and happy like this; it was almost like the summer again.

"Don't be a pig and eat all the oatmeal," she said. "I can use that corn oil—I knew I was saving it for something important—and fry up oatmeal cakes for the picnic too."

"Make them good and salty, we can drink all the water we want up there."

Andy pulled the chair out for Shirl so that she sat with her back to Sol's charging bicycle; there was no point in her seeing something that might remind her of what had happened. She was laughing now, talking about their plans for the day, and he didn't want to change it. It was going to be something special, they were both sure of that.

There was a quick rap on the door while they were packing in the lunch, and Shirl gasped. "The callboy—I knew it! You're going to have to work today. . . ."

"Don't worry about that," Andy smiled. "Grassy won't go back on his word. And besides, that's not the callboy's knock. If there is one sound I know it's his bam-bam-bam."

Shirl forced a smile and went to unlock the door while he finished wrapping the lunch.

"Tab!" she said happily. "You're the last person in the world . . . Come in, it's wonderful to see you. It's Tab Fielding," she said to Andy.

"Morning, Miss Shirl," Tab said stolidly, staying in the hall. "I'm sorry, but this is no social call. I'm on the job now."

"What is it?" Andy asked, walking over next to Shirl.

"You have to realize I take the work that is offered to me," Tab said. He was unsmiling and gloomy. "I've been in the bodyguard pool since September, just the odd jobs, no regular assignment, we take whatever work we can get. A man turns down a job he goes right back to the end of the list. I have a family to feed. . . ."

"What are you trying to say?" Andy asked. He was aware that someone was standing in the darkness behind Tab and he could tell by the shuffle of feet that there were others out of sight down the hall.

"Don't take no stuff," the man in back of Tab said in an unpleasant nasal voice. He stayed behind the bodyguard where he could not be seen. "I got the law on my side. I paid you. Show him the order!"

"I think I understand now," Andy said. "Get away from the door, Shirl. Come inside, Tab, so we can talk to you."

Tab started forward and the man in the hall tried to follow him. "You don't go in there without me—" he shrilled. His voice was cut off as Andy slammed the door in his face.

"I wish you hadn't done that," Tab said. He was wearing his spike-studded iron knucks, his fist clenched tight around them.

"Relax," Andy said. "I just wanted to talk to you alone first, find out what was going on. He has a squat-order, doesn't he?"

Tab nodded, looking unhappily down at the floor.

"What on earth are you two talking about?" Shirl asked, worriedly glancing back and forth at their set expressions.

Andy didn't answer and Tab turned to her. "A squat-order is issued by the court to anyone who can prove they are really in need of a place to live. They only give so many out, and usually just to people with big families that have had to get out of some other place. With a squat-order you can look around and find a vacant apartment or room or anything like that, and the order is a sort of search warrant. There can be trouble, people don't want to have strangers walking in on them, that kind of thing, so anyone with a squat-order takes along a bodyguard. That's where I come in, the party out there in the hall, name of Belicher, hired me."

"But what are you doing here?" Shirl asked, still not understanding.

"Because Belicher is a ghoul, that's why," Andy said bitterly. "He hangs around the morgue looking for bodies."

"That's one way of saying it," Tab answered, holding on to his temper. "He's also a guy with a wife and kids and no place to live, that's another way of looking at it."

There was a sudden hammering on the door and Belicher's complaining voice could be heard outside. Shirl finally realized the significance of Tab's presence, and she gasped. "You're here because you're helping them," she said. "They found out that Sol is dead and they want this room."

Tab could only nod mutely.

"There's still a way out," Andy said. "If we had one of the men here from my precinct, living in here, then these people couldn't get in."

The knocking was louder and Tab took a half step backward toward the door. "If there was somebody here now, that would be okay, but Belicher could probably take the thing to the squat court and get occupancy anyway because he has a family. I'll do what I can to help you—but Belicher, he's still my employer."

"Don't open that door," Andy said sharply. "Not until we have this straightened out."

"I have to—what else can I do?" He straightened up and closed his fist with the knucks on it. "Don't try to stop me, Andy. You're a policeman, you know the law about this."

"Tab, must you?" Shirl asked in a low voice.

He turned to her, eyes filled with unhappiness. "We were good friends once, Shirl, and that's the way I'm going to remember it. But you're not going to think much of me after this because I have to do my job. I have to let them in."

"Go ahead—open the damn door," Andy said bitterly, turning his back and walking over to the window.

The Belichers swarmed in. Mr. Belicher was thin, with a

strangely shaped head, almost no chin and just enough intelligence to sign his name to the Welfare application. Mrs. Belicher was the support of the family; from the flabby fat of her body came the children, all seven of them, to swell the Relief allotment on which they survived. Number eight was pushing an extra bulge out of the dough of her flesh; it was really number eleven since three of the younger Belichers had perished through indifference or accident. The largest girl, she must have been all of twelve, was carrying the sore-covered infant which stank abominably and cried continuously. The other children shouted at each other now, released from the silence and tension of the dark hall.

"Oh, looka the nice fridge," Mrs. Belicher said, waddling over and opening the door.

"Don't touch that," Andy said, and Belicher pulled him by the arm.

"I like this room—it's not big, you know, but nice. What's in here?" He started toward the open door in the partition.

"That's my room," Andy said, slamming it shut in his face. "Just keep out of there."

"No need to act like that," Belicher said, sidling away quickly like a dog that has been kicked too often. "I got my rights. The law says I can look wherever I want with a squat-order." He moved farther away as Andy took a step toward him. "Not that I'm doubting your word, mister, I believe you. This room here is fine, got a good table, chairs, bed. . . ."

"Those things belong to me. This is an empty room, and a small one at that. It's not big enough for you and all your family."

"It's big enough, all right. We lived in smaller. . . ."

"Andy—stop them! Look—" Shirl's unhappy cry spun Andy around and he saw that two of the boys had found the packets of herbs that Sol had grown so carefully in his window box, and were tearing them open, thinking that it was food of some kind.

"Put these things down," he shouted, but before he could reach them they had tasted the herbs, then spat them out.

"Burn my mouth!" the bigger boy screamed and sprayed the contents of the packet on the floor. The other boy bounced up and down with excitement and began to do the same thing with the rest of the herbs. They twisted away from Andy and before he could stop them the packets were empty.

As soon as Andy turned away, the younger boy, still excited, climbed on the table—his mud-stained foot wrappings leaving filthy smears—and turned up the TV. Blaring music crashed over the screams of the children and the ineffectual calls of their mother. Tab pulled Belicher away as he opened the wardrobe to see what was inside.

"Get these kids out of here," Andy said, white faced with rage.

"I got a squat-order, I got rights," Belicher shouted, backing away and waving an imprinted square of plastic.

"I don't care what rights you have," Andy told him, opening the hall door. "We'll talk about that when these brats are outside."

Tab settled it by grabbing the nearest child by the scruff of the neck and pushing it out through the door. "Mr. Rusch is right," he said. "The kids can wait outside while we settle this."

Mrs. Belicher sat down heavily on the bed and closed her eyes, as though all this had nothing to do with her. Mr. Belicher retreated against the wall saying something that no one heard or bothered to listen to. There were some shrill cries and angry sobbing from the hall as the last child was expelled.

Andy looked around and realized that Shirl had gone into their room; he heard the key turn in the lock. "I suppose this is it?" he said, looking steadily at Tab.

The bodyguard shrugged helplessly. "I'm sorry, Andy, honest to God I am. What else can I do? It's the law, and if they want to stay here you can't get them out."

"It's the law, it's the law," Belicher echoed tonelessly.

There was nothing Andy could do with his clenched fists and he had to force himself to open them. "Help me carry these things into the other room, will you, Tab?"

"Sure," Tab said, and took the other end of the table. "Try and explain to Shirl about my part in this, will you? I don't think she understands that it's just a job I have to do."

Their footsteps crackled on the dried herbs that littered the floor and Andy did not answer him.

"Andy, you must do something, those people are driving me right out of my mind."

"Easy, Shirl, it's not that bad," Andy said. He was standing on a chair, filling the wall tank from a jerry can, and when he turned to answer her some of the water splashed over and dripped down to the floor. "Let me finish this first before we argue, will you."

"I'm not arguing—I'm just telling you how I feel. Listen to that."

Sound came clearly through the thin partition. The baby was crying, it seemed to do this continuously day and night; and they had to use earplugs to get any sleep. Some of the children were fighting, completely ignoring their father's reedy whine of complaint. To add to the turmoil one of them was beating steadily on the floor with something heavy. The people in the apartment below would be up again soon to complain; it never did any good. Shirl sat on the edge of the bed, wringing her hands.

"Do you hear that?" she said. "It never stops, I don't know how they can live like that. You're away so you don't hear the worst of it. Can't we get them out of there? There must be something we can do about it."

Andy emptied the jerry can and climbed down, threading his way through the crowded room. They had sold Sol's bed and his wardrobe, but everything else was jammed in here, and there was scarcely a foot of clear floor space. He dropped heavily into a chair.

"I've been trying, you know I have. Two of the patrolmen, they live in the barracks now, are ready to move in here if we can get the Belichers out. That's the hard part. They have the law on their side."

"Is there a law that says we have to put up with people like that?" She was wringing her hands helplessly, staring at the partition.

"Look, Shirl, can't we talk about this some other time? I have to go out soon—"

"I want to talk about it now. You've been putting it off ever since they came, and that's over two weeks now, and I can't take much more of it."

"Come on, it's not that bad. It's just noise."

The room was very cold. Shirl pulled her legs up and wrapped the old blanket tighter around her; the springs in the bed twanged under her weight. There was a momentary lull from the other room that ended with shrill laughter.

"Do you hear that?" Shirl asked. "What kind of minds do they have? Every time they hear the bed move in here they burst out laughing. We've no privacy, none at all, that partition is as thin as cardboard and they listen for everything we do and hear every word we say. If they won't go—can't we move?"

"Where to? Show some sense, will you, we're lucky to have this much room to ourselves. Do you know how many people still sleep in the streets—and how many bodies get brought in every morning?"

"I couldn't care less. It's my own life I'm worrying about."

"Please, not now." He looked up as the light bulb flickered and dimmed, then sprang back to life again. There was a sudden rattle of hail against the window. "We can talk about it when I get back, I shouldn't be long."

"No, I want to settle it now, you've been putting this off over and over again. You don't have to go out now."

He took his coat down, restraining his temper. "It can wait until I get back. I told you that we finally had word on Billy Chung—an informer saw him leaving Shiptown—the chances are that he had been visiting his family. It's old news too, it happened fifteen days ago, but the stoolie didn't think it important enough to tell us about right away. I guess he was hoping to see the boy come back, but he never has. I'll have to talk to his family and see what they know."

"You don't have to go now—you said this happened some time ago. . . ."

"What does that have to do with it? The lieutenant will want a report in the morning. So what should I tell him— that you didn't want me to go out tonight?"

"I don't care what you tell him. . . ."

"I know you don't, but I do. It's my job and I have to do it."

They glared at each other in silence, breathing rapidly. From the other side of the partition there sounded a shrill cry and childish sobbing.

"Shirl, I don't want to fight with you," Andy said. "I have to go out, that's all there is to it. We can talk about it later, when I come back."

"If I'm here when you come back." She had her hands clenched tightly together and her face was pale.

"What do you mean by that?"

"I don't know what I mean. I just know something has to change. Please, let's settle this now. . . ."

"Can't you understand that's impossible? We'll talk about it when I get back." He unlocked the door and stood with the knob in his hand, getting a grip on his temper. "Let's not fight about it now. I'll be back in a few hours, we can worry about it then, all right?" She didn't answer, and after waiting a moment he went out and closed the door heavily behind him. The foul, thick odor of the room beyond hit him in the face.

"Belicher," he said, "you're going to have to clean this place up. It stinks."

"I can't do nothing about the smoke until I get some kind of chimbley." Belicher sniffled, squatting and holding his hands over a smoldering lump of seacoal. This rested in a hubcap filled with sand from which eye-burning, oily smoke rose to fill the room. The opening in the outer wall that Sol had made for the chimney of his stove had been carelessly covered with a sheet of thin polythene that billowed and crackled as the wind blew against it.

"The smoke is the best smell in here," Andy said. "Have your kids been using this place for a toilet again?"

"You wouldn't ask kids to go down all them stairs at night, would you?" Belicher complained.

Wordless, Andy looked around at the heap of coverings in the corner where Mrs. Belicher and the smaller Belichers were huddled for warmth. The two boys were doing something in the corner with their backs turned. The small light bulb threw long shadows over the rubbish that was beginning to collect against the baseboard, lit up the new marks gouged in the wall.

"You better get this place cleaned up," Andy said and slammed the door shut on Belicher's whining answer.

Shirl was right, these people were impossible and he had to do something about them. But when? It had better be soon, she couldn't take much more of them. He was angry at the invaders—and angry at her. All right, it was pretty bad, but you had to take things as they came. He was still putting in a twelve- and fourteen-hour day, which was a lot worse than just sitting and listening to the kids scream.

The street was dark, filled with wind and driving sleet. There was snow mixed with it and had already begun to stick to the pavement and pile up in corners against the walls. Andy plowed through it, head down, hating the Belichers and trying not to be angry with Shirl.

The walkways and connecting bridges in Shiptown were ice coated and slippery and Andy had to grope his way over them carefully, aware of the surging black water below. In the darkness all of the ships looked alike and he used his flashlight on their bows to pick out their names. He was chilled and wet before he found the *Columbia Victory* and pulled open the heavy steel door that led below deck. As he went down the metal stairs light spilled across the passageway ahead. One of the doors had been opened by a small boy with spindly legs; it looked like the Chung apartment.

"Just a minute," Andy said, stopping the door before the child could close it. The little boy gaped up at him, silent and wide-eyed.

"This is the Chung apartment, isn't it?" he asked, stepping in. Then he recognized the woman standing there. She was Billy's sister, he had met her before. The mother sat in a chair against the wall, with the same expression of numb fright as her daughter, holding on to the twin of the boy who had opened the door. No one answered him.

These people really love the police, Andy thought. At the same instant he realized that they all kept looking toward the door in the far wall and quickly away. What was bothering them?

He reached behind his back and closed the hall door. It wasn't possible—yet the night Billy Chung had been seen here had been stormy like this one, perfect cover for a fugitive. Could I be having a break at last? he wondered. Had he picked the right night to come here?

Even as the thoughts were forming the door to the bedroom opened and Billy Chung stepped out, starting to say something. His words were drowned by his mother's shrill cries and his sister's shouted warning. He looked up and halted, shocked motionless when he saw Andy.

"You're under arrest," Andy said, reaching down to the side of his belt to get his nippers.

"No!" Billy gasped hoarsely and grabbed at his waistband and pulled out a knife.

It was a mess. The old woman kept screaming shrilly, over and over, without stopping for breath and the daughter hurled herself on Andy, trying to scratch at his eyes. She raked her nails down his cheek before he grabbed her and held her off at arm's length. And all the time he was watching Billy, who held out the long shining blade as he advanced in a knife-fighter's crouch, waving the weapon before him.

"Put that down," Andy shouted, and leaned his back against the door. "You can't get out of here. Don't cause any more trouble." The woman found she couldn't reach Andy's face so she raked lines of fire down the back of his hand with her nails. Andy pushed her away and was barely aware of her falling as he grabbed for his gun.

"Stop it!" he shouted, and pointed the gun up in the air. He wanted to fire a warning shot, then he realized that the compartment was made of steel and any bullet would ricochet around inside of it: there were two women and two children here.

"Stop it, Billy, you can't get out of here," he shouted, pointing the gun at the boy who was halfway across the room, waving the knife wildly.

"Let me by," Billy sobbed. "I'll kill you! Why couldn't you just leave me alone?"

He wasn't going to stop, Andy realized. The knife was sharp and he knew how to use it. If he wanted trouble he was going to get it.

Andy aimed the gun at Billy's leg and pulled the trigger just as the boy stumbled.

The boom of the .38-caliber shell filled the compartment and Billy pitched forward, the bullet hit his head and he kept going down to sprawl on the steel deck. The knife spun from his hand and stopped almost at Andy's feet. Shocked silence followed the sound of the shot and the air was strong with the sharp reek of gunpowder. No one moved except Andy, who bent over and touched the boy's wrist.

Andy was aware of a hammering on the door behind him and he reached back and fumbled to open it without turning around.

"I'm a police officer," he said. "I want someone to get over to Precinct 12-A on Twenty-third Street and report this at once. Tell them that Billy Chung is here. He's dead."

A bullet in the temple, Andy realized suddenly. Got it in the same spot that Big Mike O'Brien did.

It was messy, that was the worst part of it. Not Billy, he was safely dead. It was the mother and the sister, they had screamed abuse at him while the twins had held on to each other and sobbed. Finally Andy made the neighbors across the hall take the whole family in and he had remained alone with the body until Steve Kulozik and a patrolman had arrived from the precinct. He hadn't seen the two women after that, and he hadn't wanted to. It had been an accident, that was all, they ought to realize that. If the kid hadn't fallen he would have gotten the bullet in the leg and that would have been the end of it. Not that the police would care about the shooting, the case could be closed now without any more red tape, it was just the two women. Well, let them hate him, it wouldn't hurt him and he wasn't ever going to see them again. So the son was a martyr, not a killer, if they preferred to remember him that way. Fine. Either way the case was closed.

It was late, after midnight, before Andy got home. Bringing back the body and making a report had taken a long time. As usual the Belichers hadn't locked the hall door—they didn't care, they had nothing worth losing or stealing. Their room was dark and he flashed his light across it, catching a fleeting glimpse of their huddled bodies, a glimmer of reflection from their eyes. They were awake—but at least they were all quiet for a change, even the baby. As he put his key into the lock on his door he heard a muffled titter behind him in the darkness. What could they possibly have to laugh about?

Pushing the door open into the silent room, he remembered the trouble with Shirl earlier that evening and he felt a sudden dart of fear. He raised the flashlight but did not squeeze it. There was the laughter behind him again, a little louder this time.

The light sliced across the room to the vacant chairs, the empty bed. Shirl wasn't here. It couldn't mean anything, she had probably gone downstairs to the lavatories, that was all.

Yet he knew, even before he opened the wardrobe, that her clothes were gone and so were her suitcases.

Shirl was gone too.

11

"What do you want?" the hard-eyed man asked, standing just inside the bedroom door. "You know Mr. Briggs is a busy man. I'm a busy man. Neither of us like you telephoning, saying someone should come over, just like that. You got something you want to tell Mr. Briggs, you come and tell him."

"I'm very sorry that I can't oblige you," Judge Santini said, wheezing a little while he talked, propped up on pillows in the big dark double bed, smooth blankets carefully tucked in around him. "Much as I would like to. But I'm afraid that my running days are over, at least that's what my doctor says, and I pay him enough for his opinions. When a man my age has a coronary he has to watch himself. Rest, plenty of rest. No more climbing up those stairs in the Empire State Building. I can confide in you, Schlachter, that I really won't miss them very much. . . ."

"What do you want, Santini?"

"To give you some information for Mr. Briggs. The Chung boy has been found, Billy Chung, the one who killed Big Mike."

"So?"

"So—I had hoped you would remember a meeting we had where we discussed this subject. There was a suspicion that the killer might be connected with Nick Cuore, that the boy was in his pay. I doubt if he was, he seems to have been operating on his own. We will never know for certain because he is dead."

"Is that all?"

"Isn't that enough? You might recall that Mr. Briggs was concerned about the possibility of Cuore moving in on this city."

"No chance of that at all. Cuore has been tied up for a week in taking over in Paterson. There've been a dozen killings already. He was never interested in New York."

"I'm pleased to hear that. But I think you had better tell Mr. Briggs about this in any case. He was interested enough in the case to put pressure on the police department, they have had a man on the case since August."

"Tough. I'll tell him if I get a chance. But he's not interested in this any more."

Judge Santini settled wearily into the covers when his guest had gone. He was tired tonight, tireder than he could ever remember. And there was still a memory of that pain deep inside his chest.

Just about two weeks more to the new year. New century too. It would be funny to write two thousand instead of nineteen something or other as he had done all his life.

January 1, 2000. It seemed like a strange date for some reason. He rang the bell so Rosa could come and pour him his medicine. How much of this new century would he see? The thought was a very depressing one.

In the quiet room the ticking of the old-fashioned clock sounded very loud.

12

"The lieutenant wants to see you," Steve called across the squad room.

Andy waved his hand in acknowledgment and stood and stretched, only too willing to leave the stack of reports he was working on. He had not slept well the night before and he was tired. First the shooting, then finding Shirl gone, it was a lot to have happen in one night. Where would he look for her, to ask her to come back? Yet how could he ask her to come back while the Belichers were still there? How could he get rid of the Belichers? This wasn't the first time that his thoughts had spiraled around this way. It got him nowhere. He knocked on the door of the lieutenant's office, then went in.

"You wanted to see me, sir?"

Lieutenant Grassioli was swallowing a pill and he nodded, then choked on the water he was using to wash it down. He had a coughing fit, and dropped into the battered swivel chair, looking grayer and more tired than usual. "This ulcer is going to kill me one of these days. Ever hear of anyone dying of an ulcer?"

There was no answer for a question like this. Andy wondered why the lieutenant was making conversation, it wasn't like him. He usually found no trouble in speaking his mind.

"They're not happy downtown about your shooting the Chink kid," Grassioli said, pawing through the reports and files that littered his desk.

"What do you mean——"

"Just that, Christ, just like I don't have enough trouble with this squad, I got to get mixed up in politics too. Centre Street thinks you been wasting too much time on this case, we've had two dozen unsolved murders in the precinct since you started on this one."

"But——" Andy was dumfounded, "you told me the commissioner himself ordered me onto the case full time. You told me I had to——"

"It doesn't matter what I told you," Grassioli snarled. "The commissioner's not available on the phone, not to me he's not. He doesn't give a damn about the O'Brien killer and no one's interested in any word I got about that Jersey hood Cuore. And what's more, the assistant commissioner is on to me over the Billy Chung shooting. They left me holding the bag."

"Sounds more like I'm the one with the bag."

"Don't get snotty with me, Rusch." The lieutenant stood and kicked the chair away and turned his back on Andy, looking out of the window and drumming his fingers on the frame. "The assistant commissioner is George Chu and he thinks you got a vendetta against the Chinks or something, tracking the kid all this time, then shooting him down instead of bringing him in."

"You told him I was acting on orders, didn't you, lieutenant?" Andy asked softly. "You told him the shooting was accidental, it's all in my report."

"I didn't tell him anything." Grassioli turned to face Andy. "The people who pushed me onto this case aren't talking. There's nothing I can tell Chu. He's nuts on this race thing anyway. If I try to tell him what really happened I'm not only going to make trouble for myself, for the precinct—for everybody." He dropped into his chair and rubbed at the twitching corner of his eye. "I'm telling you straight, Andy. I'm going to pass the buck to you, let you take the blame. I'm going to put you back into uniform for six months until this thing cools down. You'll stay in grade, you won't lose any pay."

"I wasn't expecting any award for cracking this case," Andy said angrily, "or for bringing in the killer—but I didn't expect this. I can ask for a departmental trial."

"You can, you can do that." The lieutenant hesitated a long time, he was obviously ill at ease. "But I'm asking you not to. If not for me, for the good of the precinct. I know it's a raw deal, passing the buck, but you'll come out of it okay. I'll have you back on the squad as soon as I can. And it's not like you'll be doing anything different, anyway. We might as well all be walking a beat for the little detective work we do." He kicked viciously at the desk. "What do you say?"

"The whole thing stinks."

"I know it stinks!" the lieutenant shouted. "But what the hell else can I do? You think it'll stink less if you stand trial? You won't stand a chance. You'll be off the force and out of a job and I'll probably be with you. You're a good cop, Andy, and there aren't many of them left. The department needs you more than you need them. Stick it out. What do you say?"

There was a long silence, and the lieutenant turned back to look out of the window.

"All right," Andy finally said. "I'll do whatever you want me to do, lieutenant." He went out of the office without being dismissed; he didn't want the lieutenant to thank him for this.

13

"Half an hour more and we'll be in a new century," Steve Kulozik said, stamping his feet on the icy pavement. "I heard some joker on TV yesterday trying to explain why the new century doesn't start until next year, but he must be a chunkhead. Midnight, year two thousand, new century. That makes sense. Look at that." He pointed up at the projection TV screen on the old Times Building. The headlines, in letters ten feet high, chased each other across the screen.

COLD SNAP IN MIDWEST SCORES OF DEATHS REPORTED

"Scores," Steve grunted. "I bet they don't even keep score any more, they don't want to know how many die."

FAMINE REPORTS FROM RUSSIA NOT TRUE SAYS GALYGIN

PRESIDENTIAL MESSAGE ON MORN OF NEW CENTURY

NAVY SUPERSONJET CRASH IN FRISCO BAY

Andy glanced up at the screen, then back at the milling crowd in Times Square. He was getting used to wearing the blue uniform again, though he still felt uneasy when he was around any other men from the detective squad. "What are you doing here?" he asked Steve.

"Same as you, on loan to this precinct. They're still screaming for reserves, they think there's going to be a riot."

"They're wrong, it's too cold and there's not that many people."

"That's not the worry, it's the nut cults, they're saying it's the millennium, Judgment Day or Doomsday or whatever the hell you call it. There's bunches of them all over town. They're going to be damn unhappy when the world doesn't come to an end at midnight, the way they think it will."

"We'll be a lot unhappier if it does."

The giant, silent words raced over their heads.

COLIN PROMISES QUICK END OF BABY BILL
FILIBUSTER

The crowd surged slowly back and forth, craning their necks up at the screen. Some horns were blowing and the roar of voices was penetrated by a ringing cowbell and the occasional whir of rattles. They cheered when the time appeared on the screen.

23:38—11:38 PM—JUST 22 MINUTES TO THE NEW
YEAR

"End of the year, and the end of my service," Steve said.

"What are you talking about?" Andy asked.

"I've quit. I promised Grassy to stay until the first of January, and not to talk it around until I was ready to go. I've signed on with the state troopers. I'm going to be a guard on one of the prison farms. Kulozik eats again—I can hardly wait."

"Steve, you're kidding. You've been ten, twelve years on the force. You've got seniority, you're a second-grade detective. . . ."

"Do I look like any kind of detective to you?" He tapped his riotstick lightly against the blue and white helmet he was wearing. "Face it, this city is through. What they need here is animal trainers, not policemen. I got a good job coming, me and the wife are going to eat well—and I'm going to get away from this city once and for all. I was born and raised here, and I have news for you—I'm not going to miss it. They need police with experience upstate. They'd take you on in a minute. Why don't you come with me?"

"No," Andy said.

"Why you answering so fast? Think about it. What's this city ever give you but trouble? You break a tough case and get the killer and look at your medal—back on a beat."

"Shut up, Steve," he said, without animosity. "I'm not sure why I'm staying—but I am. I don't think it's going to be that great upstate. For your sake, I hope it is. But . . . my job is here. I picked it up, knowing what I was getting into. I just don't feel like putting it down yet."

"Your choice." Steve shrugged, the movement almost lost in the depths of his thick topcoat and many wrappings. "See you around."

Andy raised his club in a quick good-by as his friend pushed his way into the press of people and disappeared.

23:58—11:58 PM—ONE MINUTE TO MIDNIGHT

As the words slipped from the screen and were replaced by a giant clockface the crowd cheered and shouted; more horns sounded. Steve worked his way through the mass of people that filled the Square and pressed against the boarded-up windows on all sides. The light from the TV screen washed their blank faces and gaping mouths with flickering green illumination, as though they were sunk deep in the sea.

Above them, the second hand ticked off the last seconds of the last minute of the year. Of the end of the century.

"End of the world!" a man shrieked, loud enough to be heard above the crowd, his spittle flying against the side of Andy's face. "End of the world!" Andy reached out and jabbed him with the end of his stick and the man gaped and grabbed at his stomach. He had been poked just hard enough to take his mind off the end of the world for a while and make him think about his own guts. Some people who had seen what had happened pointed and laughed, the sound of their laughter lost in the overwhelming roar, then they vanished from sight along with the man as the crowd surged forward.

The scratchy, static-filled roar of amplified church bells burst from the loudspeakers mounted on the buildings around Times Square, sending pealing waves of sound across the crowd below.

"HAPPY NEW YEAR!" the thousands of massed voices shouted, "HAPPY NEW CENTURY!" Horns, bells and noisemakers joined in the din, drowning out the words, merging them into the speechless roar.

Above them the second hand had finished a complete circle, the new century was already one minute old, and the clock faded away and was replaced by the magnified head of the President. He was making a speech, but not one word of it could be heard from the scratchy loudspeakers, above the unending noise of the crowd. Uncaring, the great pink face worked on, shaping unheard sentences, raising an admonitory finger to emphasize an unintelligible point.

Very faintly, Andy could hear the shrill of a police whistle from the direction of Forty-second Street. He worked his way toward the sound, forcing through the mass of people with his shoulders and club. The volume of noise was dying down and he was aware of laughs and jeers, someone was being pushed about, lost in a tight knot of figures. Another policeman, still blowing on the whistle he held tight-clamped in his teeth, was working into the jam from the side, wielding his club heavily. Andy swung his own and the crowd melted away before him. A tall man was on the pavement, shielding his head with his arms from the many feet about him.

On the screen the President's face flicked out of existence with an almost-heard burst of music, and the flying, silent letters once more took its place.

The man on the ground was bone-skinny, dressed in tied-on ends of rags and cast-off clothing. Andy helped him to his feet and the transparent blue eyes stared right through him.

" 'And God shall wipe away all tears from their eyes,' " Peter said, the shining skin stretched tight over the fleshless bones of his face as he hoarsely bellowed the words. " 'And there shall be no more death, neither sorrow, nor crying, neither shall there be any more pain: for the former things are passed away. And He that sat upon the throne said, Behold, I make all things new.' "

"Not this time," Andy said, holding on to the man so he would not fall. "You can go home now."

"Home?" Peter blinked dazedly as the words penetrated. "There is no home, there is no world, for it is the millennium and we shall all be judged. The thousand years are ended and Christ shall return to reign gloriously on Earth."

"Maybe you have the wrong century," Andy said, holding the man by the elbow and guiding him out of the crowd. "It's after midnight, the new century has begun and nothing has changed."

"Nothing changed?" Peter shouted. "It is Armageddon, it must be." Terrified, he pulled his arm from Andy's grip and started away, then turned back when he had only gone a pace.

"It must end," he called in a tortured voice. "Can this world go on for another thousand years, like this? LIKE THIS?" Then people came between them and he was gone.

Like this? Andy thought as he pushed tiredly through the dispersing crowd. He shook his head to clear it and straightened up; he still had his job to do.

Now, with their enthusiasm gone, the people were feeling the cold and the crowd was rapidly breaking up. Wide gaps appeared in their ranks as they moved away, heads bent into the icy wind from the sea. Around the corner on Forty-fourth Street, Hotel Astor guards had cleared a space so the pedicabs could come in from Eighth Avenue and line up in the taxi rank at the side entrance. Bright lights on the marquee lit up the scene clearly and Andy passed by the corner as the first guests came out. Fur coats and evening dresses, black tuxedo trousers below dark coats with astrakhan collars. Must be a big party going on in there. More bodyguards and guests emerged and waited on the sidewalk. There was the quick sound of women laughing and many shouts of "Happy New Year!"

Andy moved to head off a knot of people from the Square who were starting down Forty-fourth Street, and when he turned back he saw that Shirl had come out and stood, waiting for a cab, talking to someone.

He didn't notice who was with her, or what she was wearing or anything else, just her face and the way her hair spun out when she turned her head. She was laughing, talking quickly to the people she was with. Then she climbed into a cab, pulled the storm cover closed and was gone.

A fine cold snow was falling, driven sideways by the wind and swirling across the cracked pavements of Times Square. Very few people remained, and they were leaving, hurrying away. There was nothing for Andy to stay for, his duty was done, he could begin the long walk back downtown. He spun his club on its lanyard and started toward Seventh Avenue. The glaring screen of the gigantic TV cast its unnoticed light on his coat, putting a spark into each melted drop of snow, until he passed the building and vanished into the sudden darkness.

The screen hurled its running letters across the empty square.

CENSUS SAYS UNITED STATES HAD BIGGEST
YEAR EVER END OF CENTURY

344 MILLION CITIZENS IN THESE GREAT UNITED
STATES

HAPPY NEW CENTURY!

HAPPY NEW YEAR!

SUGGESTIONS FOR FURTHER READING

Barrett, Donald N. *Values in America*. Notre Dame: University of Notre Dame Press, 1961.

Bettelheim, Bruno. *The Informed Heart*. London: Thames & Hudson, 1961.

Boyd, Reynold H. *Controlled Parenthood*. London: Research Books, 1952.

Brown, Harrison. *Challenge of Man's Future*. New York: Viking Press, 1954.

Calder, Ritchie. *Common Sense about a Starving World*. London: Victor Gollancz, 1962.

Calder, Ritchie. *Men against the Desert*. London: Allen & Unwin, 1951.

Chandrasekhar, S. *Hungry People and Empty Lands*. London: Allen & Unwin, 1954.

Chen, Kuan. *World Population Growth and Living Standards*. New York: Twayne Publishers, 1960.

Cipolla, Carlo M. *The Economic History of World Population*. Harmondsworth, England: Penguin Books, 1962.

Elton, Charles S. *Voles, Mice and Lemmings; Problems in Population Dynamics*. New York: Oxford University Press, 1942.

Fabre-Luce, Alfred. *Men or Insects?* London: Hutchinson, 1964.

Freedman, R., Whelpton, P. K., Campbell, A. A. *Family Planning, Sterility and Population Growth*. New York: McGraw-Hill, 1959.

Fromm, Erich. *May Man Prevail?* New York: Doubleday, 1961.

Galbraith, John K. *The Affluent Society*. London: Hamish Hamilton, 1958.

Gottmann, Jean. *Megalopolis*. New York: Twentieth Century Fund, 1961.

Greene, Felix. *Awakened China*. New York: Doubleday, 1961.

Jacobs, Jane. *The Death and Life of Great American Cities*. London: Jonathan Cape, 1962.

Koestler, Arthur. *The Lotus and the Robot*. London: Hutchinson, 1960.

Lewis, Oscar. *The Children of Sánchez*. London: Secker & Warburg, 1962.

Lindner, Robert. *Must You Conform?* New York: Holt, Rinehart & Winston, 1956.

Malthus, T., Huxley, J., Osborn, F. *Three Essays on Population*. New York: New American Library, 1960.

Mills, C. Wright. *Power, Politics and People*. New York: Oxford University Press, 1963.

Osborn, Fairfield. *Our Plundered Planet*. Boston: Little, Brown, 1948.

Osborn, Fairfield (editor). *Our Crowded Planet*. New York: Doubleday, 1962.

Packard, Vance. *The Hidden Persuaders*. London: Longmans Green, 1957.

Packard, Vance. *The Status Seekers*. London: Longmans Green, 1960.

Petersen, William. *The Politics of Population*. New York: Doubleday, 1964.

Pyke, Magnus. *Automation: Its Purpose & Future*. London: Scientific Book Club, undated.

Pyle, Leo (editor). *The Pill and Birth Regulation*. London: Darton, Longman & Todd, 1964.

Reisman, David. *The Lonely Crowd*. New York: Doubleday, 1953.

Reynolds, Quentin. *Headquarters*. New York: Harper & Brothers, 1955.

Rock, John. *The Time Has Come*. London: Longmans Green, 1963.

Rolph, C. H. *The Human Sum*. London: William Heinemann, 1957.

Salisbury, Harrison E. *The Shook-up Generation*. London: Michael Joseph, 1959.

Stamp, L. Dudley. *The Geography of Life and Death*. London: William Collins Sons, 1964.

Theobald, Robert. *The Challenge of Abundance*. New York: New American Library, 1962.

Vogt, William. *People! Challenge to Survival*. London: Victor Gollancz, 1961.

Vogt, William. *Road to Survival*. New York: William Sloane, 1948.

Whyte, William H., Jr. *The Organization Man*. New York: Simon and Schuster, 1956.

PERIODICALS

Population Studies—Great Britain
Population Bulletin—United States